THE WHISPERS OF THE FALLEN

J.D.NETTO

Untreed
Reads

The Whispers of the Fallen
By J.D.Netto

Copyright 2014 by J.D.Netto
Cover Design by J.D.Netto

ISBN-13: 978-1-61187-387-0

Published by Untreed Reads, LLC
506 Kansas Street, San Francisco, CA 94107
http://www.untreedreads.com

Previously published in ebook:
Untreed Reads, 2013

Previously published in print, 2012

Printed in the United States of America

DEDICATED TO THOSE
BOLD ENOUGH TO DREAM

CONTENTS

ISAAC

"TORTURED FEAR AND STUPID
CONFIDENCE ARE BOTH DESIRABLE
STATES OF MIND..."
C.S. LEWIS

I

The deafening thunder of the storm outside awoke me suddenly. I was panting; my face was drenched in sweat. I looked at my pillow and it was soaked. I felt troubled, as if all joy had been taken from me. I headed toward the window and looked outside. The rain poured down like a waterfall and lightning ripped apart the morning sky. In my eighteen years of life, never had I seen such inclement weather.

I gasped when I saw my reflection in the mirror. My eyes were dark and heavy, as though I had not gotten any sleep during the night. Instead of their typical lively, green hue, my eyes were faded and dull. My brown hair was dripping with sweat and my mouth was incredibly dry. As I glanced down at my hands, I noticed they were shaking. I lit the candle that sat on my dresser and descended the main staircase. I was surprised to see that the house sat in darkness.

I made my way to the kitchen and saw that it was spotless. There was no bread on the wooden table and no fresh milk in the jar. This was rather odd, as my mother would always have breakfast ready before Dad and I left for the fields to work.

As I turned toward the door, I was surprised to see my father's coat still hanging behind it. Confused, I ran to their room. The moment I opened the door, I lost my breath. The bed was broken into many pieces and the sheets ripped apart and stained with drops of blood. The glass chandelier that once hung over the bed was no more, and shards of its broken glass were scattered across the entire room. Even the mirror that hung next to the window was cracked. It was clear that something was terribly wrong.

"Mom! Dad...!" I screamed, but there was no response. I made my way around the house, frantically looking for any other signs of what might have happened, but everything seemed untouched.

I lit all the candles so I could better see the entire place. The fireplace looked the same as it did from the night before. The old cedar table my dad built last year still sat snugly between the fireplace and the old clock.

Suddenly, there was a knock on the door. I stood still for a while, afraid to open it. After some time, another knock followed, stronger this time around.

"Isaac, open up!" I heard Demetre's muffled voice.

As soon as I opened it, he quickly stepped inside. His shoulder-length black hair was soaking wet. He wore the same black raincoat he had always worn during the rainy weather. The coat looked rugged from overuse.

"Why did you not answer the first time I knocked?" he asked, infuriated.

"Because...I can't find my parents," I said in distress. "I've looked everywhere but there is nothing."

Demetre's eyes suddenly seemed hollow and void. He shook his head in weariness.

"What's the matter?" I cried.

"I...I don't know what is going on anymore. I woke up terrified because of a dream I had during the night. Then I headed to the kitchen to see if Mom was there...but when I got there...nothing," he spoke in a trembling voice.

"Your parents weren't home also?" I asked, fearing his response.

"No. That is why I came. I thought they were here or you'd probably know where they had gone to."

I grabbed Demetre's arm and dragged him to my parents' room. His blue eyes widened and his face grew pale the moment he saw what had happened.

"This is what I woke up to find," I said. Demetre paced around the room with his gaze fixed on the broken bed.

"Isaac, we need to find them. I don't like this. Agalmath is such a small village, there is no way they could have gotten far! Whoever did this must be close," Demetre spoke in a hoarse voice.

My house was located in a far corner of Agalmath. I had neighbors but none that lived close enough to have heard a sound. No one would have been able to see what had happened here.

"Do you still have your horses at home?" I asked him.

"I believe they are there," Demetre replied. "I left in such a hurry, I forgot to look for the horses."

"Let's head to your house and get the horses. We should go to the fields and see if our parents are there or if any of the workers have heard from them." I knew many of them were going to be there. They had to save whatever they could from this violent storm.

I picked up a pair of old boots and put on a black raincoat. One last glance around the house was all I could bear before walking out the door. I sighed and closed my eyes. *I hope they are okay,* I thought as I made my way down the little steps and into the rain.

The howling of the wind sounded like whispers echoing in the air. Agalmath was quiet. Many houses were built high up on the hill surrounded by a dense forest of pine trees, which cast their dark shadow ominously overhead. Still, we could see a dim light flickering through the windows of our neighbors' cottages. Strangely, the animals sometimes seen grazing outside the houses were nowhere in sight.

"What was your dream about, Demetre?" I asked as the rain poured.

Demetre was silent for a while.

"It was…different. It was so vivid, I actually felt as though I was there."

Once again, Demetre fell silent and for a while, he was at a loss for words.

"Is everything alright?" I asked.

He sighed. "I dreamt I saw a huge precipice. The darkness was thick. The sky had run out of stars and the sun was no longer shining. As I stood on the edge of the precipice, I heard a voice calling my name. After some time, more voices joined in, almost like a chant. They repeatedly called me."

He took a deep breath.

"What happened after?"

"Well...I closed my eyes and I fell into the precipice. As I descended, I felt as if I was leaving my body. When I reached the bottom of the precipice, I saw..." Demetre scoffed.

"What?" I asked.

"This...this is just stupid. This has nothing to do with our situation..." He kept shaking his head.

"What?"

"I saw a man with six wings. He stood on top of a hill and his eyes seemed to pierce the very core of me. As I stood before him, I felt as though all the joy and happiness that I have ever felt was taken away. I could not see his face, only his body. Flames surrounded him. His hands slowly approached one another and once they met—I woke up."

A loud clap of thunder echoed. It was so strong that I felt the ground shake.

I was silent. What could I say to such a dream?

"Demetre...it is indeed...disturbing," I said. "Do you think it means something?"

"I don't know…I am not sure…" He couldn't disguise the trembling in his voice. I could tell he was as worried as I.

On our way, we walked right in front of McCnolle's pub. He was outside, trying to fix the broken wooden sign that hung from the window.

He saw us from afar. "Young lads," he shouted. "Where ya off to?"

Demetre looked at me, his gaze indicating that nothing should be mentioned about our situation.

"G'morning, Mr. McCnolle," I responded. "We are just heading to the fields to see if any of the workers need help."

He laughed. "Dear boy, I don't believe many of the men went off today. The storm is pretty violent. Maybe you two should just head on home, huh?"

We were both silent.

"Have your parents gone out to work today?" he asked.

The moment he did, I lost my breath. I could tell Demetre was shocked as well. To our relief, his dog ran out from inside the pub into the rain.

"Oh! 'Xcuse me," he shouted as he frantically chased after his pet.

Demetre and I immediately quickened our pace, making sure that the moment he returned with the dog, we would no longer be within sight.

"I just want to know what happened…" I mumbled. I was trying to remain calm but it grew harder by the minute.

I could finally see Demetre's house. The house was behind a small forest of trees. There was a little stone path leading to the flaming red door. His parents always loved vivid colors. Next to his house, many of the weaker trees had fallen on the ground. Tree trunks found a new resting place in the road ahead.

"The horses are in the back inside the barn," Demetre said as he made his way through a small wooden gate near his mother's quaint vegetable garden. Every time I entered this gate, memories came to mind. Demetre and I had been friends since childhood.

As we walked, I could sense heaviness in the air.

"Are you worried that the horses might not be in the barn?" I asked.

"No," he responded. "I am afraid of what is happening. I still can't quite grasp what I saw."

The old barn was visible and not far from the gate. It had lost its color due to years of inclement weather. Near the barn lay a pond where Demetre and I would fish all the time.

Demetre violently opened the door and ran inside. As I walked in, I was relieved to see the two black stallions. Their coats shimmered even in the darkness; their manes were precisely combed and graciously sat on their necks and above their eyes. The one with white spots on his back was Bracken and the other one was Midnight, named due to his coat's dark pigment. Paul Aliward tended to these horses well.

Demetre sighed. "This is a good thing." He gave me a halfhearted smile.

"Good indeed," I said.

"But also troubling…" he said as he opened the gate to get the horses out. "My parents never leave home without their horses."

I grabbed Bracken by the reins and slowly made my way out of the barn. What words of comfort could I give him in such a situation?

We left the stable in haste, setting out toward the fields. It was a ten-minute ride from where we were but under these weather conditions, I was pretty sure it was going to take us longer. Because of the muddy roads, the fallen trees and also the flying debris, we had to be extremely careful. This situation only built up my anxiety, especially because it would take us longer to get to the fields. We rode in silence. I could see that Demetre was in deep concentration, focused on the road and on the goal we had set before us.

The rain did not stop. Large raindrops poured down so hard, I could feel their sting through my raincoat.

Suddenly, the horses came to an abrupt halt—they neighed and kicked violently.

"What is wrong?" Demetre said.

"I am not sure," I replied, looking around.

"It must be the storm…it probably frightened them," Demetre said as he alighted from his horse.

"There, there…" he said, caressing his horse on the head—trying hard to tame it again.

I got down from Bracken and tried to do the same, hoping it would calm him. Weariness grew inside of me. My heart was heavy and it felt as though cold air had settled in. I sensed someone watching me. When I looked behind me, I saw a dark being approaching us. I could not discern what it was because the being merged with the tree branches. After a while, not even the rain and the trees were able to hide the midnight-colored horse and its cloaked rider. The horse was fully armored; its eyes were hollow and surrounded by spike-shaped armor. The rider's drenched cloak covered his entire body—including its head. The armor that sat on its shoulders had three spikes that stood almost as tall as his head.

The rider stopped a couple feet in front of us, still as a statue. The whisper of the trees resounded through the forest. There was so much fear coming from this one being that our surroundings seemed to dim.

"Can we help you?" I shouted.

The rider was non-responsive.

"Sir, are you alright?" Demetre asked.

Still, there was no answer.

"Something is definitely wrong here," I whispered.

"What is wrong here?" the rider said. His voice was deep and the very sound of it made me tremble.

"Um…nothing, sir…we would like to go through, please," I said.

"Isaac Khan and Demetre Aliward, it is an honor to find you out here," the rider said in an ominous tone.

"Hhh…How do you know our names?" I stuttered.

Every time this rider released a word, the horses grew even more agitated. "Many know your names and many want you. You two are very important."

13

A loud scream came from Demetre. He thudded violently on the ground with his hands pressed against his chest.

In fear, my eyes became fixed on the rider. He hadn't moved a single muscle. He didn't even appear to be breathing.

"Please, help me!" I yelled at the rider in desperation as I tended to Demetre. His skin was losing its color and his breathing was becoming heavier. The horses fled to the forest once I let go of the reins.

"Help...yes, that is all I need from you." This time, his horse slowly moved in my direction.

"Help fr-*from*-me?" I stuttered.

The rider stopped and alighted from the armored beast. The moment his foot met the muddy ground, he removed the cloak from his face, revealing a blond man with eyes so blue, they shimmered right through the darkness.

"Isaac, I simply require your services in leading me to your house. There is something that does not belong to you that has been there for a while now."

I looked at this man and back at Demetre.

"What is happening to him?" I asked in anguish.

Demetre was mumbling inaudible words.

"The pain...the pain..." he whispered.

"What about the pain?" I asked in desperation.

"Him...it's him..." As soon as he said these words, he let out a deafening scream.

Terror overtook me. I got up with trembling legs. "Who are you, sir?" I asked with a broken voice.

"Sir…" The rider sounded disgusted. "Not sir. Your mother and father did not call me 'sir' the last time they saw me in their room."

I could barely believe the words I had just heard. Instinctively, I catapulted myself in his direction. I lost ground the moment I felt a sharp pain taking me completely. Not a moment passed before the unbearable feeling caused me to lose my footing entirely. I fell to the ground, writhing in pain. My head burned and my body felt as though it was being pressed against the dirt.

"My name is Cyro. I have come for you both before another immortal finds you. Trust me when I say I only want what is good for the both of you."

I tried my hardest to pay close attention to him but I couldn't. The pain was excruciating, spreading all the way to the very strands of hair on my head.

"I will make it stop now but you have to promise that you will do as I say." His voice was void of emotion.

"I will…I will…" I tried to say it as loud as I could.

The pain rapidly released me. I gasped for air as if it was the last time I would take a breath. Startled, I got on my feet. "What is it that you want?"

Cyro smiled—his gaze encountered my eyes. It felt as though evil flowed from his blue eyes.

"Isaac, you ask too much. Lead me to your house and I myself will show you a very revealing truth about you."

I scoffed.

"Will you leave me alone if I take you there?" I asked.

"Indeed I will," he responded.

What choice did I have but to lead him to where he wanted to go? In the short time that I had stood before this rider, death itself had looked me in the eye.

"I will show you the way..." As the words drifted from my tongue, fear overtook me.

Cyro took hold of a rope that was attached to the horse's saddle. He grabbed both of my hands and tied them together. The rope was so tight, it felt as if my wrists were about to break.

My heart skipped a beat as I could no longer hear Demetre's screams. He was on the ground, lying immobile, with his face pressed against the muddy road.

"Demetre!" I yelled at the top of my lungs. Tears of desperation descended on my cheeks.

Cyro slowly approached him and gently knelt beside him. "I would not dare leave you here, Demetre. You are riding with me on my horse." He picked him up from the ground and placed him on top of the horse. As Demetre's head reclined forward I caught sight that he was still breathing. I sighed in relief.

"Now you..." he spoke as he dragged me from where I was, violently placing me in front of the horse. "You will go ahead of me, like a dog, lead the way," he said with a grin on his face. "Will you do a good job at it?"

"It amazes me how low you will go in order to achieve the desires of your lord," a voice spoke from the woods. I desperately looked around, hoping to see a familiar face from Agalmath.

I heard Cyro grunt and his teeth cringe. "I did not think you were going to find us so soon, Nephilin."

"And I thought you would have been done with your duty long before you had even arrived." His voice was soothing but powerful. The sound of breaking branches came from my left side and shortly after, a rider appeared mounted on a white horse, his garments old and ragged. His dirt-covered boots showed signs that he had been out on the road for a while now, and his shoulder-length fair hair was scattered across his face from the wind. "Cyro, release the boys," he exclaimed in a loud voice.

"I am not one to give up easily, Devin. It is a shame that you have chosen the harder path in this journey. One must be a fool to believe he can so easily neglect his own nature. You come from one of us."

I did not understand what was taking place. Why did this Devin want to help us? Was he trustworthy? Who was he in the first place?

Slowly Devin descended from his horse. From his waist he removed a beautiful sword. Surrounded by a red glow, the sword very visible, even during this torrential rainstorm.

"I will not ask you again, Cyro," he said as his hand tightened around the sword handle.

"I never said you had to ask me twice...traitor."

My eyes could barely keep up with their rapid movements. They fiercely attacked each other with an inhuman agility and precision. No human could move the way they did. I could see the raindrops touching their bodies as they attacked each other in midair, in the woods, and on the ground. I could hear the whooshing sound of Devin's sword trying to touch Cyro. From what I was able to capture, Cyro was extremely fast.

When I saw Demetre and the situation he was in, I knew there wasn't a moment to spare. I mounted Cyro's horse and galloped away, heading toward the forest. My heart knew of the risks and also consequences, but I had to do something.

I heard trees falling and branches breaking behind me, but I kept galloping through the forest, heading home. There was something that Cyro wanted that was apparently there and I needed to find it quickly. I heard Demetre's low groans as I rode through the forest's narrow path. The tree branches smacked against my face. As I made my way deeper into the forest, I noticed the noise from the fight had suddenly ceased.

I could see my house in the distance; I was almost there. I rode straight up to the door and I tied the commandeered horse to the tree. I helped Demetre off the horse and dragged his body inside the house. To my relief, the house looked exactly the same as it did when I first left.

I laid Demetre on the old settee near the fireplace. I stopped for a minute and tried to process everything that had just happened in the last couple of hours. I was so agitated that the soft ticking noise of the living room clock made me shiver.

II

I heard a knock as I covered Demetre with a blanket. It seemed that time stood still as I stared out the window, watching the rainfall. There was another knock.

"Isaac, please, open up!" a voice shouted from outside.

I gasped as I felt my senses escaping me for a while. I was not able to move. I roamed around the living room trying to find something in case I needed protection. I was startled when I heard the sound of the door being brought down by what I supposed was a really strong kick.

"We need to leave now. Grab a couple of things you might need and let's go."

"What do you mean let's go?" I shouted. I felt my body trembling.

He apprehensively paced around the house. His breathing was heavy. It was the rider that fought against Cyro in the forest. He was drenched from the rain but he showed no signs of weakness in any way. He immediately walked to the settee to see Demetre.

"What are you doing? Why are you not getting ready? Do you understand how serious of a situation we have here right now?" he exclaimed. I could sense agitation in his voice.

"As far as I remember I barely know who you are," I said.

"Right now the only thing you need to be concerned about is gathering food and supplies. We are going on a journey and trust me—we have no idea when we will be coming back."

I bowed my head and took in a deep breath.

"Is he dead?" I asked him.

"*Dead?* Those things cannot die, Isaac. They are Fallen Stars. They may vanish when touched by a blade but die, that's impossible for their kind. They quickly come back and that is why we must go."

Suddenly the horse outside neighed loudly.

"Whose horse is that?" he inquired.

"It was Cyro's. I snatched him so Demetre and I could…" Before I could finish my sentence, the rider had gone outside with his blade and decapitated the horse. To my surprise the horse did not bleed, nor did it fall to the ground, but it disintegrated into ashes, slowly taken by the wind.

"Are you ready to pack up now?" he asked me.

In fear, I trembled as I made my way to the kitchen. I grabbed one of our old bags that Dad used to bring crops in, and filled it with bread and fruits. Then I heard a loud banging noise coming from the living room. Quickly I ran to see what was going on. I found Devin breaking up the floor with his bare hands.

I gasped.

"What are you doing?" I questioned him, looking around to see a whole section of the wooden floor broken apart into pieces.

"Looking for the thing that Cyro wanted so badly. Are you done packing?"

I nodded.

"Good—do you have any spare horses?" he asked.

"I'm afraid I don't. The ones we were riding were Demetre's."

He kept on breaking everything, his eyes relentlessly looking everywhere at a rapid speed. I did not know if I should fear him or trust him.

"You…you are not human, are you?" I asked reluctantly.

He chuckled.

"How did you guess?" he said without taking his eyes off the floor, his hands briskly tearing it apart. "Am I giving that away so easily?"

"What are you? Should I fear you?" I asked. He came to a complete stop.

"Yes…you are supposed to fear me but you don't have to. Trust me, I am on your side. Now to tell you what I am…I just don't have enough time right now."

I looked at Demetre. His face was pale and his lips colorless.

"Will he be alright?" I asked.

"He will be if we keep our…" He stopped speaking and hastily reached inside the gigantic hole he had made in our floor.

"Here it is," he whispered, pulling out a golden box from the debris. The box was covered with a thick coat of dust. Strange patterns were engraved into the gold and I could make out designs of some sort. Devin used his hands to wipe away the dust. From a few steps away, I could make out a symbol etched on top of the box: a circle with a straight line in the middle. An old, rusty lock was placed on the right side of this ancient-looking object. I could tell this was no ordinary trinket.

"And what exactly is that?" I asked as my heart pounded just by the sight of this amazing object.

"Get Demetre, we are leaving now," he said, pacing around the hole in the floor.

"Leaving? Remember I told you about the horses? Are we supposed to walk under the rain until we find some sort of transportation?" His apparent lack of understanding enraged me.

"Please," he whispered as he closed his eyes. "Do you have any carriages outside?" he asked, wrapping the box with a couple of old rags he had with him.

22

"My dad has one out back but…"

He placed the box inside the old leather pack on his hip and opened the door. I caught sight of a white horse standing outside, immobile under the violent storm. It was my dad's horse, Crystal.

"Let's go then," he said with a soft grin on his face.

"How did—" I mumbled. "That's my father's horse! She ran away last week…"

"Where is the carriage at?" he asked, without taking his eyes off the horse.

"Inside the old barn," I remarked, dumbfounded as to how Crystal had gotten here.

I tried to place Demetre on my shoulder, but he was extremely heavy. I was struggling when Devin pushed me aside and threw Demetre over his shoulder.

"I saw you struggling there…thought you needed a hand," he alleged. "Can we go through the back door?"

I shivered as we once again stepped out into the storm. My clothes were soaking wet and mud permeated my boots.

"Is the horse not going to flee if we just leave her there? She's always been afraid of storms," I asked curiously.

"She won't leave unless I tell her to," he responded as his eyes avoided any contact with mine.

"So you control animals?" I anxiously waited for his reply.

"Some." He nodded his head as he tapped his fingers on his right thigh. "Can we please talk about this later?" Devin raised his voice.

I sealed my lips and swallowed my strongly worded response to his lack of understanding, but he was right. We had greater matters to tend to. The town looked deserted. All the neighbors were probably inside their homes sitting by the fire with their families, unaware of the mysterious events of the day.

The door of the stable creaked as I opened it. I shivered as my eyes roamed around the place. Even though everything looked exactly as it always had, the barn felt oddly eerie.

"There is the carriage." I pointed to my left where Dad kept it. Our carriage was a beautiful, elegant four-wheeler.

"Let us hope this does not draw too much attention," he said as he checked the inside of the vehicle.

As Devin laid Demetre inside, I caught sight of my dad's smoke pipe sitting near the window. Then it struck me. I was so caught up with everything that I forgot our parents could be dead.

"Where are we going, Devin?" I said, closing the door.

To my surprise, Crystal walked inside the barn and smoothly walked to the front of the carriage. Her white coat was stained with mud and small cuts.

"I want to know where we are going," I insisted.

He ignored me.

I was growing tired of this guessing game. "If you expect me to get on that carriage you better start to give me answers, otherwise neither Demetre nor I will be going with you."

"Then you die," he replied, climbing atop the carriage.

"What do you mean die? What is this box? Who are you? Who was Cyro? I think I deserve to know, don't you think?" I was irritated and frightened. If I was going to get in a carriage with a complete stranger and venture into the unknown, I deserved to know the truth.

"All ready. Let's go," he said.

I stood motionless, fixing my eyes on him, waiting.

"All right…Cyro was after you and Demetre because of this box. Inside it contains a book. Many think this book does not exist and is merely a legend. The fact is it has been hidden away from the Kingdoms of Elysium for thousands of years."

His answers stirred up new questions.

"How did this book end up in my house and how did you know it was there?" I asked; my eyes quickly surveyed the barn for any signs of potential danger.

"Listen," Devin snapped. "We can stay here and chat about these things and then be caught by one of those Fallen Stars or we can be on our way and I'll explain everything to you. Now which one do you want?"

"How can I trust you, Devin? You showed up suddenly, broke down my door, tore up my house, and you happened to know that a mysterious book was inside…"

He sighed.

"Diane and Dustin Khan are your parents. You were born eighteen years ago—on November thirtieth to be more precise. Your father owns an enormous field where he grows various crops such as tomatoes, carrots, and some fruits as well. Your mother is an amazing cook and an amazing seamstress… Oh—this carriage was given to your father by me to celebrate your birth." He stopped, his eyes staring straight at me. "Is this enough for you, Isaac?"

Slowly I climbed up on the carriage and we were off. Crystal calmly conducted us. Devin blankly gazed ahead, seemingly unaware of my presence.

It was hard to ride in this storm, especially because the roads were muddy and slippery. I looked up and could see we were going down the same road that took us to the fields.

"Where are we going?"

"To meet the Council," he responded with an edge to his voice.

I stared at him blankly, waiting for a more complete answer. He was silent for a while, and then he started:

"Tristar is a kingdom that has existed since before the creation of our world. Before good and evil ever battled, it stood strong and mighty. It is not here, but in a place that is far, but at the same time so close. This kingdom is also the dwelling place for the Creator and his servants called Stars. But in the ancient days, there was one Star that shone brighter than any other and had power beyond measure."

"Which I would assume was Lucifer?" I muttered.

"Yes. Under the Creator, Lucifer was the one to oversee the Stars and to keep order in place. But he had one thing the others didn't, something the Creator risked so much when he gave him this…weapon."

"What weapon?"

"The choice between good and evil. Slowly he discovered powers that were asleep inside of him, powers that would eventually spring forth. Unfortunately, the Creator believed Lucifer would ignore this gift freely."

"Why would the Creator take such a big risk? I don't understand."

"You see...the Creator never wanted puppets, he wanted beings that would choose to be part of his kingdom, not someone that tried to take over it. Yet he had to give Lucifer this choice. It is only by choice that our true nature is revealed."

I sighed.

"In secret, Lucifer deceived the other Stars. He spoke to them about this power that was stirring inside of him, a force he had never seen anywhere in Tristar. That very force was the birth of evil itself."

The events Devin spoke of daunted me. I knew my mind was too limited to fully comprehend what Lucifer started when evil was birthed out of him.

"Lucifer gathered secret meetings in the Wastelands, plotting against the Creator. Like a deceiving snake, he spoke to the others, luring them into this new power he had uncovered inside of him. Some Stars resisted Lucifer and warned the Creator of the coming of evil." He sighed softly. "Of course, the Creator was completely aware of their plans but he wanted to see which Stars would be faithful enough to inform him."

"So they also had a choice. They all had a choice," I said.

"Exactly. But Lucifer was the only one with enough power to *become* evil. The Creator and the other Stars marched to the Wastelands to encounter Lucifer. Judgment came swiftly upon those that were found with him. They were purged in fire and lost all their beauty. Inside of each one, darkness not only grew, but it became part of their very nature."

The rain finally tampered off. I looked to the sky but there was no sign of sunlight, and heavy gray clouds hovered above.

"So what happened to Lucifer and the Stars that sided with him?" I asked.

"They were sent to a place the Creator designed especially for them. He named it the Abyss. When they fell, Lucifer and the Fallen Stars continued to plot against the Creator. There were already foul creatures and other living beings that dwelled there, creatures that were forced to accept Lucifer's ideals."

"And how did this book come about?" I inquired. I felt the hairs on my arms stand on end.

"It is said by the wise men of the Council that Lucifer kept a book where he wrote the things he discovered, and the new powers that awoke inside of him. Before they attacked Tristar, he advised the Fallen Stars that if something was to ever happen to him, if he was ever imprisoned, the Diary held the secrets to his awakening."

"Awakening?" I asked as I shrugged my shoulders.

"All the Fallen Stars were sent back to the Abyss by the Creator and his servants. There had to be a complete reformation of orders and ideals in Tristar. There had never been such things as evil, or war, or an attempt to hurt one another. The hierarchies had to be reorganized."

I was trying to fully grasp this information. I pictured what it would be like to spend eternity under rules created before the world and then, all is changed because of one's choice.

"Well...what happened to Lucifer then?" At this point, my questions and doubts seemed insignificant before the mysteries he was sharing.

"The Creator damned his body, placing it into a deep coma. His body was hidden somewhere in the Wastelands of Tristar. But his spirit endures, manifesting itself in many shapes and forms, but never in its entirety. Lucifer's spirit visits our world of Elysium every now and then."

We were silent for a moment. I stopped and tried to let everything sink in. I was looking around and finally noticed how quiet the forest had become. The trees were still dripping with dew from the rain.

"How did the Diary end up with my parents?" I asked reluctantly.

"When Lucifer and the Fallen Stars fell, the Creator already had plans to create Elysium and all that you see here. During this process of creation, after the waters were separated from the land, the first humans were born. To that first group of humans, he entrusted them with a book recovered from the Abyss by Leethan, one of the Higher Stars of Tristar. He wanted to know that his creation was...trustworthy. He gave them a choice as well, choice between the light and the darkness. Those first humans were immortals with amazing powers. Many went on to be kings and queens in Elysium."

"Sort of like you, right?" I said.

"I will get there…trust me," he said. "The humans kept on spreading throughout this earth, having children, grandchildren, and started civilizations. Until one day one of their daughters was roaming around alone—she was young and curious. The Fallen Stars kept their eyes on creation, looking for any gaps that would allow them to infiltrate it and damage it in any way. Mordred, one of the Fallen Stars, entered Elysium through the Gates of the Fourth Dimension. The girl found him as she walked about, lying on the forest floor. His clothes were ragged and old, his eyes were red, and he seemed weak. The girl took him to her village and there, they offered him help and shelter. No human would have ever thought of the darkness that was to come about. As time passed by, he and the girl grew fond of each other…"

His face grew sorrowful as agony flowed from his voice.

"Mordred seduced the young girl with his charm and beauty and lay with her."

I was shocked. His eyes showed such agony and hate that I was feeling remorse by asking him all these questions.

"Um…you can stop if you want to, Devin. I didn't mean…"

"It's alright," he said. "You will have to know this sooner or later. Let's take advantage right now that we are alone and it is calm. The future holds much war and perilous journeys for all the inhabitants of this place." He bowed his head and breathed in deeply. "As soon as the act was over, Mordred disappeared right before her eyes. She stood still, trying to comprehend what had just happened. A few moments later, she felt a sharp pain in her stomach. As she laid her hands over it, she noticed her stomach had grown in a short amount of time and she felt something kicking inside."

"She was pregnant?" I was pretty sure he could see how surprised and awestruck I was. I could not fully grasp the disturbing idea of a young girl getting pregnant and seeing body changes in such a short amount of time.

"Well...yes, she was. Then, all around the village, Whispering Lights appeared."

"Whispering Lights?" I asked.

"Small lights that can enter the brain and cause great distress. They are usually sent out by a Fallen Star. They have rhythms of their own. It is said that they sounded like drums beating in perfect harmony."

I gasped.

"As the sounds grew louder, the screams also echoed. Other Fallen Stars invaded the village and for the very first time, humans were murdered. She also noticed how strong her body was becoming, how her senses grew keener, her heart was beating faster. She was becoming one of my kind—a Nephilin."

"So they were no longer immortals after what happened?" I asked.

"Only those chosen to guard the book remained immortal, along with the young girl. They all lost this privilege because of one that fell. The Fallen Stars wanted the Diary so they could discover the words their lord had written. But they were not able to find it. They left proclaiming that one day they would strike Elysium with all their might and would relentlessly search for the book. But the Diary can only be unlocked by one of those that descend from the Council. Only through blood can it be opened."

"What was the book's location before it ended up here in Agalmath?" I asked, burning with curiosity.

"The Council kept the Diary hidden away; they were wiser than many since they had been appointed to protect the Diary."

"Was this the only book Lucifer wrote?" I asked curiously.

"Many are the rumors that other books were written by Lucifer, only these books were never found," he replied.

"Wait...wait...wait...how do my parents come into play?"

"After these happenings, darkness was able to enter Elysium. Starting with the baby that young girl was carrying inside of her...she carried my kind." His voice broke at the saying of the last word. I could feel that he resented being whatever he was.

"What are you?" I asked.

"I am a Nephilin, the cross between human and Stars. That's what the young girl became after she had lain with the Fallen Star."

We were both silent for a while, then he continued.

"As time went by, other Fallen Stars slept with humans, causing them to give birth to my kind. Years passed, tales became legends, legends faded into fables and humanity forgot the Creator and where they had come from. Nephilins remained hidden in the shadows as humans populated the world. As humanity thrived, many were the men that were drunk with the idea of power."

"The Diary remained hidden throughout all this time?" I asked.

"Yes…the Council faithfully kept it hidden away in Justicia. Until one day the Fallen Stars commenced an attack on the small villages of Elysium, murdering many innocent men and women. They started an army that no human could stop with mere weapons. These humans became something called Shadows. You see, the darkness had so deeply infiltrated into Elysium that humankind lost all the knowledge about the Creator. When one dies without knowing light and darkness they cannot cross over to Tristar, so they become Shadows—insane, uncontrollable souls, with an unexplainable urge to kill anything that stands in their path. They do not have a mind of their own and are controlled by the Fallen Stars."

"What do they look like?" I asked.

"They still resemble humans but they are deformed. Their eyes are bright gold, and their skin colorless. They move like wild animals when hunting," Devin said with eyes fixed on the road.

Devin sighed. I was immobile, my breathing faltered. All this information overwhelmed me.

"I thought you wanted to know where your parents come into play…"

"Yes…what happened?" I was so appalled at the story Devin was sharing that I found it hard to have any reaction whatsoever.

"Eighteen years ago the Fallen Stars found the hiding place of the Diary. During the perilous battle between the Fallen and the Council, your parents, Diane and Dustin Khan, along with Paul and Lune Aliward were able to escape with the book. They made their way to Agalmath and there they settled down, keeping the Diary hidden in a place no one would ever suspect."

I nodded slowly as I looked at the sky. Heavy drops of rain hit us with force once again.

"How did you know where we were?" I asked.

"The Council has been watching both of your families for a while. The Fallen Stars will come after you both, especially Demetre. We knew that when you reached your state of maturity they would no longer wait to attack. You both were the ticking of the clock. As soon as you both turned eighteen, the war started."

It had finally hit me. We were the reason for their coming.

"Why us? What is so special about us?" This was the sort of question where you knew you would not get a pleasant response.

"Your parents were part of the Council. Many say that you two are the only direct blood descendants. Rumor is that the only way for the Diary to be opened is if both of you choose to shed your blood for it. But they had to wait eighteen years until your blood matured."

I was looking back at the carriage and through the small window behind me I saw Demetre lying down. He was still unconscious. Due to the lack of pigment on his skin, I could tell he was weak. Just a couple of hours ago we were both ordinary kids that had to work with our parents to earn our living. I felt the weight of the situation.

"Are things going to get better, Devin?" I asked, looking at the trees ahead.

"Not for a while, I'm afraid, Isaac."

I sighed. My heart pounded in my chest.

"I'm going to go inside the carriage and rest a bit. I feel tired. Will you be alright?" I asked reluctantly, knowing that he might also be exhausted.

Devin chuckled.

"Oh, don't worry about that. Go rest. I will wake you up when we get to the borderline."

I was clueless on what he meant when he said borderline, but I was losing the battle against my eyelids and their urge to close. I lay down and closed my eyes, waiting for sleep to come to me. It wasn't long until I heard Devin humming a very mellow tune as the sound of a soft breeze blew against the carriage window.

III

I saw a young girl, eyes as blue as the midday sky, hair as golden as the sun. She was clothed in a fine red dress, standing against a white wall. She brought me great fear. Somehow I could sense she was one of the immortals: a Nephilin. She slowly walked toward me with a piercing gaze. My body shivered with every step. I heard whispering voices as she approached. She laid her right hand on my shoulder.

"Isaac…Isaac…can you hear me?" I woke up with what appeared to be Demetre calling me.

I leaped up quickly. "*Demetre!* You are finally awake. How are you feeling? Do you feel any pain?"

Demetre looked out the window.

"I am fine," he replied in a tremulous voice. "Where are we? Is…is this your father's carriage?"

"Do you remember anything?" I asked.

He paused for a minute. I could tell he was deep in thought, trying to remember any of the incidents of today.

"The rider…my chest…Isaac, what happened to that rider in the fields? Our parents…what happened?"

Patiently, I explained to Demetre all the events that had preceded us until now. By the look on his face, fear was overtaking him with every word I spoke.

"Are our parents really dead?" Demetre asked with fearful eyes.

I shivered at the question. "I'm honestly not sure. I'm not sure about anything right now," I replied sincerely.

"Are you sure this Devin is trustworthy?" he asked.

I shrugged. "We have no choice as of right now but to trust him. He has been right so far about everything, and the story he told…the events he spoke of, they make sense."

"So the Diary is in our possession?" he asked.

"It has been for eighteen years but our parents never mentioned it to us. They wanted us to not have any part in this."

We came to an abrupt stop. I immediately opened the door of the carriage and both Demetre and I walked out. I saw Devin standing next to the horse, looking out at the woods.

"Nice to see you are doing well. Isaac was worried," he spoke with eyes firmly gazing at the woods ahead.

"What are you looking for, Devin?" I asked him as my eyes scanned my surroundings.

"We are being followed. A while ago something picked up our trail. I can feel them," he affirmed; his eyes never swayed away from the trees.

"Who picked up our trail? What is going on?" Demetre sounded desperate. Abruptly he placed both of his hands on his knees and bent down, hurling violently.

"Are you alright?" I asked. He was taking big breaths.

"I am feeling weak. I feel as if I haven't eaten for days," he managed to reply, despite the hurls.

As I turned to Devin, I saw a dark shape standing in a tree right on the other side. I blinked and then the dark shape had disappeared. For a moment I thought it could've been the tiredness of my mind, but then I looked again, and I saw the dark shape standing, this time in another tree.

"Devin, right there!" I pointed but the dark shape was gone.

"Demetre, you should probably head back to the carriage," I instructed.

"It is useless. They have found us. Be calm and no sudden moves," Devin whispered.

Right above us on the tree branches stood three dark shapes. My stomach dropped, and I couldn't breathe. They were so close that when I looked up, I could see the creatures much more clearly. They were eerily humanlike, but the darkness emanating from within them was supernatural. Although they stood upright like humans, their bodies were deformed. Their fingers were crooked and twisted, and their arms dangled lifelessly in front of their bodies. These dark creatures wore nothing but ragged and torn cloth resembling what might have once been proper clothing, and their talon-like feet were bare. The last thing I noticed before catching my breath was their piercing yellow, catlike eyes staring right through me.

"What are they?" I whispered.

"Shadows. Stay close," Devin advised us.

They acted similar to wild animals when hunting. They were drooling; their body movements were swift and agile. I could clearly see the female and male resemblances in all of them.

"What do they want?" Demetre mumbled.

"To devour us—that is the only thing these creatures want," Devin replied in a breathy voice.

Then, as I turned my head to look at Demetre, Devin leaped up, took out his sword from his waist and ran toward the woods. Two of the Shadows followed him while one attacked Crystal.

"Come on. To the woods! Let's go!" I exclaimed.

I did not look back as I ran. We escaped deep into the forest without the slightest clue of where we were going. The eerie silence of the forest spiked fear inside of me.

We ran as fast as our legs could carry us, leaping over fallen trees, navigating through the thick brush, and trampling anything in our path.

We came across a beautiful torrential river. The bottom of the river was visible even under the cloudy gray skies.

"We swim across," I instructed, trying to measure the distance to the other side with my eyes.

"Across? Do you see how strong this river is? We'll drown, Isaac," Demetre insisted, trying to catch his breath.

Once again the growls echoed around.

"We don't have time, Demetre." I stepped inside the river; the water was up to my waist. Just as I started to take another step I felt something grab my leg and pull me down with a strong force.

"Isaac!" I heard Demetre's muffled screams as I was dragged to the bottom of the river. I opened my eyes in the crystal water and I could see the same Shadow from minutes ago. Its eyes glistened under the water. Terrified, I tried to swim back to the surface, but it continued to drag me down. My adrenaline kicked in and I tried pulling myself from its grasp, but it was too strong.

From behind the Shadow I saw Devin approaching at an amazing speed. He drew his sword and violently pierced the creature in its head. Its body slowly vanished into ashes, which floated like a cloud up to the surface.

In haste, I made my way back to the surface, gasping for air. Devin leaped up from the water into a tree, while Demetre stood near the riverbank in shock.

"I told you it was a bad idea...why didn't you listen?" Demetre said the moment he saw me coming out of the water.

"Isaac, the Council is not far from here. We must keep on running so we can cross over the borderline," Devin yelled.

We ran as fast as we could. Devin went ahead of us, leaping from branch to branch and tree to tree. His agility was mesmerizing; my eyes were hardly able to keep up with him.

"Stop!" Devin shouted.

"What is it?" Demetre asked in a loud voice.

Devin quickly descended from the tree and stood at our side. He looked frightened. He was so still that even his breathing was barely noticeable.

"There are more, many more coming our way from the clearing up ahead," Devin said.

It did not take long for me to get a glimpse of them. Their numbers were probably in the hundreds, all walking in our direction. They came out from the trees, some leaped out from the rocks, others even from the ground. But ahead of them, there was one that appeared to be the leader. He wore a black cloak that extended all the way to the ground.

"You really thought you had gotten rid of me, didn't you?" he said. I had not easily forgotten his voice. It was Cyro. My eyes widened. I looked at Devin.

"Why do you keep protecting them, Devin? What is your gain in all this? You know you were born from one of us. There is no redemption for you," Cyro calmly spoke.

"You know there is always a choice, Cyro, even if I am damned regardless."

The Shadows growled ferociously. They seemed to be waiting for the simple order to attack. Cyro slowly walked to us. He looked at Demetre and smiled.

"Pity to see one so young enduring so much pain." He laid his hands over him. I was afraid Demetre was going to suffer again. I froze. I saw no action coming from Devin either.

"I hate to tell you, Devin, but sooner or later your nature will come out." He smiled. "A wild beast can never be tamed."

He walked back to where the Shadows were.

"I could just release my puppies over you three. It would be such a delight to see them devour and feast on your flesh." He spoke the last words with such excitement and disturbance, it caused my breathing to falter.

"Consider this an act of mercy. You may go to wherever you are heading, but know this—we will find you again and take what belongs to us. I know there are people that you must see now. Farewell," he said with a malefic grin.

Like the mist, they all disappeared right before our eyes. I was confused. Did we not have what they wanted? Weren't they after Demetre and me?

"What just happened?" I asked Devin. There was no reply. "I take it you are as confused as I am?"

Devin nodded slowly. Judging by the expression on his face, I could tell he was trying to piece everything together.

"As Cyro spoke to me, I saw...I saw a blond girl. Her eyes were blue...she smiled at me," Devin grumbled. I felt compelled to tell him about my dream earlier, but not right now. It could not have been the same girl, at least not in a dream.

"Did she say anything to you?" I asked.

43

Devin still seemed awestruck. "No, she never said a word. She only smiled. Interesting that…as I gazed at her, I felt as if every joyful moment I had ever experienced in my life was just about to vanish," he replied.

"Who are they?" Demetre asked, looking ahead.

I looked up and saw four horsemen. They had red capes and were clothed in silver armor that, even without any direct light, shone brightly. I noticed they had brought an extra horse with them. As soon as Devin saw them, he walked in their direction. The four horsemen came down from their horses only a few feet away from us. As I watched from afar, it appeared as if Devin knew these men really well.

"Are you sure this Devin is trustworthy, Isaac?" Demetre asked me once again.

I sighed.

"What choice do we have, but to trust him?" I whispered.

Demetre grabbed my arm and dragged me away so we were out of hearing distance. He led me behind an old tree trunk.

"Isaac, he is one of them," he whispered. "He is a Nephilin, a son of the Fallen. You heard Cyro—his kind is also against us, evil runs in his veins. Why would he be protecting us? He has the Diary with him right now and he has us—two boys who are completely dependent on him."

"I guess you will have to trust me and I will have to trust myself," I replied as I made my way back to where Devin and the four horsemen were.

"Isaac!" Devin shouted. "Come here. I'd like you to meet a couple of old friends."

I took another look at those men. Their armor alone would frighten any ordinary human. As I got closer I could see them better. Their armor did not have a single scratch. I could easily see my own reflection on them.

"This is Dantes." He pointed to the one in the middle. He had grayish hair, seemed to be in his mid-forties.

"This is Aleen." He pointed to the one that stood to Dantes' right. He looked younger; his flaming red hair glistened, his eyes greener than the greenest spring leaves.

"This one is Alestin." He was blond, skin almost as pale as Devin's. He was the one that stood on the far right.

"And this," he pointed to the one that stood to my far left. "This is the chief and commander, Vladmir."

"It is a pleasure," Vladmir said. The others bowed their heads as soon as he was done speaking. Vladmir seemed to be a very experienced warrior. He had a scar that started right above his right eye and went all the way down to his chin.

"And who is this other young man?" Vladmir asked. I did not even notice that Demetre was standing a bit far behind me.

"Demetre Aliward, sir," he replied.

"Well, you all seem like great young boys. The Council is ready to receive all of you. Come, the borderline is not far from here." He spoke with softness in his voice, but the authority in his tone could not be masked. As soon as he took his first step, the other men followed.

"Oh! Where is your horse, Devin?" he asked with a grin on his face.

"We lost her when the Shadows attacked our carriage," he replied.

"Not a problem. We have spare horses that we brought along." He turned to Demetre. "Can you ride?" he asked.

Demetre nodded his head. "Of course I can."

"Very well—you and Isaac will ride one and Devin will take the other. Now let us go. We must leave this forest."

He climbed on his horse and led the way.

IV

Demetre and I rode in silence. Devin and the other riders were ahead of us, chatting. Demetre glanced over at me occasionally, checking to see how I was doing.

"We are here!" I heard Vladmir shout as he and the others brought their horses to a halt. A vast field of grass dressed with colorful fruit-laden trees appeared before us. I searched the landscape, dazzled by its splendid view.

We slowly rode to the clearing. A thick mist formed around us as the air grew moist and damp.

"What is going on?" Demetre asked. "Is this the Council?"

"I don't know. It's not like I have been here before," I responded, mesmerized at the sight.

The mist followed us as we walked. I stretched forth my hand, trying to touch the white cloud of vapor, but I couldn't. The mist shrunk back, avoiding my grasp. As I pulled my hand toward me, the mist returned again. I curiously looked down, realizing the ground we treaded on had been hidden by the fog.

Slowly, the mist began to dissipate, losing its power; it then evaporated altogether revealing a majestic paradise. To my surprise, I was now standing before a gate which opened onto a luxurious garden under a canopy of bright blue skies. With every step, I could see strange and colorful creatures leisurely roaming the grounds. Some resembled ordinary rodents such as squirrels and raccoons, but their vivid colors captured my attention. The sweet smell of what seemed to be lilac permeated the air. Birds sang all around us in a concert of perfect harmony. It seemed as if they had rehearsed their peaceful melodies. Their bodies were covered with feathers that glistened in a prism of colors under the sun.

Ahead of me I saw a colossal castle surrounded by a river. The monument was breathtaking, unlike anything I had ever laid eyes on.

"You thought you had lost me, right?" Devin asked as he and the other horsemen approached me.

"Can't really say what was going through my mind right now…" I fell short on words as I gazed at the azure blue sky. I closed my eyes and was immediately lost under the rays of the sun.

"What is this place, Devin?" Demetre asked.

"This is Justicia. It is not part of Elysium, even though the only way to get here is through one of the invisible gates. We just crossed over one of the borderlines into the Fourth Dimension."

I raised an eyebrow with a concerned look. I believed he immediately got the message.

"This is the realm where the Creator lives. This place is located in the northern part of Tristar. The Creator, his kingdom and servants are located in the middle—the Heart of Tristar; a place forbidden to the living. The Heart of Tristar is secluded from all others. Only those who died with knowledge can enter there."

I once again turned my attention to the castle and, gazing in awe, I marveled at this exquisite beauty. No creature in Elysium could've built something so majestic. White stones made up the walls, precisely placed throughout the three monumental towers. The middle tower stood higher than the others, with a golden lion statue mounted at the very top. There was a moat to be crossed before we reached its massive gates.

As we approached the moat, a man walked out to meet us. The closer he came, I was able to catch a better glimpse at his appearance. He wore a black tunic with a multicolor cloak over a beige linen shirt and a pair of black knee-high boots.

"Welcome to Justicia!" he said, greeting us with a cheerful voice.

"Vladmir, take your men now and go back to your posts. There is much to be done on this momentous day."

Vladmir turned around; the other three men were at his heels.

"Devin." The man approached Devin's horse. Devin alighted from his horse and met the man with a hug. "It has been so long. Where have you been? You don't come to visit," the man said with a cheerful smile.

"Time has been my worst enemy lately," Devin happily replied. The man turned his gaze to me. "Oh, these young ones must be Isaac Khan and Demetre Aliward. Am I right?"

"Yes, sir," I replied.

"Well, my name is Athalas—lord of the Council here in Justicia. Come down and give me a hug, young ones. Your parents are very dear to us all here."

We dismounted from our horses and hugged him. This was the most comfortable I had felt in the past couple of hours. Athalas gave me such comfort the moment he mentioned our parents.

"Let us go inside. The moon is about to take its place in the sky and we have something very special prepared for you on this night," he spoke with great expectation.

As we made our way inside the castle, my eyes could not quite believe what they gazed upon. White marble was used to build the floors; tall white columns rose up to the ceiling. A gigantic glass dome stood majestically above us. Ahead, a staircase; it swayed as though suspended in midair, glistening beautifully.

We were led up the staircase into an immense hallway. To our right was a glass window with a magnificent view of the front garden and the moat. Draped along the window was a gorgeous satin curtain. Statues were scattered along the hall; many canvases with decorative hand-painted landscapes hung on the walls.

"Did you sculpt these?" Demetre asked Athalas, closely examining the statues.

"Well, yes—some of them. We have many fine artists here." Athalas' right hand lovingly touched one of the statues as he answered.

"They are incredible," Demetre whispered as his eyes drank in the indescribable glory of this place.

"I am just glad we are safe and sound," I said, resting my left hand on Demetre's shoulder. "And that you are alive and well."

We finally came to the grand wooden door that stood at the end of the hallway. When Athalas opened the door, we caught a glimpse of a massive room artfully decorated with black and satin artifacts.

"Here are your accommodations, young ones. Inside are two separate bedrooms so you may each have some privacy. Don't forget, dinner is at seven. I will send someone to personally escort you both to the dining hall," Athalas said cheerfully.

"Thank you very much," I replied. "This is the safest we have felt since we left home. We really appreciate it."

"You are in a safe haven, young ones—many out there know your names. Many have been waiting for this very day. Know that here you will find security and peace. You have done well—bringing the Diary here." His lips curved into a gentle smile. He then made his way out of the room.

"How are you holding up?" I asked Demetre the moment the door closed. After all we had gone through, I wanted to make sure all was well with him.

Casually, he strolled over to one of the three windows. "I am alright. This is all confusing to me still. I can't hide that I am sickly worried about our parents."

The haunting reality had once again settled in. Despite all the things we had discovered on this day, the location of our parents was still unknown.

"What about the pain?" I inquired. Every word seemed to be followed by a strong urge to weep. With great restraint, I held it in. I needed to be strong right now.

He sighed. "I'm scared that it might come back. If you ask me what that pain was, I still don't know."

I rested on the settee that was placed next to the window. "What did the pain feel like?"

"Like something was crawling inside of me, desperately trying to get out." His eyes widened as he spoke. "It was as if someone was alive in me." He pressed his right hand on his chest.

The thought of witnessing Demetre suffer such pain enraged me. Ever since we were kids, I always looked after him. His dad was never one to mess with. His short temper caused Demetre to grow farther from him as the years passed. He was often alone and never one to blend in with the other boys in Agalmath.

"Remember, I am here for you. Despite all those that we meet, let's make sure our friendship is untouched. Our trust goes beyond the darkness," I affirmed.

"Yeah, I know." He nodded; a smile spread softly across his face.

After we freshened up and were dressed in clothes that seemed to have been tailored to fit us perfectly, there was a knock on the door.

Demetre reluctantly answered. Although this was supposed to be a safe haven, we were not entirely sure whether our new acquaintances could be trusted.

"Athalas is calling you all to come down for dinner. Are you ready?" It was a beautiful woman. Her beauty was enchanting; her physique was statuesque and her presence breathtaking. She spoke in a sensual tone, soft and mellow. Wavy golden hair cascaded down her back. Completely enamored by her beauty, I could not take my eyes off of hers. They were a deep blue color. I recognized these eyes; Devin had these very same eyes.

"Umm…Yeah—we…umm…we will be right down," I replied, barely able to speak.

She gave me a halfhearted smile. "Well, come on then. I have to show you where the dining hall is." Another smile followed.

"Right…" Demetre nodded in agreement. I could not help but notice her lovely garments. She wore a thin silver tiara on her head with a small red rose in the middle, a marvelous red wool coat that hung down to her knees, revealing a blouse underneath that was embellished with precious jewels, and heeled boots.

She waited politely at the door as we passed by her. She quickened her pace ahead of us, leading the way. The only sound that I could hear was her boots clicking against the marble floor. She made no attempt to make conversation whatsoever.

"Do you think Athalas really sculpted all of these statues?" Demetre whispered as we once again crossed the hall.

"I believe so. Well...that is what he said," I answered with a whisper.

She stopped suddenly.

"Well...most of them." She turned around. "I am sorry to be so impolite and not introducing myself. My mind is off somewhere else. My name is Adawnas—I am part of this Council. Forgive me if I disappoint you, but Athalas did not sculpt all these statues."

"Re-really...were you one of the sculptors?" Demetre inquired with a timid voice. Her beauty was so entrancing, it intimidated us.

She chuckled.

"No, young one, I am afraid those are not one of my accomplishments." Her eyes closely surveyed the scattered statues throughout the hall. "There are a couple of statues here that I don't recognize."

"What do you mean?" I asked, surprised at what she said.

"I do not often come to this side of the castle, but a couple of days ago, I noticed Athalas had been out for quite a long time. The members of the Council cannot stay out for too long. They must constantly keep watch over the Gates of the Fourth Dimension for any activity. Well, Athalas was out for two days, and then Timothy came to me and filled me with questions." She sighed. "He claimed that he saw new statues in this hall that appeared out of nowhere." She was silent for a moment, measuring each word carefully. "As I came to escort you to dinner, I also wanted to check on the new statues. I was stunned by so many new ones appearing so fast."

I could sense doubt behind her words. She seemed reluctant and I sensed that she was hiding something.

"So nobody knows where they came from?" Demetre asked, creasing his forehead in a sign of confusion.

She laughed softly. "This dinner tonight will be very special for you. Now let us keep on going. We cannot be late."

We continued walking, but my mind remained focused on the fact that no one knew the origin of these new statues.

"Might I ask you a question?"

She glanced over her shoulder.

"Of course…" She nodded.

"Are you also a Nephilin like Devin?" I choked as soon as the words drifted from my mouth. She gave me a melancholic stare and continued walking.

We came to another large wooden door. Intricate designs covered it from top to bottom. From all the beautiful ornaments, the two golden knobs stood out the most. Adawnas did not knock, but simply opened the door and walked right in. We followed. She bowed her head, greeting the other seven who were also here. They all bowed their heads in return. Devin was also present, dressed in similar attire as to the Council members.

There were two seats reserved for us in the far left side of the table. Adawnas sat next to Devin. There was something about Adawnas' behavior that seemed incredibly mysterious to me. I could see anxiety stamped on her face.

The door opened and everyone rose to their feet. It was Athalas. He was dressed in a regal black robe that covered his entire body.

"I must say, I love having a full house!" he exclaimed, spreading his arms to greet us two newcomers. He sat in the first chair at the head of the table.

We were respectfully silent for a while when he suddenly clapped his hands and shouted,

"Bring in the food!"

The doors of the dining hall immediately burst wide open and servants entered carrying enormous platters. At least the servants appeared to be ordinary humans. The platters were lavishly layered with a variety of meats, vegetables, fruits, desserts and pastries.

"Is this elaborate dinner all because of us?" Demetre whispered, looking at me from the corner of his eyes.

I looked around at the table and simply smiled. "I don't know, but I must say…I really don't mind." A soft laugh followed my answer.

To our surprise, a very merry tune started to play. To my left, there were two masters of music dressed in very colorful costumes. Their hands used a bow to skillfully play their instruments, which were etched with floral patterns and inlaid with precious gems.

"It is an honor to meet you both, Isaac and Demetre," a raspy deep voice spoke from behind. "Allow me to introduce myself to you both. My name is Ely. Are you finding our accommodations suitable?"

"Yes, very much!" Demetre replied with a mouth full of pork and chicken. I shook my head and scoffed.

"Yes, thank you very much for your concern. Where are you from, sir?" I asked him, taking a nibble from the pork.

"I have been everywhere. I am one of the very men chosen by the Creator to guard the Diary from the beginning of all things. It's amazing to observe how the world is starting to change so radically because of a wee little book."

"Little?" I asked, incredulous. "From what I have seen today, this book is anything but little."

"Little to those who have more power than others. Trust me when I say this—once you encounter true power, the big things grow strangely dim before your eyes."

"Who are you talking to, Isaac?" Devin asked from the other side of the table.

"To this gentleman, of course!" Demetre replied.

Devin was perplexed.

"What is wrong?" I asked, looking around.

"There is no one here...no one here but us," Devin replied with a confused look. Adawnas shot Devin a cold stare and bowed her head.

I looked again and there was nobody.

"I am sure someone was here." I stared at Demetre, confounded.

"I saw him, Isaac…with my own two eyes. I know there was someone here!" Demetre affirmed.

"Attention!" Athalas shouted as he clapped his hands. "It is a delight as always to have dinner with all of you here tonight; members of this Council who since the dawn of days have been guarding the Diary and those who keep it. Tonight, we have three very special guests with us. I would like the Council to personally meet Isaac Khan and Demetre Aliward, and to greet once again our old son, Devin." They all applauded.

"Brave ones that have come here to bring the Diary to its rightful place. It might be a surprise to the both of you, but we have been guarding you for eighteen years."

I surveyed the dinner guests and Adawnas' fearful expression caught my attention. She sat quite still, her eyes fixed on Athalas.

"Through our mighty gifts, we have been able to protect you and the safety of the Diary."

"Yeah…they have done a terrific job. Look at where our parents are…" Demetre mumbled.

"In order to honor you, we have personally prepared a rare delicacy. It is the Purple Soul, the purest wine you will ever find!" Two servants approached us. They brought in two golden grails with the emblem of a dark lion and handed them to Demetre and me.

"Now a toast—to the brave ones!" He lifted up his glass of wine; the other members raised their glasses in unison.

"Do not drink it!" Adawnas shouted suddenly.

Everyone froze.

"Do not drink it," she repeated.

"I beg your pardon, Adawnas." Athalas spoke in a harsh tone, completely opposite from the soft, kind voice I had heard before.

"I will not allow this to take place, Athalas," she explained.

"Are you to do something you might come to regret later?" His voice was dark and foreboding. His face had become flushed; the veins on his neck were now visible.

"I am not going to regret this in any way." She turned to face Demetre and me. "This wine is poisoned. He—they want to destroy you. You are here because they want to destroy you both!"

"That is absurd!" Athalas fiercely pointed his finger at her. "How dare you come against us in such a way? You should know better, Nephilin. No wonder your kind has been hiding in the shadows of the world for all these years. Guards!"

Guards clothed in black armor marched in the moment Athalas was done speaking.

"Tell them first! Tell them how you have fallen," she yelled as the guards surrounded her. "Tell them how you sold your soul years ago!"

"Why must I do anything you order me to do? Who are you before me, incompetent creature? Have you not seen or understood that you are an aberration? Your kind was never meant to be born." As Athalas spoke, his teeth clattered. His hands moved in a strange, serpent-like manner.

I was in a complete state of shock. Not only was Adawnas a Nephilin, but the place I had thought to be safe was the darkest yet.

"You will regret this choice, Athalas," she said as the guards pressed her down. I looked closely at them. There was something familiar about them. I realized they were also Nephilins. Their vibrant blue eyes were the clearest evidence of this fact.

"Regret? Do you not see the ones that hold you down? They are just like you!" Athalas contested.

"Other Nephilins in Justicia," Devin mumbled in a somber voice.

"Yes, servants of the Dark One," Athalas roared.

"What are you doing?" I protested, rushing toward Adawnas.

"You better stay where you are," Athalas commanded with a hiss. The other members that were seated rose up quickly and charged toward Demetre and me. My teeth cringed with desperation.

The color of Athalas' face changed to ashen gray, and his eyes turned a crimson red. Slowly he reached out for the knife that lay on the platter of pork roast.

"You know, Adawnas," he spoke, slowly moving toward her, measuring every word. "Your beauty is indeed something out of this world, but it is nothing that I cannot destroy. You should have been wiser." He held the knife near her throat. His other hand caressed her face.

I looked around and noticed the other members of the Council as motionless as the statues in their grand halls. I looked at Devin as he stared at the scene in shock.

"Do something." I mouthed the words to him but there was no response.

Adawnas let out a terrifying scream. Athalas held the knife against her shoulder, deliberately carving deep into her flesh.

"Immortals only until something wounds this pale, silky skin...unlike me, of course," he spoke as she shrieked in torment.

"Stop it!" I yelled in agony.

Athalas' gaze met mine.

"Guards, take her to prison. I believe she will be tantalized by the entertainment we offer in the dark places of this castle." Athalas scoffed as he approached Adawnas' wounds and kissed them.

The guards bound her with thick metal chains. I looked into her frightened eyes as the tears were streaming down her face. Devin's eyes glimmered as he bowed his head and closed his eyes.

"Pity...I did not want you to find out like this. I swear I was going to be somewhat merciful, I really was," Athalas uttered in a malefic tone.

"My chest...my chest..." Demetre screamed without warning. I shot him a look, only to find him pressing his hand on his chest once again.

"Long have we played this game, haven't we, Demetre?" Athalas growled menacingly and then hissed once again.

"Please, stop! He does not need this!" I tried to go to his aid but one of the Council members violently grabbed my arm and held me back. I did not struggle for I knew it was useless.

"Long have I watched you, chased you in your dreams, and taunted you. But the time has finally come. Bring the box."

One of the human servants that had helped serve the food approached Athalas with a box that looked very similar to the box that housed the Diary.

"Where did you get that?" I questioned.

"Remember, you all came here seeking a safe hiding place for the Diary? Well, Devin handed it to me the moment after you were accompanied to your rooms," Athalas answered with a peculiar smile. "Have they told you yet, Isaac?"

I was very confused. "Told me what?"

"Nephilins are damned. There is no redemption for their kind whatsoever. They were conceived because a human and a Fallen Star had lain together. In their veins, betrayal runs freely. Devin and Adawnas are what I call 'peculiar exceptions.' They seem to struggle against the will inside of them to serve the darkness daily—especially Devin. He has wanted to kill you both since the first day he found you in the woods. That is why they were the only Nephilins here. Because I had to pretend to believe that their souls could actually be saved."

The screams coming from Demetre grew louder.

"My beautiful puppet here has kept me much informed." He approached Demetre and gently laid hands on his shoulder. "Oh, how I love you like a son, young one. For eighteen years we have been apart. I had to stay here, isolated, waiting for your blood to mature so it could be shed." Athalas' eyes narrowed. "Your parents were really special." He emphasized the last word with a malevolent tone.

I could see Demetre's gaze. Utter horror consumed him. He struggled unsuccessfully, trying to get out of his grasp. Athalas continued to caress him, but not long after, Demetre fell unconscious.

"You look so much like your father, it really is a shame he died," he hauntingly spoke.

Died? I was shocked, frozen. I felt anger rising up in me, but I was held captive by its power, unable to release its sting

"Died? How? When?" I cried.

Athalas chuckled. "Don't worry, Isaac, you are no exception. They all died peacefully together in the fields near Agalmath. Their bodies were well hidden from all of you."

Time stopped. I stopped. Thoughts rushed into my head—confusion became resident in my mind. Sorrow fought the rage within my heart. Both of these emotions were demanding my attention, controlling my whole body.

"You…in…insolent…coward!" I screamed. I could not control myself. I wanted to kill him, chop him up into pieces and throw them to some wild beast.

"Why are you doing this, Athalas? I thought you were a protector, a lord!" I exclaimed adamantly.

Athalas' expression was undecipherable momentarily, until suddenly it came forth.

"I simply realized eighteen years ago that the enemy is stronger than any power in this universe," he said, his voice booming throughout the hall. "I realized that if the Creator is as powerful as they proclaim, then how come not all of this is gone?" His voice intensified. "How come evil has been allowed to thrive underground for so long without any…intervention?"

"Mankind suffers now through their own choice. Humans chose to surrender to the darkness the day they betrayed the Creator," I contested, struggling to break free from the grasp of the one who had ahold of my arm.

"It was the best choice they ever made," Athalas replied; his eyes were red with fury. "I will show you what a foolish thing it is to oppose us."

Athalas got ahold of the box. His eyes widened and a dim light shone from his pupils. The box cracked slowly until it violently exploded. Athalas let out a perplexing laugh.

"Beautiful! We have done well, men. The fake Diary worked wonders, wouldn't you say?" He clapped his hands. His sinister sneer sent chills down my spine. The other seven laughed in unison.

"Fake?" I fell short on words as I tried to understand what was happening.

"This box was cursed by me the day I sold my soul to the Dark One. Your parents carried a fake when they left to go to Agalmath. I kept the real one here because I knew one day you would walk up to my doorstep and come to me. Bring in the real Diary," Athalas commanded with a hiss.

The room grew darker, the candles went out and a very dim light emerged. My eyes were fixed on the light, trying to comprehend its source. My breathing accelerated as I saw the light shaping itself into what appeared to be a man. Of course, I would be fooling myself if I really believed that this was an ordinary human. It did not take long for me to see who it was.

"Athalas, I must say after waiting all these years, my heart rejoices on accomplishing our first task." Cyro's voice echoed as the light revealed his distinct figure. He glared at me coldly.

"So this is why you showed 'mercy' unto us—you knew we were going to come here," I retorted. He ignored me.

Cyro cleared the table of all food and utensils with one swipe of his arm. Gently, he bent down and picked up Demetre and laid him on the table. Athalas seemed ecstatic.

Demetre's voice ripped through the atmosphere.

"No!" he cried, writhing in pain on the table with eyes as black as the night sky.

"Finally, he will come to us in flesh and blood." Cyro rubbed both of his hands as his eyes examined Demetre. "Long have we waited, long have we stayed in the shadows of the Abyss—but no more." Cyro removed the dagger he carried on his waist.

I closed my eyes. Memories flashed in my mind. It killed me to know that I was defenseless and could do nothing to help Demetre. Despite my fear for my dear friend, I could not understand one critical fact: how could they have the real Diary?

Everything came to an abrupt halt when the walls began to shudder. I heard bangs and thuds coming from the outer parts of the castle.

"What is going on?" Cyro questioned.

I looked up to discover the ceiling cracking slowly. The walls whirled, trembling violently. Large portions of the ceiling began to crumble and crash down on us. At that moment, I saw an animal crawl through the opening. Its eagle-like wings fluttered around, its face resembled a lion's. By the looks of the animal, it seemed to be an Aquila, a legendary creature believed to be nothing but a myth.

It flew directly to the table where Demetre lay. The moment its eyes met Cyro's, the animal hissed and leaped upon him. He tried to flee from its grasp but the Aquila had Cyro by the throat, detaching his head from the rest of the body. I knew he was not going to die, I knew this was just going to be a delay, but it was one that had come at the perfect time.

"Isaac, make for the hall!" Devin yelled as he deviated from the falling debris. I looked around and tried to locate the door. The dust rose like mist on an early morning. I glanced back and noticed Demetre's body was no longer on the table.

"Devin!" I called repeatedly but there was no response. More and more Aquilas came crashing through the ceiling and attacked the other Council members. I slipped out unnoticed through the same wooden door I had entered from just hours before.

Running through the hall of the castle, my rapid footsteps echoed amidst the loud sounds of rubble and muffled screams that came from the dining hall.

"Devin!" I shouted, running frantically in search of my ally.

I looked over my shoulder only to see an evil black shadow taking Athalas' shape.

"Yes, run, little boy. You cannot hide!" he shouted ferociously as his body disintegrated like a black vapor back into the air.

My arms were restrained and I could feel my face being held by a firm grasp. My feet abandoned the floor beneath them as the nerves of my body were in excruciating pain. Out of the dust of the falling debris, he appeared.

"Please, we both know it only takes a wink for me to destroy you," Athalas spoke. "Had you not had a greater purpose, I would have killed you the moment you set foot in Justicia."

My breathing got heavier, my heart pounded violently, and my hands trembled from fear. I looked deep into his eyes only to find that they were as dark and void as the midnight sky.

"At least you have already destroyed your own self," I muttered with difficulty.

"Let him go, Athalas!" I heard Devin's voice boom. As I looked over my shoulder, all I was able to see was Demetre's body lying on the marble floor. Seconds later, my body landed with a thud as Athalas' body was tossed halfway around the hall by Devin's merciless attack.

Soon after, they broke off with powerful attacks. My eyes struggled to keep up with their swift and agile moves.

To my surprise, three Aquilas had found us. They watched the fight and positioned themselves very close. They were alert, poised and ready for an attack. Devin had a grip on Athalas' arm and with a simple twist, he tossed him upward. A vicious attack followed. The Aquilas immediately attacked his body as it was suspended in midair.

"What happened?" I asked with heavy gasps.

"I had to call some friends," Devin said with a grin.

Devin carefully picked up Demetre's body. Bruises and cuts were scattered all over his face; his shirt was ripped right above the shoulder. My heart ached to see my friend going through such distress.

"You called the Aquilas?" I asked, surprised.

"Yes. I was lucky that these Aquilas were here still. Now, let us go. Adawnas is being held captive in the prison of the castle. We must get to her and make our way out of Justicia immediately."

The agonizing screams of the other Council members had grown fainter. The Aquilas destroyed the hall as we made our way down a flight of stairs. I glanced at Demetre only to see that he was still unconscious.

"Why would they need a prison on this side of Tristar?" I asked.

"I would assume that after the fall, precautions were necessary," Devin responded.

Not long after, we stood in front of an old iron gate with the word "Justice" engraved on its corroded surface.

"Is this it?" I asked. Fear slowly crept in as I stared at the gate.

"Yes, this is it." He carefully laid Demetre on the floor, opening the gate with his bare hands.

"Couldn't she do that herself?" I asked in disbelief, seeing how easy it was to open the gate.

"I am assuming that this will get a bit more complicated," he replied, picking Demetre up from the cold floor.

A putrid odor permeated the atmosphere. The prison was dark and one could hear the never-ending drops of water that dripped from the ceiling. There was also a river inside the prison. The sound of the flowing waters resounded all around the place.

"Adawnas!" Devin shouted as we ran through the winding chambers, desperately searching inside every cell. I was astounded to see torture chambers and chastity rooms here in the castle.

We stumbled across a gigantic cell; its bars were wrapped in a red, incandescent light.

"What do you suppose is this foul smell?" The pungent smell made my eyes water.

"Who is there?" a broken voice spoke from inside. "Devin?"

"Adawnas?" Devin shouted vehemently. "Is that you?"

I heard her rapid footsteps approaching the red bars. The moment she touched them, she was brusquely thrown back, hitting the wall.

"It is protected," I muttered.

"I must find a way," Devin said, decidedly.

He laid Demetre on the cold floor. The moment Demetre's body was laid, the bars quaked and the red light vanished within seconds.

"Did you see that?" I asked in surprise.

"Yes, but I don't understand..." As he pondered on the reason the bars had trembled, I pushed Demetre's body closer to the cell.

"It's his body...I suppose it is the energy inside of him," Adawnas spoke in a quivering voice. "Devin, we must leave. They are building an army. The bodies are all in here, rotting in this dark hole."

"Bodies," I mumbled. "Try breaking the bars now, Devin," I said as I looked at Demetre's unconscious body and the effect it had against the red lights. What kind of strength was in him that could cause the bars to weaken?

Devin tossed his own body against the lightless bars. They broke apart instantly. Adawnas was free.

"The stench is of human corpses. The Council was secretly murdering humans from small villages in Elysium in order to build a Shadow army. That is why Athalas was out of Justicia for so long. They have been left here to rot," Adawnas sobbed.

"Killing humans," I mumbled. "The Council was murdering them...and bringing them here...my parents...." I was slowly overshadowed by my thoughts when I felt Devin's hand pressing on my shoulder.

"Now is not the time. We must flee from this place. Demetre needs aid."

I nodded slowly, took a deep breath and composed myself.

"Which way should we go?" I asked, trying to spot a way out.

"If we follow the river we can probably find a way out of here," Adawnas replied.

"Adawnas, carry Demetre," instructed Devin. "Isaac, let me carry you so we can gain more time."

I wasn't too fond of the idea but time was our adversary. The moment Adawnas had Demetre and Devin had me, we took off at an amazing speed. I held on firmly, trying not to lose my balance. I could feel the adrenaline rushing through my veins; my cheeks were flapping rapidly.

"Stop!" Devin yelled. We came to an abrupt halt as a wall burst out of the ground in front of us.

"What is this?" Adawnas asked in confusion and awe.

I looked to my right and saw the shadow of a man standing near one of the cells.

"Over there!" I pointed in the shadow's direction. "Do you see it?"

"What do you see, Isaac?" Devin asked, confused.

I climbed down from his back and walked toward the shadow.

"Isaac, where are you going?" Devin asked as he followed.

"I know I saw something—or someone. He is right there." I tried to show him where the shadow was but he could not see it. A thick gray mist gradually rose around us. It touched my face, hands and neck.

"Do you see this now? Any of you?" I shouted. Judging by Devin's surprised expression, I knew that this time, he saw the mist—it emerged into the form of a man.

"Ely?" I asked as the mist shaped the traces of the face.

"You have not done well by coming to this place." His voice sounded more like a whisper and his eyes were hollow. I noticed he did not have legs, but he stood above the mist.

"Ely?" Devin asked. "What are you doing here?"

"I am being held captive. I have been here from the time you went out to help Isaac and Demetre. The Council discovered that I had informed you about the Fallen Star that sought you. Immediately I was thrown in the Prison of Despair."

Devin's eyes widened. He bowed his head slightly, shaking it with disappointment.

"Who arrested you, Ely?" Adawnas asked.

"A blond girl—beautiful but wicked. Her face was as sweet and kind as a summer morning, but her heart is as evil and as dark as Athalas' soul."

"What exactly is this Prison of Despair?" I asked.

"Why, dear boy." Ely's voice was cold. "You are in it as we speak."

My breathing failed. My eyes met Devin's.

The mist, along with Ely's color, changed from gray to dark red.

"You only see here a part of me. I have mastered the ability to communicate by sending a part of me out, but the place that I am in is not in this world. We are now near the entrance of the Abyss where the Shadows and the other foul creatures of the world are. The Creator constructed this prison only for those who willingly gave up their lives to serve the Darkness. I am locked deep in the dungeons. Athalas sent me to the darkest place so I would not be able to reach you. I was lucky to have never mentioned to him my ability to transport myself."

I looked at Adawnas and Devin and could see the anguish on their faces as they listened to their friend's account.

"You have not done well by coming this way." As Ely spoke, a brick barrier sprung forth from the ground. "Have you not noticed how there are no soldiers guarding this prison?" he asked. "The prison guards itself."

"It…self?" I muttered.

"When the red bars were destroyed, a curse was placed upon you by the prison. It was appointed to follow the orders of the head of the Council, Athalas, whatever they may be."

Silence loomed over us for a moment. We could no longer hear the cry of the Aquilas or the rumble of falling debris.

"What are we to do?" Devin asked, his voice filled with despair.

"I apologize, but that I do not know," Ely replied. Unexpectedly, the mist slowly began to vanish.

"What is happening?" I asked him. "Where are you going?"

"My body cannot support the transport for long. I must go back to my body or I might turn to dust and ash." His voice cracked. "Good tidings to you and may the Creator guide you." As quick as a breath, the mist dissipated.

Loneliness came over me. Despair knocked on my heart's door, trying to make its way in. A million thoughts tried to invade my mind and I was trying with great difficulty to resist.

"What to do now?" Adawnas asked softly. Her bright blue eyes did not blink; they focused on the spot Ely had just vanished from.

Devin sighed. "I have not the answer to your question now," he admitted, standing like a statue, barely breathing.

"Visitors? Do we have visitors?" a broken voice reverberated around us. "Where d'you come from, eh?"

None of us replied.

"Oh, I do see now. Visitors don't answer. Pity to know ye will rot hea'," the voice spoke once again. Devin looked at Adawnas and me.

The ground shook violently.

"Why do ye fea' desperation, eh? I can be your closes' friend. Do not judge I becoz you can't see I, eh."

I heard rumbles coming from behind me. When I turned, I saw a door being drawn on the mildewed wall.

"I show you way out of hea'. Desperation will never betray ye. Now answer, what are your names?" This time, the voice sounded loving, yet malefic.

"My name is Isaac," I responded. "These are Adawnas, Devin, and the sleeping one is Demetre."

There was no response from the voice.

"It vanished," I murmured as I looked at the door.

Footsteps were then heard, coming in our direction. We were on high alert as they quickened their pace.

"Do you see it?" Devin yelled. "Do you see it?"

I looked around but was unable to see anything.

"See what?" I asked. I looked behind me and saw a disfigured being standing in front of the door, its skin as shriveled as an old prune, its eyes as golden as the rays of the sun, its teeth glistening in the dark. I looked at its arms and hands and saw that they were disproportionate for its size. It had no legs, but the tail of a snake, covered with thin gray stripes.

I stood there paralyzed with fear. The creature's low snarls sent shivers down my spine.

"My, my, who do we have hea', eh?" the creature whispered. "Isaac, son of Dustin and Diane Khan." After it had finished speaking, it dragged itself toward Devin. "My, my, and hea'? An immortal at the entrance o' death?"

"We have not died," Devin replied, enraged, under heavy breaths. "Adawnas was sent here by Athalas. We came to rescue her."

The creature hissed softly.

"Amusing thing—the human heart, eh? It'll get so caught on things of passin', no? Shame to know his heart died. I felt it comin' but I could not say much."

Devin took a step forward.

"What are—"

"Devin Analiel, born from..." the creature interrupted Devin, its eyes gazing at the door. "This one...hard choice..." It made its way toward the door and banged its head against it.

"I cannot see...No...can't see parents of he, eh..." It stopped abruptly and looked at Adawnas. "What about she? What might ye be?"

"As immortal as he," she coldly responded, her fingers tightened into fists.

"No, no, immortals no. Give me dead, dead ones, eh?" it snarled as it approached Demetre.

"Demetre Aliward...this one...dead...eh?" It smiled.

"Not dead. This one is not dead!" I yelled.

The creature laughed hysterically and then quickly wrapped its tail around my body.

"Young one, this one died...in his heart, eh? You cannot sees what Death sees," it hissed as its tail released me. "Death sees the heart that no one can. You sees outside as I see in."

"So you are Death?" Devin questioned. "That is your name?"

It once again growled, its eyes meeting Devin's. "Indeed, I is."

"Why have you come to encounter us?" Adawnas asked.

Death looked at Adawnas and leered at her with a grotesque smile.

"This immortal, not so fool, eh? Death comes to show ye this door. Secret, dark ways behin' it, eh?"

"What is behind it?" Devin asked. Death looked at all of us with inviting eyes. With a churlish tone, it started to sing a dark song.

"Oh eyes, for those who don't see.

Poor, little, witty hearts that cling to ye

Through the darkness they shall go

Let darkness take them whole."

As Death sang the sad, short song, the door burst open. Screams of agony and pain resounded from the other side. My soul weighed down inside, a weight much too unbearable to carry. My heart felt as heavy as a rock. Devin screamed, Adawnas cried bitterly. Demetre did not wake up, nor did he move. I approached the door to investigate what was on the other side. The screams were deafening.

Looking down, I saw many bodies aligned, resting against a dry wasteland. They were all in deep sleep; their features were hard to discern. I could see their cracked, dry skin, their bodies clothed in old rags. The demographic was mixed: men, women and children, forming a straight line as far as the eye could see.

I felt my body descend toward the bodies. I struggled not to go, trying desperately to find a way to stop, but I could not.

"Ye must sees, eh? Ye must sees where they are," Death's voice whispered in my ear as I continued my descent. "Their bodies lies in this prison, eh?"

My feet touched the dry ground. A putrid smell lingered. I was immobile, not knowing what to do or where to go. In front of me was a man, with pale skin and dark purple bags under his eyes. He had no hair on his head, but a full beard. I noticed his breathing was very shallow. To my right, I heard a rattling noise. I saw a dark snake approaching the body. I did not dare move.

The snake dragged itself among the bodies, carefully making its way. Its scaly dark skin shimmered with every movement. I did not understand why it was here or how it could survive under these harsh conditions. I stepped back as the snake approached the man, its yellow eyes fixed on his face. It gazed at him for a while and the moment he took a breath, the snake hissed. A little dim light sprang forth from the man's slightly closed mouth and made its way inside the snake's mouth. The man's breathing stopped and his skin lost its faded color.

"Their bodies lie in cold places while spirits sleep. The souls are mad with hunger and vengeance. Ye needed to see," Death spoke.

"Who is doing this?" I asked in a trembling voice.

Death slowly bowed its head. "Master not good 'nymore, eh. Heart as cold as ice, eyes as hollow as night." After it spoke, it let out soft sobs.

"You mean to tell me Athalas is your master?" I asked, frightened of the answer I was about to get.

Death slowly reached out to touch my face; I recoiled resentfully.

"Yes...yes indeed..."

As my eyes were set on the man, a soft breeze blew and everything followed it. Like a morning wind that comes over a field of dandelions and carries them along, the Prison of Despair, and everything else, was taken by the wind, slowly fading away. A loud explosion echoed and I was sucked back to Justicia.

I was shocked when I saw the magnificent castle set aflame. The beautiful columns were all destroyed by the fire, the garden polluted by the smoke. The roars of the Aquilas were loud and ferocious. Behind me I saw Devin, Adawnas and Demetre.

"We are out!" I yelled. "We made it."

"How did we...what happened?" Devin asked as he composed himself. Adawnas wiped away her tears.

"Isaac!" a hollow voice echoed in the atmosphere. I glanced over my shoulder and recognized Athalas and the other Council members stationed at the entrance to the castle. Devin clasped my arm and immediately we were on our feet, running as fast as we could. They transmitted guttural sounds as their bodies vanished into shadows. They were acting more like animals now. The ghastly screeches sounded terrifying, like wolves howling at the moon.

Ahead, we saw the mist that had brought us to Justicia. Without a moment's hesitation we entered the mist. There was lightning inside, bright flashes that crossed from one place to another. It was as though the mist could sense something evil was coming. Shortly after we entered it, misshapen shadows appeared. They moved rapidly through the mist to the point where my eyes failed to keep up with them. I began to hear the same rattling sounds I had heard before.

The mist darkened and the shadows became invisible. The only thing that hung in the air was the terrifying rattling sound.

I felt branches from the trees brush against my face; we were back in the forest, back in the same place where Cyro had spared us. The moment we stepped foot outside of the mist, I felt pain strike my body. Not only did I feel it, but Adawnas and Devin fell flat on the ground, writhing in agony as well.

"Insolent fools. Did you really think you could flee from us?" Athalas spoke. I looked at him and noticed how different he looked. He was clothed in shades of black and gray, bearing the symbol of a dark lion on his chest.

I rolled on the ground in desperation. My body was afflicted from head to toe by his power. I was defenseless.

"Beautiful thing, isn't it? To see one like you being taken by one like me. You will not die tonight, but you will be taken to them—the ones that badly need you. You are just like your parents."

Athalas swiftly looked at Adawnas. His eyes were filled with rage. He stepped closer to her and slapped her across the face.

"Insolent fool! You knew I did not intend to kill our guests. I just wanted to put them to sleep so the Dark One could have his way with them!"

I heard footsteps approaching.

"Ah! My friends have arrived." Athalas stood to his feet and laughed. "It really is pitiful to know that this is how it all will end, isn't it?"

"Shadows," Devin whispered; his body lay pinned to the ground.

"Yes—all wanting to devour *you*. Honestly, the only thing standing between you and death right now is me."

After he spoke, the Shadows let out a series of screeches. Some were high pitched, others low, but they were all ghoulish.

"I am pretty sure you know the reason why I am here," Athalas said as he let out a laugh.

"I am not giving him to you, Atha—" Devin protested, but before he could finish, one of the Shadows attacked him with a bite on the neck. Another one swiftly arrived and stole Demetre's body away.

"Before you finish that sentence, I would carefully consider your words. If you want, you can freely and willingly come with me," Athalas spoke as he walked toward me. "I promise you won't come to any harm," he said with a sneer.

Hastily, Athalas retrieved his sword and swiftly cut a small incision on my chest. I was paralyzed with fear. The pain from the blade was excruciating. "I would consider the option, young one. You do not know what lies ahead."

"Your power is temporal, Athalas. You know it," Adawnas spoke in a halting voice.

"Are you sure of this, Adawnas? How could my power be so temporal if the Darkness has endured this long? How temporal will it be if I am the conqueror of Death?"

Devin struggled, but managed to raise himself up with a wound on his neck.

"Because"—Devin could barely speak—"of people...like you...fools like you." He tried to attack Athalas, but was much too weak.

"The immortal Nephilin is finally damaged!" Athalas clapped his hands gleefully.

Athalas' eyes turned red and opened wide as he slowly turned his head to my direction. I was still bleeding from my chest, and I knew my blood was what he needed to open the book. He did not speak a word, but I sensed that he was penetrating my thoughts, speaking into my mind.

The pain increased. My vision dimmed and I visualized myself burning in a lake of fire. My flesh was detaching from my body and slowly melting away. I could not die in the fire, nor could the pain be stopped. As I burned, I felt something crawling on my neck. I reached for it only to find maggots eating at my flesh. My heart was pounding violently in my chest, almost exploding. I felt the maggots crawling over my organs, feasting on my burning flesh.

Seconds after it had begun, the vision faded. My sight gradually returned to me. I heard muffled screams, footsteps and the clanging of metal. My surroundings fell silent and the temperature dropped quickly. I had no control over my body. All sound faded into a deathly silence.

V

My body returned to life. Slowly, I felt my senses return to me. My eyes opened to see that I was locked in a beautiful room. There were enormous black curtains hanging down over large glass windows, a regal bed with two lions carved on the bedside dresser. The carpet had a delicately crafted floral pattern and a sweet fragrance lingered in the air.

I noticed my clothing was different: clean and ornate. I wore a black waistcoat over a black leather vest, a gray overcoat that fell to my knees with solid black boots. As I turned, I approached the mirror hanging on the wall to my left. Reaching for my chest, I could feel that the cut Athalas had made was still there.

I realized I was completely alone. I ran toward the sturdy wooden door, knocking desperately.

"Anyone there?" I yelled, hoping someone would find me here. The room was fully lit by torches.

I turned around to open the curtains so I could see where I was and I discovered a marvelous city under the gray skies. The beautiful houses all had very similar architectural characteristics, with huge pillars and gigantic windows.

I was alone and without the slightest idea of where I was. Eventually, I heard the door creak behind me. As I turned, I saw a man standing there. He was very tall with long blond hair, a fair complexion, and his eyes were such a brilliant blue that they seemed to shimmer.

"Please, come with me," he instructed, gesturing the way with his right hand.

"Where am I?" I asked apprehensively as I studied him. His height was intimidating.

"Please...come *now*." He ignored my question completely. Without contesting, I followed. As I walked down the gigantic hall, my mind raced, trying to recognize this place. The structure of the hall was breathtaking. Red veins stretched up to the ceiling on the marble walls. An ornate fireplace was situated on my left. It was quite obvious that it hadn't been used for quite some time.

We came to a sudden stop. An eerie moment of silence followed.

"This is Billyth, located in the northern part of Elysium. Now, no more questions."

I was silent and fearful of what was about to happen. My heart beat wildly and drops of sweat dripped down onto my shirt.

From behind us, a door opened and a beautiful young girl sauntered in. She had blond hair with the sparkling blue eyes, and her ivory skin was flawless. She wore a red overcoat stamped with designs and patterns. I could not see anything else but the familiar red coat. Then it struck me—I was in complete shock. She was the girl from my dream.

"Please, what is taking so long, Azaziel?" Her voice carried a soft melody. As she spoke, it was as if I was listening to a beautiful song.

"I apologize, Nephele." He turned his gaze to me. *"Please come now."*

He turned around and kept on walking. I followed. Nephele waited until I walked past her. I felt fear rushing through my veins. These people were intimidatingly beautiful, powerful and from another time and place.

We arrived in a crowded throne.

"Please follow me. You are one of our honored guests," Nephele whispered in my ear.

I hesitated.

"Why would I do that?" I asked.

She giggled softly. "Do you remember what Athalas did to you and to your friends?" The very thought of it made me shiver. "Trust me when I say to you that I can make that feel like a small tickle. Now please, *kindly* follow me."

The people that were present all had the same characteristics: blue eyes, pale skin and undeniable power. As Nephele, Azaziel and I walked down the aisle, everyone bowed their heads. I suppose they were paying tribute to these two beings. Before us stood a sublime dark throne. Azaziel and Nephele took their place on the right side.

"Please stay on the left side of the throne, Isaac," Nephele spoke gracefully. She fixed her eyes firmly toward a small door to our right.

Though no one spoke audibly, it was clear that they understood each other.

From a distance, I saw three people walking down the hall. I could tell it was Devin and Adawnas, but the other one wasn't very clear until they were closer—it was Athalas. My heart leaped when I realized Athalas carried Demetre's body. Devin and Adawnas had their heads bowed as they walked in, their faces expressionless.

"Ah! The prodigal children have come home! While some of us hide here, you two are brave enough to go out on your own and try to live a life never chosen for you," Nephele said.

Neither one of them replied with any gestures or words. They looked frightened.

"I must say, I really admire you two. Denying your nature like that—leaving Billyth and joining with the Council for so long, only to see it fall afterwards… To think that you both left in secret, believing in the foolishness of a new life for our kind." She looked at me. "May this be a lesson to *all* who oppose the Darkness!"

All the while, the only thought that permeated my mind was one—*my friend is not dead.* Most importantly, the Diary hadn't been opened then.

Athalas walked to the middle of the group and dropped Demetre down on the floor. Demetre wore only a white cloak and his pants. His chest was completely bare. Demetre's body landed with a thud. Nephele shot a piercing glance toward Athalas. Without warning, Athalas let out an agonizing scream.

"Be careful how you handle him. You have made him suffer enough already," she declared.

Athalas fell to his knees; the pain subsided.

Those present in the room created a circle around Demetre's body.

I was confused more than ever now. First, they all wanted us because of our blood, but now they wanted to protect us? Why did I have to stay next to this black throne alongside Nephele and Azaziel? What was going on?

Nephele reached behind the black throne and removed a box. Engraved on the front was the symbol I had seen before; its ornate design and detailed jewel work closely resembled the box that carried the Diary.

Upon opening the box, a soft voice whispered in the room. None of us were able to understand what the voice said. She removed the book from inside, letting the box drop to the floor.

"Isaac, I hope this opens up your eyes to so many things you were unaware of." She came closer to me, leaving Azaziel on the other side.

"I don't assume your guardians have told you about Demetre, have they?" She kept her eyes firmly on Devin and Adawnas.

"I am afraid not…but I've known him my whole life."

"That is what your foolish mind thinks. Demetre is not to be this fragile, innocent little man." She stepped down the small staircase, approaching Demetre's body. She knelt next to him, her hands caressing his face slowly, her eyes gazing at him adoringly.

"You are probably wondering why you are standing next to this throne, in front of so many of us."

"Can't say that I am not," I said, my gaze fixed on hers.

"Well, your friend Demetre is actually a lot more important than you think. You see, the pain he felt on his chest was actually the Fallen Star waking up inside of him."

My eyes widened as I heard the word that caused so much fear in me.

"What do you mean? Fallen…what…Demetre?" I stuttered as I tried to make sense of things.

"Yes. One of the Fallen Stars—one of the generals of Darkness to be more precise." Nephele stood up and walked back up to the throne.

"It shocks me your friends did not tell you. You did not only think they were protecting you two only for your blood, correct?" A malefic smile appeared on her face.

I closed my eyes, my fists tightened firmly. "I still don't understand why I am standing here still."

"We are to give you a choice. One that we hope you will honor," Azaziel responded quickly.

Devin and Adawnas set their eyes on me. I guess they knew what he was going to ask me.

"You probably don't know this but your abilities will soon awaken. Not only do you descend directly from the bloodline of the Council, but your maturity will also bring forth special gifts."

"What do you mean? I also have special abilities in me?"

Azaziel shot a cold stare at Devin and Adawnas. "What great friends you have, Isaac! I suppose they did not tell you this for their own protection," he said sarcastically.

"Isaac, please don't listen to him." Devin approached me, only to be restrained by two Nephilins that grabbed ahold of his arms. Seeing Devin and Adawnas so confined was something that was hard to comprehend.

"Please, stop being so insolent. You two are already a disgrace to our kind. This could have taken place a lot earlier if you two were not so incompetent," shouted Nephele. "Let us continue, please."

I did not know whom I could trust now. Was there a special reason I was not aware of the true meaning of their protection? Were they *really* protecting me? These Nephilins hadn't killed me yet; did that make them trustworthy?

"We want to give you the choice of becoming one of us," Azaziel said with a crooked smile.

"You mean...becoming a Nephilin?" I asked, afraid of the answer that was to come.

"Precisely," confirmed Nephele. "You could be as strong as we are. And of course, it would be my pleasure to turn you."

"And how would that take place?" I asked eagerly.

She put both of her hands together and walked closer to me.

"I would sleep with you, Isaac. It would not be painful at all, but immensely pleasurable. Trust me," she said, smiling.

I looked at Demetre lying on the floor. Life was almost leaving his weak body.

"How can that be if Athalas has not become one of you?"

Nephele smiled.

"Athalas sold his soul to Lucifer directly. Thus, there was no need to turn him. As for you, you can't do that. Your only way is to become what we are, Isaac."

There was a pause. I was troubled and weary.

"It seems you still have to think about what we are offering you," Nephele said, stepping back to her previous position. "Well...while you think...Athalas."

"Yes," he replied.

"Get the sacrifice ready. We must start."

Nephele laid the Diary next to Demetre's body. He gasped and opened his eyes. He screamed in pain.

"My chest...my chest...please no!" he shrieked.

I ran from where I was to come to his aid, but my legs felt stuck and my whole body was burning. My heart felt as if it was going to explode. Nephele looked back at me.

"Do not be a fool. Please use this time wisely so you can make the right choice, Isaac." Azaziel dragged me back to the left side of the throne.

My body was not responding correctly. I could only stand straight, in a single position. This feeling killed me inside.

Nephele kissed Demetre on the lips and whispered something that I was not able to understand. The other Nephilins stood near the walls, heads bowed, and silent. I could not tell if they were communicating with each other in their minds or if they were just waiting for the Fallen Star to come out of Demetre. The sound of his screams relentlessly echoed in my mind.

Why would she kiss him? I wondered.

"It was about time for you to come back to us. I could not bear to be away from you any longer than I've already been—especially now," she whispered ominously, then looked at Athalas and nodded.

In a split second, Athalas grabbed his dagger and pierced Demetre on his chest. This time, his scream was so loud and desperate, my eardrums hurt. Devin and Adawnas looked at him with tears rolling down their faces.

Athalas repeatedly pierced him in the heart. Demetre's blood was oozing out, flowing like a stream, making its course to the Diary. Nephele had her cold eyes set on him. Her face did not show even a glimmer of compassion.

As quick as a breath, my eyes opened and I found myself in a sort of chamber. The place was simply macabre. Around me I saw walls that were covered in mildew, iron bars placed at every window around me. I looked out and I saw the ocean, the waves crashing angrily against the outer walls. Where was I? Had I passed out and been taken to some prison? I had the feeling that time had come to a complete stop.

There was a door in front of me. I pounded on the door with all my might, but there was no reply. I turned around and saw a man seated on a chair on the corner of the room. Interestingly enough, I felt no fear. His garments were very similar to the Nephilins, only his garments were glorious, covered in small particles of light that shimmered with every slow breath he took. His eyes were not blue like theirs, but a brilliant gold that glimmered vibrantly in the dark. He had his legs crossed, hands resting on his knee, and he was staring out the window.

"I suppose you are probably thinking two things, young one." Like the Nephilins, his voice was musical.

"Try me," I replied. I waited for fear to strike me, but to my surprise, it did not.

"You want to know where you are and who I am obviously," he replied, chuckling.

"Well, of course! I was just in the middle of what seemed to be some sort of sacrificial ceremony and—"

"You are weak, Isaac…too weak," he interrupted abruptly. "That is why I brought you here, under the orders of the Creator."

The weakness he mentioned was of no surprise to me.

"I assume you already know what is happening," I asked.

"Don't think that only this world feels the change. The Fourth Dimension also feels it. It now has its gates unguarded.

With the Council being broken, Tristar has also felt this change."

Silence reigned over us for a moment. A soft breeze was coming in from the ocean, blowing through the window, filling the room with a sweet aroma.

"I know Nephele has given you a choice, Isaac. Think of it as an offer. But you need to know why you were made this offer, and not the others."

"You have my complete attention." I frowned. "But before we go on, what is your name?" I asked.

"Forgive me. My name is Raziel, a Star." I felt peace reach out to me every time he spoke. There was something about this being that stirred me inside. I did recall some old stories my parents used to tell me about Raziel. In the stories, he was an announcer, bringing messages to humans.

"They fear you, Isaac." He took a deep breath. "Fear of what you might become if you deny their offer."

I smirked. "How threating can I be, Raziel? I am just a mere human who happens to descend from those that guarded the Diary. I have no powers of my own."

Raziel let out a soft laugh. "That is where you are mistaken."

I felt my heart skip a beat. "Mistaken..."

"You are the son of Diane and Dustin Khan. Of course you have gifts of your own. You inherited them from your parents. You were unaware of them because of your age," he said in a soothing voice.

I roamed around the room, astounded at what he said. "Then why have you brought me here? Will I not be able to fight with these gifts of mine?" I asked, looking him in the eyes.

"This time, the Creator himself wants to offer you something." He calmly walked toward the window, his gaze set on the ocean.

"What would this offer be?" I approached him.

"The Creator himself wants to awaken powers inside of you. Apart from these inherited gifts, he wants to deposit in you more." He smiled. "You are indeed very special, Isaac."

I felt my eyes twitching as he spoke; my hands were suddenly shaking. "What is happening?" I fearfully asked.

"I have brought you to this place so you could physically feel the awakening of your inherited powers. The transformation would have been invisible to your naked eye but here, they are as real as the air you breathe." He circled around me. "The gifts are in your blood. They run in your veins."

My head felt as if it was going to explode; my heart burned and my body ached.

"Please make it stop," I cried. When the words came out of me, my voice sounded different.

"You have to choose which path to take, Isaac. I cannot choose your road for you. I can only enlighten your choice," he said as he touched my shoulder. "You can settle for your powers or you can choose what the Creator has in store for you."

"What does he want from me?" I asked in a broken voice, eagerly waiting for an answer. This pain was unbearable.

"Let him give you powers. It is a much narrower road but it will be a road worth taking." He smiled. How could he smile in a situation such as this one?

"What do I have to do?" I screamed. My body trembled intensely.

"All you have to do is ask me to take you to him." He smirked. "Keep in mind that your powers are in your blood. If you choose the Creator's powers, your blood will change and so will your heart."

The pain that was in my chest was excruciating, but the decision that I now had to make seemed even worse. Many thoughts rushed in my head. Finally I found the strength to speak.

"Yes," I said.

Raziel quickly stood next to me. "Yes to what?"

"Take me to him," I spoke with quivering lips.

"Very well," he whispered, closing his eyes slowly. At that very moment, my eyes saw something that left me breathless. A surprising set of wings gently sprang forth from Raziel's back. They were marvelous. Light emanated from them in colors that I don't think I had ever seen anywhere in Elysium. Slowly, he flapped them toward me. A mighty wind blew in the room. The macabre walls melted away like ice in the heat of the day. The waters of the ocean rushed in, rising all the way to my waist. The pain ceased.

I splashed the water to see if it was real. The temperature was perfect; even the taste of the water was different. I looked around and noticed that I was standing in the middle of the ocean. When I looked up, I saw a picturesque mountain range lying before me. I could hear birds singing and whizzing about the gorgeous sky. Was this the pain Raziel spoke about? If it was, I would take it anytime.

My body already felt different. Something here gave me strength. It seemed as if nothing could touch me.

I looked down and I could see the fish swimming.

Where am I? The moment the thought came to my mind, someone answered,

"The same place you were before." The voice that spoke brought me amazing comfort. It was unlike anything I had ever heard before. My heart did not fear, nor was it hesitant.

"Isaac. I am glad you have made this choice of your own will. Many would not have done so, considering the benefits of being a Nephilin in Elysium."

I could hear the voice, feel the strong presence, but I could not see the body of this person, or creature. I looked around earnestly, trying to see the face of the one that gave me such joy.

"Where are you? I can't see you," I asked frantically, spinning around feverishly, seeking to lay eyes on the owner of this magnificent voice.

The voice laughed.

"I am here." When the voice said *here,* it sounded as if many voices had come together and formed some sort of choir. The voice resonated everywhere.

"I am in everything that you see. I am the Creator." Instantly, I tried to think of things that I could say to him, but I was short on words.

"All that you see here carries a part of me. Of course I do have a body, a shape. But you are not ready to see me in my full form. Regardless...I am delighted you have chosen to receive my gifts!"

I took in a deep breath. "I am glad you came to me to speak. I have so much to ask...to say. Long have I thought you were distant," I said, comforted by the peace that came from this voice.

"Distant?" The voice sounded preoccupied. "That was never my intention...to be distant from you. In order for me to come to you once again, some will have to willingly choose to fight for a greater cause."

I noticed the water growing darker and the sky grayer as the voice spoke.

"I know you are aware of the pain that is to come with this choice. Not only when receiving these powers, but also on your journey ahead, but the pain is necessary." There was a deeper, mysterious tone to the voice now.

"Know this, I am watching your every move and will be with all of you until the end. Do not let your heart be troubled with the turmoil of the future. Be sure of one thing: the future is already written in the hidden stones of the hearts of those who said 'yes.'"

The entire scenario around me changed according to the mood of the voice. They were all directly connected, synched as one. "I hope you are ready," said the Creator.

I inhaled deeply. "Yes. I am," I replied.

My eyes were shut firmly.

"When you go back to Billyth, they will not have noticed that you have been gone this long—time in the Fourth Dimension is quite different. Go and find the others who will fight next to you. Humanity chose the fall, now it is up to you to redeem and rise."

"Why me?" I asked with tearful eyes. "What do I have to offer?"

"You had your heart, now you have given it to me. That will be enough." The voice echoed louder this time.

There was silence. The water dropped in temperature and was slowly rising. I opened my eyes and the sky was no longer beautiful. The fish were no longer swimming, and the mountains were not visible anymore.

The water grew so cold that it felt as though knives were piercing my body. I could not move. I shivered so much that I thought I was about to have a seizure. Not long after, the waters covered me. I tried to swim, to go to the surface, but I couldn't.

In my head, the pain had once again shadowed the beauty and peace I had just experienced. As my body was being exposed to these conditions, I felt it shutting down. Somehow, in the silence of these waters, my heartbeat was louder than ever. I knew I was dying. Was this the pain Raziel meant? I had to overcome death somehow? Was I supposed to die? Maybe it would be better for me to die here. I agonized, trying so hard to stay alive. Somehow I knew I had to die. Death seemed the right way to go.

So much for feeling immortal in this place. That was my last thought before I felt myself rise away from my body as it sunk to the bottom of this ocean, isolated somewhere in the Fourth Dimension. I hovered over the dark waters, watching all that was happening around my fragile body. To my surprise, the water level lowered. The bottom of the ocean turned white and my garments turned blood red. I did not know how, but I knew I could feel that part of me was still inside that body that now struggled to survive, but another part of me had left it.

I heard loud footsteps approaching. I looked around and saw nothing but the white nothingness that had surrounded me. In the midst of nothing, red smoke formed. But the smoke seemed different. Every move it made was synchronized. The smoke grew wings and paws. Then a mane formed. The red color faded away, revealing white fur. I was astounded at what I saw. A white lion with six wings approached my body. I felt a sudden connection with this creature. His red eyes brought me peace. Flashes of light surrounded his body. The majesty that came from this being was something unheard of. The lion gently approached my body and stood there, looking at me. I wondered what it was going to do. His eyes never stopped staring down at me.

The lion graciously walked around my body; his wings moved in a beautiful manner. The grand mane gently bounced, though no breeze was blowing. The lion stopped. Without hesitating, it attacked, violently biting my neck until blood poured out. The lion held my body in his jaws for a few seconds and then released it. I watched my own body being slaughtered as a burning pain embraced my neck. As the lion saw me bleeding, his red eyes filled with tears. I could hear low sobs coming from him.

The lion bent down and blew something on my face. A mighty wind could be heard. As I looked at the scene, I felt the wind blowing strongly against my body and as it blew, the wounds on my neck closed and my body slowly came back to life. I opened my eyes and noticed I no longer watched the scene but I had returned to my body. I leaped up in the hopes that I could see the lion but he was gone.

"A corrupted body and a corrupted soul need to die so righteousness won't fall." I looked to my right and saw Raziel standing next to me. The ocean waters rose once again, all the way to my waist.

"Say goodbye to your old body and to your old man." In a friendly gesture, he laid his hand on my shoulder. "How do you feel?"

I took in a deep breath. "Better than ever!" I responded happily. "Even though it was quite an experience to watch it all. To see me die…"

"Your soul looks a lot more peaceful now, don't you agree?" Raziel asked with a grin.

"My…soul?" I asked.

"Your soul was weak and fragile. That soul belonged to a boy, this one belongs to a man," replied Raziel. "This was the prison of your soul. That is why you were inside that room with me. You were imprisoned, locked from the knowledge of your true destiny. Now that the walls have been brought down, you can walk in freedom. Soon you will realize that you will be able to read people's thoughts. Your powers will evolve with time. When you go back, it may seem that your body hasn't changed before ordinary eyes, but you will feel the strength inside of you burning."

As his wings flapped, the ocean and the beautiful landscape disappeared.

VI

I was back in the throne room once again. Like Raziel mentioned, time hadn't passed here. The scene once again was visible to me: Athalas bleeding Demetre alongside Nephele, who just glared at him. I looked at Devin and Adawnas, weakness stamped on their faces.

"Will this be enough time to take up on our offer?" Nephele spoke as she dawdled up the stairs. I reached out to touch my face and noticed that my body did not show any external signs of change, but inside I felt as if a fire burned relentlessly.

"Yes, it will," I boldly replied as my fingers moved impatiently, tapping against my legs.

"Very well! I think I can guess what your decision is, correct?" She clapped her hands in a delightful manner. Athalas swiftly came from behind her, touching her on the shoulder. The moment he extended his hand, I could not help but see that not only his hands but also his garments were covered in blood. I had to compose myself. Even if the pain was immense, somehow I needed to find the strength to not allow this to sink in. "He is dead. The blood has all been poured over the Diary," said Athalas under heavy breaths.

"We will tend to his body in a minute," she replied, still keeping her eyes fixed on me.

"So, do you care to tell us your decision?" She smiled anxiously.

I knew there was some sort of strength inside of me, burning. But I had no idea how to use it. I looked around the room. The others all had their heads bowed; all were silent.

"Do you really think you can fool me, Isaac?" Azaziel grunted.

"I am not trying to fool anyone," I replied, looking at Nephele. "As appealing as this offer may seem, I cannot accept it."

I could tell the moment I replied, Devin and Adawnas became very apprehensive. Nephele's eyes slowly changed. Her face twisted up with anger.

"Pity. You would be so useful here," Nephele replied, touching my face.

She took a couple steps back. "It is a shame you won't get to see Demetre in his full form."

I was silent, looking deeply in her eyes. What Raziel had mentioned was coming true. My eyes were able to see inside her mind. I saw her inner thoughts about me; her deep fear of who I was. I supposed they couldn't read my mind, since none of them had proceeded to do anything against me. She stood motionless, eyes fixed on me. I knew of her abilities to cut off senses and kill others. Pain crawled under my skin. My eyes began hurting, my heartbeat accelerated. I could hear cracks inside of myself, as if she tried to break me inside. Somehow, I did not feel threatened. I was feeling stronger than ever. I could read her soul and mind. She was becoming frustrated due to her inability to take over me.

The others murmured amongst each other. A sudden ferocious growl surprised us all. Nephele ceased her efforts to kill me and looked back. She frowned as she walked toward Demetre.

"You would have suffered less if you had been killed by me," she grunted.

Many Nephilin guards jumped onto me, trying to chain me down. There were at least twelve of them on top of me. Out of pure instinct, I was able to push them back using only my mind. Like birds they flew away. A throbbing pain took over my head.

"Surprising!" exclaimed Azaziel. "Yet not good enough."

"Leave him," Nephele ordered coldly. "Allow him to get a good glimpse of what is to come."

She picked up the bloody Diary, looked at it, and tossed it around the room. She then turned to me with a ferocious look.

"He came to you, didn't he?" she whispered.

"Who did?" I asked, suspicious of what she had discovered.

She slapped me in the face. Rage had stirred inside of her. "Do not toy with me now—*the Creator*. Did he come to you?"

I did not answer.

"You have become impure...now we must wait for the purity of your blood to be restored." She seemed distant in thought, probably thinking of ways to lure me into accepting their offer.

"So close...so close," she mumbled in disappointment. "Never mind! You are no good to us anymore. Now you will have to suffer in the hands of your old friend—or what remains of him, anyway."

Demetre wriggled around like a fish out of water. He screamed in pain, beating himself on the ground. Red eyes and pale skin appeared. After a while, he stopped moving.

Nephele's eyes glistened as she contemplated Demetre's transformation.

"Finally, it is complete," she whispered with tears in her eyes.

Demetre rapidly stood to his feet. His face still had traces of the Demetre I knew, but he was changed. He stood still for a while, breathing. The room fell into complete silence.

"Corbin...Corbin...can you hear me?" Nephele whispered softly.

He opened his red eyes. I immediately realized he was no longer the friend I knew.

"Oh my love, how do you feel?" Nephele seemed to be hypnotized by him.

"It feels great to be here in flesh and bone once again, Nephele," he replied in a somber voice. After a brief pause, he continued, "Is the Council still guarding the Fourth Dimension's entrance?"

"No, my lord...all of the Council members have betrayed the Creator, and have sided along with us," replied Nephele.

Corbin smiled. "They will be very useful in our hands, won't they? We must have as many Shadows as possible to be trained in destroying this world." He looked around, ignoring our presence.

"I suppose these are the innocent Nephilins?" Corbin approached Devin and Adawnas. As he moved, a shadow followed him. His presence carried emptiness—an unexplainable void.

"Why do you deny who you truly are? To know that you went out of your way for the mere hope of being redeemed is quite amusing to me." He quickened his pace.

"You know that you will be destroyed soon!" Adawnas shouted, keeping her eyes fixed on him.

Corbin laughed. "And you think you won't? Your bloodline is doomed, Nephilin. You are hopeless. As for me—look at me. I finally have a human host to live in. Do not dare speak as if you are one worthy of redemption."

In an instant, he raised his hand and slapped Adawnas. She was thrown to the other side of the room, falling on top of the other Nephilins. There was a sudden change on his face—he was infuriated.

"If you were not so insolent, this Diary would have been opened by now. Do you realize that?" Hastily, Devin leaped up and fell on top of Corbin. He took up his sword and tried to wound him. Devin's agility was no match for Corbin's.

"It will be a treat to watch you all die by my hands," Corbin grunted. He effortlessly dodged every move Devin made. There was an urge in my body to attack. This new strength burning inside of me seemed to have its own will of when to come out.

As he dodged and swayed Devin's attempt to strike, I attacked him. I did not use a sword or a spear. Somehow I was able to use my mind to stop him. I focused all of my attention on him, and he immediately halted. I was not able to detain him for long due to the sharp pain that invaded my head. All the room muttered, not in their minds but with spoken words. It seemed as if I had done something that was too impossible or dangerous to do. Nephele intervened.

"What did you just do, Isaac? Do you have any idea what you've just done?" she asked, shouting at the top of her lungs.

Immediately I was able to see what her mind desired. Fear was the only thing that was stopping her from ordering the Nephilins to attack me.

Corbin closed his eyes. Everyone fell silent.

"Azaziel!" Corbin called out. Azaziel hastily went to his aid. "Let us leave Billyth tonight. Allow the bodies that are spread outside to rot—do not bury anyone right now. The Nephilins need to remain hidden for a while, at least until the greater attacks commence. We will deal with this one later." Corbin looked deep into my eyes.

He nodded. "What do we do with them, my lord?" he asked.

Corbin ignored the question. He grabbed Nephele's hand. A shadow enveloped them and as fast as a heartbeat, they disappeared.

"Coward!" I yelled. "Where are you off to?"

Did he doubt that I could defeat him? How could he turn away from me in battle? As fast as I could blink, the others also vanished from the room.

I was infuriated.

"Why would he suddenly spare me from this battle? Is he afraid?"

"Be glad that he did, Isaac. Be glad for many things that have happened tonight for they could have been a lot worse," said Adawnas as she stood to her feet.

"How could it be worse, Adawnas? They have the Diary." The thought provoked fear.

"They don't have you, Isaac. You've chosen wisely." She gave me a crooked smile, and then groaned in pain.

I walked to the window to look out at the city. As I looked outside, I understood what they meant by *the bodies*. They were scattered everywhere, as if they had been strategically placed around the city like special ornaments.

I don't know where this strength was coming from. Somehow, in some way, I had to overcome the sadness of my loss. All while I gazed at a city populated with corpses. Demetre had always been with me since birth. I did not recall a single significant moment in my life where he wasn't present. I was always there to protect him from any situation he couldn't get out of by himself. Now I found him fighting against me.

From the window, the sight I saw could not solely be described by words. My only urge was to desperately go out there and try to find survivors. Since the awakening of these powers, my vision had become clearer, allowing me to see a lot more than before. Seeing those bodies scattered around brought within me a great rage and fury.

"We must look for survivors. We cannot leave without looking around," I affirmed.

Devin, Adawnas and I started toward the window, broke through the glass and landed right on the street below.

I looked up and saw how incredible the castle looked. A mesmerizing clock tower majestically rose between two colossal columns. The high triangular roofs seemed even taller from the ground. The windows were adorned with ornamented frames.

Near the castle were many houses. Inside each one of them, I saw the bodies of the families who just happened to live in this city, ruled by some sort of underground government.

"So the Nephilins hide underground?" I asked Devin, enraged with what my eyes saw.

"They…um…we used to," he murmured in a soft, shy voice. "Since the Fallen Stars started to create the army of Shadows, we have remained hidden. Not only underground but also on mountains and in caves."

I looked at Adawnas and it was clearly visible how much seeing this destruction brought her pain. She quietly looked around at the bodies. She could not mask her overwhelming sorrow.

In one of the houses, we found a child lying on the floor. He had been shot in the chest by many arrows. As I approached him, I felt a sharp pain in my head; my eyes stung immediately. I closed them only to see a vision. I saw Nephele killing with her vile and repulsive gift, along with Azaziel.

"No!" I screamed as soon as the vision vanished.

"What is wrong, Isaac?" Adawnas asked. It took me a while to find reason again.

"I can see what they saw, the last image in their minds before they died," I explained. My hands shook uncontrollably as Devin approached us.

"Your gifts, they are quickly developing. Still, we must go on." Devin looked at the bodies, shook his head in a sign of disapproval and left.

We walked out of the house, my heart feeling as heavy as stone. We continued walking along the dark streets of Billyth. Looking around, the thought that I had tried to hide away for a while knocked on my door again. The picture of my father's and mother's faces appeared in my mind, only to be destroyed by the terrible truth that they had been killed.

A tear strolled down my face. I was trying to stop it, to not let this thought take over me now, but I was not able to contain it. After the first tear another followed. I was overwhelmed by all the emotions I tried to ignore. The thought of having lost my parents and my best friend was tormenting.

Continuous sobs followed the tears, and soon, I was a wreck. So much went through my mind, all the things I thought I could hide away somewhere in my heart. Devin and Adawnas kept walking ahead of me. They noticed I had stopped, and after a while, they both looked back and walked toward me. None said a single word as they stood by my side. That was good enough for me; their presence alone brought me some comfort.

After I cried and grieved for a while, I was somewhat able to compose myself. I did not mention the reason for my crying; I did not want them to know. Not now.

"There is no one left," Devin whispered. The feeling of a causeless death and of an ever-growing will for power filled my cup. No longer was my heart beating for fear or because I thought I was too fragile to face the darkness. My heart was now beating for justice.

"Did you know about the offers I was going to receive?" I asked as I wiped away the last tear.

They looked at each other silently.

"Yes, Isaac. All along I knew you were going to receive the offer. I was almost lured into letting you drink the wine, but I simply couldn't." Adawnas was the one to respond. She sounded shameful and disgusted. "I have been with the Council for many years. The moment my heart felt the Darkness enter Tristar through Justicia, I had to pretend to be like them. Otherwise, spears and swords would have been used against me."

I sighed.

"And you, Devin...Did *you* know?"

He walked closer, laying his hand on my shoulder.

"All along..." He could not look me in the eye when he answered.

"Did any of you ever think about mentioning that to me?" I was trying really hard not to doubt them anymore. I longed to know that I could trust them. After facing death right in the eye, having gone through so many perilous moments, and witnessing my best friend become one of the Fallen Stars, I would have appreciated some type of warning.

"We couldn't, Isaac. The decision needed to have been wholly yours, and no one else's," Devin replied.

"And how did you know about all of this?" Instantly I wondered if they had any special gifts similar to mine.

"Well...Devin was...visited," Adawnas mumbled.

I turned to face them both.

"The day I came to you in the forest, Ely had warned me about the future...and of the urgency of finding you before your natural abilities were awoken. How do you think we have been able to withstand all of this for so long?"

Truly I hadn't thought of this concept before. They were both beautiful and perfect Nephilins, with many abilities. Yet, neither gave in to what the others said.

"By doing what we did—leaving our...hiding place and coming to the Council, we felt as if we could possibly be redeemed from being who we are. Hope was stirred inside of us," said Adawnas.

"Hope of what?" I asked ingeniously.

Adawnas sighed.

"Hope of salvation, Isaac," she responded.

"Even though evil runs through our veins," Adawnas continued. "I refused to take part of their plan—to have creation die without knowledge, thus creating a gigantic, thoughtless army that would be able to strike Tristar and dethrone the Creator."

"The Shadows..." My voice trailed off as the grotesque image of their faces invaded my mind.

"And what of Demetre? What did they do to him? He did not choose such fate," I asked. The tears tried to return.

"They performed the Soul Exchange. Demetre was offered to the Darkness when he was an infant. This offer gives liberty for any chosen Fallen Star to take over his body upon his blood maturation. Therefore, Demetre's fate was chosen for him." Devin sighed. "This is a dangerous thing, given that a Fallen Star is now hosted in a human body. Their tissue, skin and blood have intertwined. They are one."

I placed both of my hands on my face, closed my eyes and once again cried bitterly. Demetre, the person I had known throughout my entire life, the person that knew me best, died without having a choice. A part of me wanted to refuse to believe that this was true, but deep inside I knew the truth had to be embraced now.

"I am sorry, Isaac," Adawnas whispered.

"And what of his soul?" I replied in a hoarse voice. I feared the answer to my question.

"He died knowing the truth. One must assume that he will not become a Shadow, but I cannot answer that question for you, I'm afraid," Devin replied. "Our kind has caused great damage to this place. We are an abomination to the laws of the universe. We were never meant to be born or created. Our race is doomed by birth." He scoffed. "I am sad to say that what happened to Demetre is a small part of the many things already taking place in the deep places of this world."

He turned to face me once again. "Still, I promise you, even if I am already doomed to an eternity of darkness, I will protect you. I will not be one to give in to the disorder that has come."

VII

We kept on walking around Billyth under the cold torrential rain. The air had become very moist and thick and the atmosphere felt even heavier. The architecture of this place was breathtaking. The houses seemed to have been taken from a painting. They were stacked up like stepping stones, one on top of the other. The city had been built upon many small hills, making the cobblestone streets uneven.

As I walked along the masterfully constructed streets, I heard the distant growls of Aquilas. Adawnas and Devin were immediately on high alert. I spotted their shadows in the rainy sky. The flock flew together, crossing over the city. While my eyes followed their every movement, I gazed at something majestic. As they flapped their wings, small light particles scattered in the air like dandelions carried by the wind. The lights hovered and then slowly disappeared. From where we were standing, the twinkling lights looked more like stars. Soon, other black figures appeared in the sky. Their silhouettes were so dark, they merged with the dim clouds, making them difficult to see.

I was startled by the roaring sounds of thunder. A dreary feeling overtook me. It was something I had not yet experienced. Like in a vision, I watched Shadows marching in our direction. They were gathered in massive formations, heading toward us with one purpose.

"Corbin did not spare us." I sighed with trepidation. "They were going to destroy the city."

The dark figures approached the Aquilas. They collided and instantly, a fight broke out. With every strike incurred by the Aquilas, more particles of light were emitted, sprinkling the sky with golden colors.

My mind filtered the thoughts of the Shadows as they approached us. Every impulse from these beings was transmitted to me; I could feel every urge they had.

"We have to leave *now*…please…I see the Shadows. They are coming to annihilate this city. We cannot withstand this onslaught," I declared.

Devin and Adawnas looked startled.

My eyes were firmly fixed on the battle between the Aquilas and the shadowed beings.

"Damn traitors!" Devin shouted. "Now that the Council has fallen, the Gates of the Fourth Dimension are unguarded and Fallen Stars and Shadows can freely cross over."

"We can make it to the mountains. We can take the river and head to Mag Mell," Adawnas said.

Devin seemed to disapprove of Adawnas' idea. I had never heard of the Kingdom of Mag Mell, but right now the only thing that concerned me was leaving.

We tried to make our way out of the city, hoping to go about unnoticed. At that moment, a mighty growl echoed, one that sounded extremely close, causing Devin and Adawnas to stop.

We all fell silent, trying to listen closely. All I could hear was the rumbling thunder of the rain clouds in the sky. At once, the loud sounds of the battle vanished. No longer could I hear the Aquilas or the shadowed beings.

As we continued our effort to escape the city, we reached a small courtyard surrounded by many houses. There were four benches, arranged neatly in a perfect circle around a tree. Underneath the tree, water flowed from a beautiful water fountain. The beauty of the courtyard faded against the stark sight of the numerous dead bodies of its citizens.

From the street that was directly before us, I heard a predatory roar, followed by pounding thuds on the ground. The houses around us were being destroyed as the creature's wings toppled them all to the ground. It was one of the shadowed beings that fought with the Aquilas. The stench of putrid flesh that came from the creature was unbearably nauseating. Its black skin glimmered in the dark. Six small horns protruded above its eyebrows. A seventh horn grew right above its nostrils. The creature's teeth were long and unevenly shorn. We all remained very still as it sniffed the corpses around us. I tried to read its soul, but the creature did not seem to have one. Adawnas stood right next to me, frozen like a statue. From the sky another beast swooped down, this time right next to me. Neither creature seemed interested in us; the corpses were what grasped their attention. Violently, they shook them around, tearing them into pieces and devouring them. As I watched them feast on human flesh the sight repudiated me. Blood gushed from their mouths and trickled down their thick necks, coating their claws with the sticky thick substance.

After they had satisfied their hunger, they took flight.

"What was that?" I asked as I tried to breathe, which was almost impossible, due to the intensified stench of human remains. I was surprised with the vivid impressions of the Shadows clouding my mind, their evil presence once again capturing my heart. They were coming fast, now approaching the mountains.

"We have to keep moving on, Devin. They are pretty close," I declared.

We moved hastily, crossing through the city as fast as our feet allowed. I was amazed by the stamina I had to race alongside the Nephilins. This served as more proof that I was no longer the same boy. I was still astonished as these visions and other powers awoke within me, but I knew this was only the beginning. The adrenaline rush that pumped through my veins as we ran was incomparable to anything I had previously experienced. With each step I took, I could sense that I was evolving.

It was foolish of us to think that the beasts had disappeared before trying to get rid of us. Shortly after we began to run, the beasts were right at our backs. Their yellow eyes glowed eerily in the darkness and their teeth glimmered like the moon.

"Separate!" Devin ordered.

I immediately fled to my right as Adawnas veered to the left. Devin continued on, going straight ahead of us, toward the mountains. One of the beasts charged at me while another darted toward Adawnas. Through my new powers, I was able to see all the houses and judge with precision how I was going to jump over and dodge the oncoming structures. The beast flew above me, attacking savagely. Its movements reminded me of an eagle diving down from the sky to catch the prey it spotted from above.

I continuously swerved, dodging its every move. From tree to tree and rooftop to rooftop, I leaped as I tried to escape its attack. Though the beast was amazingly swift, I was faster. Just as the creature thought it was gaining on me, I turned and with a simple thought, I was able to dominate the beast, making it come to a brusque stop. The beast let out a mighty growl.

My eyes were transfixed on this abominable creature. Issuing another order with my mind, I inflicted lethal pain into its heart. The beast howled as the pain consumed its body, causing it to thrash about as it fell to the ground moments later.

Without delay, I went to Adawnas' aid. After a quick search, I spotted her and the beast fighting. When I approached her, I discovered that Devin was already there, fiercely thrashing the beast. The grotesque creature howled as its body landed with a heavy thud to the ground, dilacerated due to Devin's violent attack.

Devin took out his sword and decapitated the beast. A foul smell erupted from the blood that spewed out of its body. Despite the treacherous state we were all in, Adawnas mustered the strength to gracefully stand up.

"What are they, Devin?" I asked as my eyes remained fixed on the body.

"Desert Dragons. That is why Corbin did not want them to remove the bodies from the city. The stench of dead flesh is guiding them here."

With increased urgency we continued our escape. The marching sounds of the Shadows were audible now. The sounds of thunderous stomping from a great army mightily shook the ground. Their growls rang out; the roar of more beasts resounded around us. The rumble of the crashing of buildings collapsing filled the atmosphere. I could feel their anguished souls as they commenced to destroy the city. I tried to avert my focus away from them, but it was extremely difficult.

As we fled deeper into the mountains, I could still hear their souls crying out. I stopped and turned around, but Devin quickly rebuked me.

"Are you insane, Isaac?"

I ignored him. Something was drawing me to run back to Billyth, against my will.

The impulse was unexplainable. Somehow the tormented souls of the Shadows were fascinating as well as horrifying to me. I hastily turned back, without understanding why.

In a dark corner at the foot of the mountain I stopped where I could watch the city burn. It was intriguing to see the

Shadows screaming, growling, howling and destroying everything within seconds. What took men many years to build had quickly been turned to ash and dust. The stench of burnt flesh was everywhere. Ahead, I could see dark figures in the sky; Desert Dragons roamed throughout Billyth making sure none were left alive.

"Have you gone mad, Isaac?" Adawnas whispered from behind me. I was so caught up watching, I had not noticed I had been followed.

Silence overshadowed.

"I can see every thought their souls are having, every idea...is loud and clear to me now," I said in a quivering voice. "They are lost inside of themselves, being controlled by other forces. It is indeed sad to see them like this—an army of the living dead."

She walked closer.

"So now you understand why the Diary must never be opened. This is just the beginning—the beginning of the destruction that is to come upon Elysium. Even though you refused to give your blood to open the Diary, they will destroy the kingdoms. One by one they will fall to the Darkness. They will try to seduce kings, queens, stewards and armies of this world into joining them."

I turned my gaze to her. "What is the purpose of destroying the kingdoms of this world?" I asked.

"To rid the world of the Creator's creations, and now it has become a relentless chase for blood...*your* blood...*your* kin."

My blood and kin? Did I have any other relatives I was not aware of? I wondered what remained of my bloodline, besides my now dead parents. The thought of their death was still difficult for me to comprehend.

Devin approached from the woods.

"Are you two in the mood to die tonight? We must hurry," he said, walking closer to us.

"But there is no one left, Isaac," Adawnas continued. "Since you refused to give your blood, they will have to wait for your human will to be at its highest again. They have tried this in past ages, but never with this intensity."

"Tried in past ages?" I asked as I turned my eyes away from the burning city.

"They have searched for the one to open the Diary before, but never with such vigilance."

"Will these powers ever leave me?" I asked as I made my way back into the forest.

"They will never leave you, but they cannot contain your human will. Even though your inner man is strong, you won't be able to completely rid yourself from desires such as pride, greed and the longing for power. They may be sleeping within you now, because of your excitement for being so powerful, but soon they will spring forth. You are still human nonetheless," said Adawnas.

Devin sighed.

"We should not linger here. Why are we here anyway? If I am not mistaken you are the one that urged us get away from this city," Devin alleged as his eyes were fixed on the burning buildings.

The thought of succumbing to temptation seemed incomprehensible. After seeing all of this, living, and breathing these abilities, why would I want to give in to Nephele and Azaziel?

"Are we leaving?" Devin was getting irritated.

Somehow, I felt a certain satisfaction while looking into the tormented souls as they burned the city with their bare hands. Their minds were locked in a constant battle. I knew they were being controlled by evil, but at the same time, they wanted freedom from this control. Sorrow filled them with a constant void, possessing every member of their decayed bodies as they destroyed everything along their path."

"I am not waiting on either of you any longer. Let's go!" Devin was enraged.

"Isaac, we have to leave. They will see us here..." Adawnas motioned gently.

"Yes. Let's," I mumbled.

The moment we started to head back toward the forest, I was able to refrain myself from watching the Shadows destroy the city. The farther we distanced ourselves from Billyth, the easier it was for me to block out their feelings from my mind. I figured I could resist reading Adawnas' and Devin's souls, because I hadn't yet been curious enough, but I found the thoughts and feelings of the Shadows fascinating.

"Let us rest awhile," Devin said the moment we were at a safe distance from the kingdom. I supposed even those with great powers still needed to rest. I reclined near a tree, Adawnas sat next to me, and Devin sat next to a small river that was nearby.

"What if the Shadows come back for us here?" I asked.

"I am sure you will be able to see them even with your eyes closed," Devin replied as he made himself comfortable near the riverbank.

From where I was sitting, I saw the thick darkness of the night sky hovering above us through a small gap in the tree branches ahead of me. As I gazed into the sky, I heard a tune coming from the river. I lifted my head to see Devin looking at the darkness that hovered over us. He was softly humming a song. He sang of a woman from the past that had lost her heart in war and lived forever in grief.

...Dear one who has walked by

My heart you've stolen, it is no longer mine

From the shadows you came,

but I shall not come to thee in vain.

One day I hope to find the heart,

the heart that was once mine.

As he sang, my eyelids grew heavier.

I saw a staircase that led to a long dark hallway. I was chained to two gigantic pillars and my body was completely bruised. A snake was wrapped around me; its eyes were as yellow and bright as the morning sun. Its tail rattled as its tongue touched my face.

We are coming from the shadows. We have risen from the ashes to find you. I heard many voices whispering as the snake tightened its grasp around my chest. I was unable to move and my mouth refused to obey my command to speak.

As I looked at the snake, it was transforming itself, slowly taking shape. As I blinked, I saw Demetre standing before me, his eyes dark, his skin pale, his clothes looking completely disheveled. His body slowly deteriorated and flames surrounded him.

I woke up gasping for air. I was sweating profusely; it seemed as though I had gone swimming in the river. I surveyed my surroundings only to find Devin and Adawnas sound asleep and the forest in complete silence. The sound of the murmuring river brought me some peace. I reclined my head and closed my eyes, wondering if I would be able to fall asleep again.

VIII

I was awoken from a deep sleep by a violent shaking from Devin.

"Let us be on our way, Isaac. It is already late," he admonished.

Slowly, I opened my eyes. I still expected to see sunlight when I woke up, but that hadn't happened for some time. Adawnas appeared like a breath of sunshine with three apples in hand.

"Here is breakfast!" she said as she tossed the apples to Devin and me. As we continued with our walk, I saw a remote village surrounded by an old rugged wall in the valley of the forest from atop one of the hills. Smoke swirled in circles from the chimneys of the housetops and I could hear the faint chatter of the residents.

"What is this place?" I asked Devin.

"The Valley Hills—a small village near Mag Mell. Many small villages surround the kingdom. Kings use them to signal an oncoming battle. If these regions endure the preliminary attack, the kingdom is alerted beforehand of the enemy's approach. It is said that Mag Mell is the kingdom with the strongest army amongst humans. If there are any in the human world that can call all other human kingdoms to battle, it is Mag Mell."

I looked at the small village again.

"And how are mere humans supposed to defeat these…things…that are coming after the Diary?" I asked curiously.

"If the human kingdoms unite, they may have a chance to win this war." Devin placed his hand on my shoulder. "Humanity can still be redeemed. All that is needed is the will to fight. We must warn all of the kingdoms before the Shadows have the chance to spread," Devin said hastily.

"Remember, they seek to kill as many humans as possible so that their souls are unable to cross over, thus adding numbers to their army," Adawnas added. "The Shadows will not cease to attack Elysium until all humans are killed. Inside the Abyss, the enemy is planning another attack. We must all be ready."

Flashes and images appeared in my mind. Sorrow grew in my heart as I looked at every single one of the faces that emerged.

"I can see—feel what they are feeling," I mumbled. "They have doubt, pain and loss. Some have recently lost loved ones," I said in a hushed voice.

The moment I finished speaking, we started to make our way down the hill, toward the village.

"The weather is growing colder. Do you feel it, Adawnas?" Devin asked.

"Yes. There hasn't been any sunlight. This sudden change in weather will surely bring surprises," she said, shaking her head in a sign of disapproval.

We found ourselves at the wooden wall that guarded the village. Two watchtowers stood next to the hoary old gate, both guarded by two guards holding spears.

"Who might you all be?" one of them asked.

"We are travelers looking for a decent place to rest our heads," Devin promptly replied. I knew that even though we had gotten some sleep in the forest, we still showed signs of weariness.

"And the young traveler…who might he be?" the other one contested.

"We found him in the forest. He claimed he was lost and his mother would be waiting for him here. Now please, may we enter?" Adawnas answered in an assertive tone.

"Hey! There is no need to get feisty, young lady. We are on high alert. There is talk of strange happenings and creatures, and we have not seen sunlight for many days. It seems as if this storm will never pass," the guard on the right quipped sarcastically, as he gestured to the other to let us in.

The wooden gate was opened. Upon entering, we found ourselves in a courtyard with a beautiful statue located in the middle. Its form was in the likeness of a king riding a horse with a sword in one hand and a spear in the other. Trees enveloped the statue within a picturesque garden filled with a floral bouquet. The small homes and quaint little stores made the town feel warm and welcoming. After witnessing so much violence, I was surprised to capture the beauty on some of the windowpanes that were dressed with flowers and plants, which reminded me of happier times. Judging by what I had encountered, all seemed placid in this paradise.

"It does not look so bad," I said in a cheerful tone.

"Well, this is one of the most peaceful places we have come across lately. Let us hope it stays that way," Adawnas said as she studied all the people around her.

Many children were playing on the streets. All of them were laughing and running without a care. Their mothers watched them, but their faces did not express the same carefree joy. I noticed there were no men around. Could it be their husbands had left? Was this why I felt the loss in their hearts?

"No men are present here, Devin. Don't you find this peculiar?" Adawnas asked.

"We must talk to the overseer of this town. Maybe he will be able to give us some answers," he replied.

We hurriedly made our way through the crowded narrow street.

"We have no royal status—we have no right to ask for a meeting with their overseer. How are we ever going to get a chance to talk to him? Who will we say we are?" I asked.

"The overseer will be able to tell us why the men are missing. No order is passed on to citizens without being approved by the overseer first. We must assess the possibilities of what can be accomplished here before we head to Mag Mell," Adawnas said with an edge to her voice.

As we walked, I experimented with my newly acquired gift and focused my mental powers on the women's souls to see if I could discover anything that might help us. The mixed emotions and thoughts I could read did not reveal any important information.

Like a fine-tuned instrument I discerned that their hearts were apprehensive, worried about what could have happened to their men. Some were pensive with thoughts of deserting the village and heading to Mag Mell. After wandering through the village, I was no longer able to restrain myself from asking someone about the latest happenings.

I approached a woman sweeping her front porch. She looked quite plain, wearing an old dress, her hair pinned at the nape of her neck in a tight bun. The wear and tear of the old dress indicated she was a hard worker. I came to a sudden stop.

"Excuse me, ma'am," I said in a soft voice as I took a few paces toward her. "We are distant travelers and we would like to ask you a few questions if you wouldn't mind?" Devin and Adawnas stood by my side, unresponsive to my recent action.

"I am sorry, young ones; I don't do business with outsiders. Now please, if you would kindly leave..."

"Please, ma'am. It is only one question, one simple question and we will be on our way," I tried again, hopeful.

"Find another to answer to your blabber. My time now is very limited, can you not see that?" she responded as she continued sweeping the floor; her eyes never gazing in our direction. I sighed.

"But no one is willing. Please, ma'am, it is just one question," I persisted.

She stopped her sweeping, laid her broom against a wall and commenced to walk in our direction.

"One question and then you must be off—otherwise I will call the guards on you three," she replied bitterly. I looked around cautiously for anyone that might be suspicious. I did not want to let my guard down here, not even for a moment. Now that my gifts were maturing, I could easily view my surroundings.

"Where are your men? Your husbands, your fathers, where are they?" I asked reluctantly.

Immediately, her gestures changed from defensive to those of a weak and insecure woman.

"I...I don't know. The king requested the men go to Mag Mell. The reason is unknown to all of us." Her eyes swam in tears; her voice was quivering softly. "Now please, take your leave. If you want to know more, head over to Mag Mell. I strongly advise you against going. There have been rumors of a shadow growing there."

"When did this take place?" Devin asked.

The lady scoffed.

"They were all called to leave last week, a little before the sun was hidden by the clouds," she responded in anguish.

"Do you know where we can find the overseer of this town?" Adawnas questioned her. I could sense she was afraid of the Nephilins. It was obvious, if one took a good look, that Devin and Adawnas had noticeable differences, but they were still able to pass as mere humans.

"The overseer is located in the Over Hall, just a couple of streets ahead. It is the white building with six columns. I highly doubt he will be available to speak to anyone, especially outsiders," she said as she grabbed ahold of her broom.

"What is his name?" Devin asked her.

"Anatolio, sir—that is his name. My husband is very close to him, and he did not even tell me the reason why all of the men were called to Mag Mell. He did say it was for a worthy cause." Her hands tightened their grasp on the broom. A soft breeze whispered.

"Thank you, ma'am. You have helped a great deal," I said.

She nodded and resumed her sweeping.

"They are indeed clueless to what is happening," Adawnas said. "How can the humans be so negligent, so disconnected?"

"It was their choice," Devin responded. "They chose to fall and now they live in ignorance of the truth. Still, we must warn Anatolio of what is happening. He needs to know about the spreading of the Darkness."

135

As we walked toward the Over Hall, screams echoed around us. A familiar feeling rose within me; an urge empowered me once again. Some of the women were running in the opposite direction from where we were headed. Some stood petrified, frightened at what lay ahead. Within me, I already knew what awaited us.

"Shadows," I said, making my way through the scampering crowd.

"They have found this place," Devin said. We quickened our pace. Every time the Shadows were near, it felt as though a stake was driven into my heart. I was greatly abhorred by their presence, but a part of me also wanted to keep watching them as they moved.

We then came upon the scene that had frightened all of them. A Shadow stood on top of a man, his body desecrated, his innards scattered over the courtyard. This catastrophe occurred directly in front of the Over Hall. I was able to connect to his last image just prior to his death. I relived the images of the Shadow leaping on top of him, ripping open his stomach with its teeth, slashing his neck with its claws, and ripping him apart. Indeed, it was Anatolio's body.

"It's him, Devin, it's Anatolio," I reported, approaching the mutilated body.

"Someone wanted him dead," Adawnas answered in a somber tone.

The Shadow turned to face us, its face smothered with blood, its garments ragged and filthy. I could hear low grumbles emerging from the hollow being. At that very moment, Devin took up his sword and hastily pierced the

Shadow through the chest. It growled as it faded into ash. The crowd stared at us and at their overseer, whose body lay torn apart on the ground. They all muttered amongst themselves, wondering who we were.

The moment I turned around, I heard growls all around us. Instantly, my heart grew weary. It would not take a mastermind to determine the next plan of attack.

"There are more approaching. They would not send only one of them," I concluded.

"You must all leave...now!" Devin shouted; the veins on his neck were now visible. "Head for the trees, the trees, now!"

Commotion erupted. The screaming of children and women filled the village. Some attempted to head back to their homes to retrieve what they could from their belongings.

"There is no time!" Adawnas shouted. "Please, you must all leave at once! Don't wait."

Loud thunder rumbled through the sky. Rain immediately followed. The growls grew louder, closer. Clamorously, the people fled, heading in the direction of the wooden gate.

"We cannot linger," Devin said. "They are coming. We must leave also."

"And leave these people helpless?" I asked. "I thought our duty was to save people, not to allow them to be slaughtered."

"Isaac is right," Adawnas agreed. "We must help them."

Devin placed both of his hands over his head, sighed and looked up at the rainy sky.

"How many?" he asked.

I closed my eyes to concentrate at a deeper level, to better feel the presence of the Shadows. After I was able to push beyond the impulse of tuning into their feelings and thoughts, I was able to see them.

"I see many, Devin—*hundreds* of them coming our way," I mumbled. I felt the cold sweat dripping from my hands.

"We will not be able to defeat them all, Adawnas—you know it!" he yelled.

The people fled in despair, the children cried hysterically, mayhem was on every side. Out of the commotion of the people, a man dressed in silver armor unexpectedly sprang from the shadows and walked in our direction. He held a sword decorated with silver jewels; its blade was long and its black cross-guard had a lion engraved. In his left hand he held a dark spear with a silver tip. The engravings of the lion were also etched on the spear's handle.

"Yes, we will." The man exuded complete assurance. These three simple words seemed to carry the certainty of our victory. He looked back.

"Underwarriors!" he yelled in a commanding voice. The ground trembled and from under the Over Hall, soldiers arose. They also sprang out from underground, from inside houses and from under the trees.

"Who are you?" I asked. Devin and Adawnas seemed confused as well.

"Would you rather converse right now, or do you want to fight these creatures and send them back to the Abyss?" he asked as he placed a sword in my hand.

"Use it wisely," he said, making his way toward the woods.

His exquisite armor appeared to be created from an ethereal material fashioned in silver with golden stripes. It shimmered with a celestial brilliance, even without the presence of sunlight.

At last the Shadows had reached us. They leaped onto the women, biting flesh anywhere they could. The moment the Shadows began to attack the people, the Underwarriors violently struck from the rear. They were not as fast as the Nephilins, but right away I noticed that they were highly skilled in combat.

I wielded my sword with such agility, it appeared as though I had been fighting with one my whole life. I pierced as many Shadows as I could; some through the chest, others I struck in the head. Though our efforts proved triumphant versus the Shadows, many women and children were still devoured. I tried to keep as many alive as possible, convinced that their fate was doomed if I was unsuccessful.

The Shadows continued scaling the walls, climbing down from the trees and appearing out of the houses. With all of the passion that ignited in me, I did not want to waste any time. I had to make certain that I would send as many of them to the Abyss as possible.

I relentlessly pressed through the Shadows, slaying them mercilessly. My body felt invigorated, stronger in so many ways. As I attacked, I could see the Shadows clearly. My heart was still filled with fear for the women and children, who were feeling despair and defenseless from the attacks by these foul creatures, and the knowledge that they would never see their husbands or fathers again.

One specific Shadow caught my eye. It held a torch and it was sniffing the ashes of other Shadows that had been defeated. Quickly, the Shadow cast the torch onto their remains and a fire began to spread throughout the town.

"They are flammable!" I yelled in despair. "Their ashes are flammable!" I kept on shouting, hoping Devin or Adawnas would hear me. I tried to find something that would stop the fire, but there was nothing. Some of the Shadows fled toward the inferno and cast themselves into the flames. Each time one walked into the fire, an explosion took place.

I leaped from rooftop to rooftop, tree to tree, trying to find Devin and Adawnas. The Underwarriors were still battling; some lay dead on the ground. As I forged ahead, I finally caught a glimpse of Devin fighting. Hastily, I went to his aid. There were two Shadows mounted on top of him, one on his neck and the other on his leg. With their razor-sharp teeth, they bit him violently. Instantly, I pierced one right through its back. It hissed as soon as the blade touched it. Devin swung his sword and decapitated the other. He seemed weak; wounds were scattered along his arm and neck. I pulled him inside one of the houses.

"Devin...the Shadows are setting the town on fire with their own bodies!" I declared. "The town is being destroyed."

His eyes widened, boring deep into mine. He looked outside to see the dark cloud of smoke rising.

"Isaac, we must leave at once," he affirmed in a strong voice.

"Lea...leave?" I mumbled. "What about the people...the children that are still alive? We are just going to leave them here?" The thought of forsaking these people brought me despair.

"There is no other way. If we stay, we die here, along with them." The moment he was done speaking, he slowly rested his back against the dirty wall and sat on the floor, groaning in pain.

"*No!*" I yelled as I grabbed his shoulder. "I thought our duty was to not only protect the Diary, but also the people of Elysium. They are unaware that many others will soon share their fate." Desperation finally burst forth from me. My face reflected the gloom, which quickly spread throughout my entire body.

"People will die in this war whether we like it nor not. Trust me, if we die, all will be disastrous." His voice was cold. "We must look for Adawnas. We must leave this place at once," Devin insisted with utmost urgency.

"But if we can prevent their deaths—"

"*We will!*" he snapped, shouting at the top of his lungs. "We are destined to prevent the deaths of many. If we stay, we die now and our journey ends. I am so sorry, but we have not gone through all of these perils to die here. It is a hard choice but on this journey, hard choices are fated."

I could no longer argue with him. He was right. My eyes filled with sorrowful tears. I knew they were going to die; their fate awaited them on this day. I knew there was one thing Devin could not understand; one thing he did not know. He did not have the power to see the people's souls. I could see them, feel their hearts as they died around me. The experience was overwhelming, disheartening.

"Let us be courageous now and head out!" he charged as he struggled to get up. I inhaled a deep breath, wiped away the tears and nodded, reaching out to him, helping him to stand. As he stood to his feet, I was surprised to see the wounds on his neck and legs were rapidly healing.

"Devin!" I heard Adawnas' voice. She appeared out of the woods "We cannot linger any longer. The Shadows are going to turn this place into ash. I saw their army. There are many of them coming…still coming," she panted. I was not able to miss the scarlet stains on her clothes. Seeing the blood was in some way a confirmation that the citizens of Valley Hills would be dead soon.

"I am sorry, but we have no choice now," he said, displaying no emotion on his face. I understood what he meant. We had to leave the people behind.

At that moment, the faces, thoughts and emotions of the people flooded my mind. Their deaths would be intolerable for me—at least for some time.

In the midst of the explosions and the destruction, we ran with all the speed that our legs could carry. It was foolish of us to think that we would escape unnoticed by the Shadows. The moment we caught sight of them, they immediately followed us.

I separated myself from Devin and Adawnas and headed toward a huge monument that was to my left. It was covered in pure white, surrounded by many golden columns. On top there was a statue of a woman holding a scale. Aside from the monument's architecture, something else grasped my attention; there was a sentence written above the columns:

"Justice and Vengeance Come by the Measure of the Scale"

I broke through the monument's wooden door. The moment I walked inside, I knew what this building was used for. It was a courthouse. Behind me, many Shadows followed. Exactly what I wanted! I wanted to take advantage of every single moment I had before I actually had to leave. I wanted to annihilate as many Shadows as I possibly could. And the recompense of being able to destroy them inside of a courthouse caused my heart to burst into joy.

My heart wanted vengeance; vengeance for the people that were dying outside. With my sword, I slashed every one of them. The more Shadows I decimated the more Shadows appeared. Some descended from the ceiling, while others came from the door. I continuously wielded my sword around, wounding as many as possible. Then my body slowly trembled; my eyes widened. With a simple thought, I was pushing the Shadows back, away from me. They growled contemptuously.

They still tried to assault me, but their onslaughts were ineffective. With my mind I created a shield around me. I noticed as my hunger for justice increased, the shield gained more strength, instantly causing the Shadows to burn.

Inside of my shield, a cloud of smoke formed. My heart felt heavy, almost as if falling from my chest. I noticed the Shadows' movements decreased in speed, slowly stopping. The world around me stopped. I heard low groans.

A voice echoed behind me.

"Isaac, you have come to my chamber." After the voice spoke, it hissed like a snake.

My breathing quickened.

"Who are you?" I asked, hesitant.

The voice laughed malevolently.

"I am the nightmare of your soul. It has been so easy to play with your head, Isaac. You fell right into my trap." Again it hissed slowly, with deliberate contempt.

"Lucifer?" I held on firmly to my sword as I spoke the name. The very sound of it sent a chill down my spine.

"Yes," a hollow breath countered. "It is I." A shadow appeared and slowly transformed itself into human form.

"Your mind is a vast field of information and excitement for me, little Isaac. I have learned a lot from watching you lately. I must say, the Creator has not been training his...puppets well." His shape did not seem to be symmetrical; his shadow moved like rising smoke.

I tried to speak but I couldn't. My mouth failed to respond, as did my body. My sword thudded loudly on the ground as my hands unwillingly released it.

"What you are doing is absolutely senseless. My body might be asleep, but my spirit moves unhindered over these lands. It is not hard to find you, Isaac...your thoughts are...really loud." A portion of his shadow shrouded my face in the shape of a human hand, dimming my view. My teeth chattered and my breathing faltered as I felt the frozen cold soul he possessed touch my face.

"You cannot hide from me. I still control you. You still belong to me. That is why I must tell you a secret, little Isaac."

The weight I felt inside of myself was overwhelming. It was as if all of the wickedness of the world had been birthed into me.

"Oh—I don't think I should. You will see it very soon. You shall see that the Diary does not stand alone."

My eyes constantly averted his stare as his vileness was intolerable to me. I felt that his presence would pollute the very core of my being. Not only did I hear the hissing of a snake, but now there were also rattling sounds reverberating throughout the chamber, and hollow voices echoing.

"Isaac...what are you doing in here?" I faintly heard Devin's voice in the midst of the other voices. After quickly assessing my immediate surroundings, I soon realized that Lucifer had slowed down the dimension of time.

"Isaac, what is wrong with you?" This time it was Adawnas' voice. The moment the voice echoed again, Lucifer disappeared, along with the rest of the Shadows that had entered the courthouse. Instantly, time resumed to its normal pace.

"What are you doing here? Why didn't you follow us? Are you incapable of listening?" They kept on mumbling, but I paid little heed to their preoccupation with the nonessential matters of the present moment. My mind and body had been devoured by this evil being and it was in a complete state of shock.

The disaster around me was incomprehensible. To witness so many innocent lives that had perished by the most profane and merciless murderer drained my soul.

After we jumped over the wall that encircled the village, we headed deep into the forest. As we fled, the screams of the people slowly faded, but their thoughts and feelings didn't. My mind was obsessed with the recent slaughter from the Abyss—thoughts of their fate lingered inside of me.

At last, we were far from danger's path. My body was extremely weary. I pondered whether or not to mention the visitation I just had to them. We were all silent. Devin headed to a nearby oak tree and sat by its side, not speaking a word. Adawnas climbed up one of the trees and relaxed there. I remained in the same stationary stance, gaping at the dense, black forest.

My mind was crowded with the desperate cries and screams for help from the villagers; helpless to protect them as the Shadows plundered and killed the innocent ones. The images of the village being completely destroyed by fire were vivid in my mind.

I rocked my body back and forth; my breathing became much labored. I tried to make sense of it all, especially the reason why Lucifer had shown himself to me...why did he withhold the secret...the reason why he said I was still his? Could this have anything to do with the visions and dreams I had been having?

As a feeling of loneliness crept inside of me, I found myself weeping over all of the things that were bottled up inside until now. My parents, Demetre, those people...it all happened so fast. Some things I had gained, but I had lost many others. The tears rolled down my face and this time, I was just too exhausted to hold them back. My soul was so wounded. I laid my head down on the tree and wept bitterly, releasing all the emotions that had drained me mentally, emotionally and physically. It was time to rest.

IX

With the darkness that covered Elysium, the only way to discern that morning had arrived was when the darkness of the clouds was washed away by the rays of the sun that shone behind them. The moment I opened my eyes, I immediately felt the change of temperature. To my surprise, I saw flurries of snow falling. Quickly I rose and glanced at the gray sky.

"Strange, isn't it?" Adawnas asked. "I have never seen snow fall at this time of the year. It is indeed quite unexpected."

"Anyone hungry?" I heard Devin's voice echo from within the woods. Shortly after, he appeared with a deer in his arms.

"I have food," he said with a grin on his face.

I shook my head. "Have I slept for long?" I asked Adawnas.

"One hour probably…not that long."

Since our journey, the forest had been very quiet and it surprised me when I heard the chirping of birds and the faint squeaks of rodents stirring from their holes among the trees.

"You know, I tried awfully hard to ignore your weeping but I couldn't," Adawnas spoke with her mellow voice. "It is alright to grieve over those who have passed, but you must not allow grief to rule you."

Unexpectedly, from afar I saw some men heading in our direction. I felt the strength of their hearts, the indomitable courage they had within. Devin looked ahead and smiled. He seemed relieved.

As the men drew near, I recognized one of them. It was the same man that approached us in the Valley Hills, the one that led the Underwarriors. Four other men had joined with him. Their armors were broken, their swords and shields shattered.

"I am glad to see you all made it out alive," the man I recognized spoke.

"I am relieved to see you have survived. We didn't get a chance to talk," I replied as I walked closer to him.

His skin had burn marks all over it. "Unfortunately, many of the women were killed, the children were taken, and we lost many men," he added. Their faces looked weary, their breathing hard, even their hands trembled.

"Please, sit down. I am pretty sure you are all tired and hungry. We are about to have deer," Devin said as he prepared the meal.

"What is your name?" Adawnas asked.

"My name is Alexander, head of the Underwarriors. These here are Adamo, Gluglielmo, Nathan and Lino. We are the only ones who survived the attack of the Shadows," he said as they sat on one of the broken logs.

"How did you find us?" I asked. My eyes analyzed the wounds scattered throughout their bodies.

They all looked at each other and then set their eyes on Devin and Adawnas. "It is not hard for us to find your kind."

Devin immediately released the deer.

"I suppose you are here to destroy not only Shadows, but my kind as well?" Adawnas said sharply.

"But they are not like the others," I contested. "They have been nothing but brave and loyal on this journey."

"We are not here to kill any of you—not even your kind," Adamo spoke. "We noticed you were different the moment you walked into Valley Hills. That is why we joined with you in battle."

Devin had already started the fire. The temperature continued to drop as we spoke.

"What are Underwarriors? I have never heard of your kind in all my years of existence," Adawnas affirmed.

"Which I assume you have many long, well-lived years on this land, am I correct?" Gluglielmo added. We all chuckled softly.

"Well, where to begin?" Alexander scratched his head. "We do not differ from your kind in many ways, but we have something that…" There was a sudden pause, and then he continued, "Privileges that you were not given."

"You mean the opportunity to be redeemed?" Devin interrupted. At this question, Alexander became apprehensive.

"We are humans now, but this was not always the case," he stammered. "We can even consider ourselves to be related, if that is even possible."

Silence fell.

"We were sent from Tristar in human form long ago, shortly after the fall of the Brightest Star. We do not age, and we cannot die."

"But you're still wounded and many of you *did* die," I affirmed, my eyes boring into his. "How can this be?"

"Our bodies have retained vulnerability to war and the slaying of swords, but we do not die once these bodies are corrupted. Our souls return to Tristar where we stay until ordered elsewhere."

As my eyes examined the severity of the Underwarriors' wounds, I noticed they possessed a few traits resembling those of the Nephilins.

"I can see you are also wounded," Adamo spoke as his eyes gazed at the bite marks on Devin's arms and neck. Even though they were quickly healing, they were still very visible.

Devin placed the deer on a wooden stick and set it over the fire, ignoring his comment.

"What is your objective, exactly?" I asked them. "You sprung out of the ground like ants, came to our aid, eradicated the Shadows, and then you found us. What is it you have been charged to accomplish?"

"We have come to aid the humans and the Council in protecting the Diary." Alexander's words fell heavy and weary from his lips. "They have chosen their own ruin, and yet the Creator still gives them a chance for redemption."

"It might upset you to know that Nephele has the Diary," I said with grave distress.

A smile began to curve at the corners of Alexander's mouth. "They may have the Diary, but they do not have you, young one," he said.

"I will assume that you are on our side then—all of you, that is," Devin said hotly. He began tapping his fingers against his arms in a sign of impatience.

Alexander smiled again and placed his right hand on Devin's shoulder.

"Indeed, indeed we are." There was a slight pause. "Who would have ever thought that we would see Nephilins and Underwarriors working together? Who knows...there might be redemption in the future for your kind, after all."

"You say that you are from Tristar—does that mean you have met Lucifer?" After my horrifying encounter with him in Valley Hills, I couldn't resist the impulse to ask him.

Silence hung in the air momentarily. Nathan scoffed.

"Yes, we have seen him. Better yet, we served him in Tristar for thousands of years. He tried coercive persuasion to defect over to his side, but we did not approve of his evildoing nor his malevolent intentions," Nathan answered with a strong and authoritative voice.

"Have you also seen the Creator?" Adawnas asked.

Alexander smiled. "Why, yes! We have seen him many times. I clearly remember the day we came to life through him. We are created differently than humans, or your kind. Humans he molded with his bare hands—us he breathed upon the shining stars of the night sky and out of each star, we were born."

As they spoke of the Creator, their faces lit like torches. Of course, as they spoke, I could not help but recall the divine moment when I first heard his voice in that ocean. To hear them speak of him brought me a serene peace.

Afterward, we sat by the fire, eating deer, enjoying the silence. I attempted to read the Underwarriors and I could discern that they were indeed not from here. Their thoughts were difficult to see and understand. It was like listening to many men speaking at once and trying to understand what each one was speaking.

"We must be off," Alexander said, wiping his hands against his legs, cleaning his fingers. "We will be heading to the Gates of the Fourth Dimension to see what can be done there."

"Just the four of you?" Devin asked.

"Yes." Alexander walked closer to Devin. "You know, I really hope that your kind will find redemption from the Creator. I never thought that I'd meet a Nephilin with such an amazing soul. I still wonder why you are so different from the others."

Devin was speechless. His eyes glimmered with joy as he peered over at Adawnas, but his joy was met with coldness. She remained stoic, arms crossed.

"I am really glad we met, Alexander," I said. "I do hope our paths will cross again soon."

"Don't worry, we will," he affirmed as they all stood to their feet.

Slowly they walked to the woods, disappearing in a matter of seconds. After this visit, I felt hope springing forth once again within me.

I was so absorbed with our conversation that I failed to notice that the landscape around us had been completely covered with snow.

I was amazed to see how fast the snow covered the trees. A never-ending white road leading us deeper into the heart of the forest appeared ahead of us.

We walked in silence. I could tell Adawnas and Devin were as apprehensive as I was, entering the unknown depths of the forest. We did not know what to expect. Even Devin and Adawnas, who had been alive for so long, were completely oblivious to what was in store for us.

"It does not even feel like this is Elysium anymore." Devin broke the silence. "So many changes taking place..." he mused as we walked.

"How difficult will it be to convince Mag Mell of everything that is going on?" I asked.

Devin shrugged.

"Well, from what I remember you were not thrilled to know our journey was leading us there," I added. He shot me a cold look.

Devin's silence implied that he was thinking of an answer to give me—one that would not expose his pride and morals.

"The bigger kingdoms here in Elysium are all very proud, holding dear to their hearts their traditions and cultures. To bring down these walls will not be easy," Devin said, breaking his silence.

"Especially the people from Mag Mell," Adawnas spoke in her soothing voice. "They are proud, Isaac; they have conquered territories, brought war upon many and proved victorious. Their thoughts will probably invade your mind as we approach the kingdom."

As we continued on, pieces of broken concrete were scattered along the ground. Not long after we stumbled onto the concrete, towers rose from the ground of the forest.

"What is this place?" I asked, astounded at the sight. It was quite apparent that once a stately city had thrived amidst these old ruins.

"This marks the beginning of the Mag Mellian territory, and is only one of the many ruins that are scattered around this area—remnants of kingdoms that have been destroyed and their people enslaved."

Throughout my journey through Elysium, I discovered that I truly lacked knowledge about this place. With every new mystery revealed, I felt like an outsider in my own land. A soft cool breeze blew and the still-soft snow was slowly blown away from some of the monuments, revealing faded colors, broken designs and unique patterns.

Neither Devin nor Adawnas seemed to be surprised at the sight. They had probably been here before, or expected to see these ruins.

"We have to keep on moving—there is no time to linger," Devin affirmed, carefully analyzing our surroundings.

The snow once again commenced to fall. The dense forest was becoming nearly impossible to travel through. To our surprise, we came across a river. It had not yet been frozen by the cold, but it would only be a matter of time before it succumbed to the bitter conditions.

"I don't think we should travel any further. The snow is getting too intense here," Adawnas alleged as we stopped at the river bank. The visibility was barely perceivable to see what lay ahead of us.

"Devin, let us rest. We will continue our journey in a short while," I said, my teeth chattering due to the frigid conditions.

Devin sighed, obviously disapproving of the idea. I also found no delight in stopping again to wait out the storm, but we needed our full strength where we were heading.

In the woods near the river, we picked up some old tree bark and leaves to build a shelter. Once inside, Devin gathered some wood and built a small fire. We all lay near the burning flames, trying to warm up our bodies. I tried my best to relax and rest for a while, but as time elapsed I found it difficult to get a wink of sleep.

A loud growl broke the silence. Adawnas hastily headed outside to investigate the commotion; Devin and I followed.

Unfortunately, the visibility was poor, making it impossible to see anything clearly since the storm had not weakened.

"Can you see them?" she asked us as her eyes frantically searched for the creatures that growled.

"What is it?" I asked, but no one responded.

Shortly after we began searching, we spotted them. They were Aquilas. Adawnas in haste headed toward them. As we approached the animals we realized that they were all walking, their wings frozen solid from the storm. Once they saw us, they recoiled, afraid of our presence.

"They are not equipped for this type of weather...they will not last here," she said as her voice broke.

"Unfortunately, they will not be the only ones to die here." Devin caressed one of them. The Aquilas were struggling to move. Their heads were down and their wings were completely torn. Some of them also had deep wounds covering their bodies.

Adawnas looked at them with gloomy eyes.

It was the first time that I had seen Adawnas weeping. She laid her head against the ground and repeatedly beat her clutched fist against it, screaming in desperation.

"Adawnas, please, let us not lose our focus right now," Devin tried calming her.

"It is not about losing our focus, Devin," she screamed. "Look at them—and many more will surely come. Is there really hope for this situation? Let us face the facts now: they have the Diary, and the world is completely covered with this dark cloud blocking us all from the sun. You know this will not be the only disaster, but it is the beginning of many to come."

Devin bowed his head and moaned.

"You feel it, don't you?" she asked as she wiped the tears from her face.

In haste, she stood to her feet.

"And us? Why do we fight? Why should we care? Even if we make it, and we get all the kingdoms to unite in this battle, what hope do we have? Are we really anticipating that a human army has the strength to stop Lucifer's army?"

Devin's expression was cold; no sign of any emotion came from him. His eyes were fixed on her every movement.

"Adawnas, you need to control yourself!" I said in a feeble attempt to calm her.

She turned her head to gaze at me.

"What do you know? *Nothing!* You should be the one going on this journey throughout the kingdoms, not us. There is no hope for us, even if there is victory."

"You know that is not true." Devin's tone of voice was bitter.

She scratched her head as she again turned to face the Aquilas. They all lay on the snow-covered ground, their very breath weakened by the moment.

"We are damned just like this land, Devin. Our kind has been damned since the dawn of time." Devin remained silent. "You remember those days just as well as I do—the days of darkness after the war where we lingered in Elysium without any direction, being disdained by our fathers."

"Please stop speaking all of this rubbish." Irritation was evident in Devin's voice.

"You know this is not rubbish. You can be enraged all you want, but you know I am telling the truth. We were damned by birth. Don't you remember how we had to grow up alone because our mothers were turned into Shadows and we were left to wander the world in solitude? Soon after, Lucifer attacked Tristar and was put to sleep. That was until Nephele decided to gather our kind."

"But *we* are not them, Adawnas—*we* are not our parents." He tried to calm her down but she was too desperate, too distraught to listen. This was not the time for comfort, she was too angry.

"The need to deny my natural urges...the need to refrain from catering to my own will is overwhelming." She bore her eyes into mine, her fists tightened as she walked closer. "It would've been a lot easier if you had chosen Nephele's offer Isaac, we would have all been part of the covenant with them, conquering this world right now."

I was shocked at her allegation.

"Adawnas, I do not regret my decision and if given the chance I would never go back on it," I affirmed in a strong voice.

"Do you not see what is happening? *Look around you now!* What we are trying to do is to change an eternal mindset of concepts. We are attempting to reform an entire generation's frame of mind to believe in something they always thought was a myth."

"Still, we carry proof that these things exist!" I contested.

For a moment I looked around and saw my companions in a state of discord, confused. The Aquilas were dying in this subfreezing temperature, buried in the snow that had covered the entire land. Was this also going to be my demise?

"We are all damned, just like this place..." She sobbed with tears rolling down her cheeks.

"But the Creator came to me—"

"He came to *you*, Isaac...not to me," she yelled.

I shot Devin a look and I could tell he was as disconcerted as I. In the few moments of stillness that hovered over us, my mind was overtaken with memories of our journey. Had it all been in vain? Had our arduous efforts to protect Demetre been useless? The Creator had indeed come to me, but if his power was far superior to the Darkness, why was the Darkness spreading swiftly throughout the land?

"Adawnas, please, you know we must be in agreement on this matter. We cannot lose you now," Devin whispered to her while holding both of her hands.

"I can't do this anymore, Devin. I cannot pretend to believe in this anymore...I am so sorry," she said, gasping.

She was once again screaming hysterically, her hands over her head.

"I am sorry," she lamented, taking off at great speed. In a couple of seconds, she had vanished into the woods.

I quickly panicked, my body paralyzed from the shock of her departure.

"Devin, we need to go after her now!" I declared as I positioned my body to start running.

Slowly he turned his back, head bowed; he walked back toward our shelter.

"You mean we are not going after her?" I shouted, shocked at his actions.

He sighed. "No. This choice is not ours to change. Let us get some sleep now."

I looked around and saw the blanket of white that covered the landscape in every direction the eye could see.

"Sleep? How can you think of that now? She left!" I yelled at the top of my lungs, hastily making my way to him. "How do we know she has not sided with the enemy?"

He quickly moved his body toward me, his eyes penetrating deep into mine.

"I hope you understand something. I have been fighting against my nature for such a long time now. I wasn't always this strong, Isaac. She decided to align herself with me the moment she discovered Athalas' plans. Don't think for a split second that this is easy...or cheap. How would you feel if you were starving and someone presented you with a succulent turkey breast? After a while, that same person tells you that you cannot eat it, but you must only drink the wine that is set at the table? The wine will quench your thirst, but it cannot satisfy your hunger. I am doing this because I want to believe. I need to believe." With that said, he turned about, continuing his walk to the shelter.

I was speechless.

What else could I say or think of? I felt groundless, as though I was floating around some insecure invisible space that would soon drop me into an abyss. I could not turn back; neither did I want to go forward.

I reclined against a tree and stared up reflectively into the sky. The snow had stopped falling. The Aquilas had fallen silent. I turned to them and saw their frozen bodies buried halfway in the snow.

"There is still hope," I mumbled to myself. I continued to remind my soul, rehearsing the things Raziel had confided to me. *They fear what you will become.* Right now, I had no other choice but to believe. I closed my eyes and softly sang a tune.

Night star in the sky, how marvelous you shine
Above me you stand. In the darkness, you are the only lamp
Even if small and dim
Night star, in the darkness you bring light from within.

After I sang, my heart and mind drifted back to happier days tucked away in my thoughts. I pretended that everything was simply a nightmare; that I would wake up in the morning and once again find my parents in the kitchen, head out with my father to the fields, and afterward, return home to a nice cooked meal. I took a deep breath and shivered from the harsh blow of the frigid air.

I headed back to the shelter and found Devin sitting down, tears strolling down his face. It shocked me because I had never seen him cry.

I lay down on the opposite side of the shelter. He uttered not a single word. I fell asleep as I listened to Devin's low sobs and muffled groaning.

X

I awoke to find myself in a white room with a gigantic glass window. I used my powers in an attempt to read my surroundings, but there was nothing.

I headed to the window and peered up into the sky. The moment my eyes looked upon the scene that was repeated before me, tears began to form. As I scanned the heavens, stark images of my entire journey passed before me. My heart was filled with great turmoil as I viewed the faces of those that had died. I saw the women who died in Valley Hills, the mutilated bodies scattered around the premises. I experienced once again the anguish of witnessing my best friend change into a beast as I stood by helpless, unable to protect him.

"You should have been smarter, Isaac."

I instantly recognized the cold voice, which sent shivers down my spine. I turned around to see Nephele standing right behind me.

"When I offered you the choice, it was simply because I knew of the destiny that awaited you," she stated with an icy smile.

"I am no fool, Nephele! I offer no regret for the choice I've made," I affirmed without flinching.

"A fool you are, Isaac. The diminutive enhancement of your abilities is insignificant in comparison to what could have been—actually, what can still be."

A rush of adrenaline coursed through my veins. A sudden change was taking place inside of me. My body grew weak. My vision was getting blurry, and my head began to spin.

Could this be the moment of weakness Raziel warned me about? I wondered as weakness overtook me. Could this be my human will trying to break out? Every part of my body weakened as thoughts rushed through my mind. My body became limp.

"Where are we?" I asked, not sure if this was a dream or reality.

She smiled.

"This is reality, Isaac—nothing else."

"Reality…" I was confused. My breathing grew shallow.

She walked toward the glass window; her eyes were fixed on the memories that played out in the sky.

"I can see some of these events hurt you deeply, but there is still time to change all of these events, Isaac," she said, gently laying her hands against the window. After a short silence, she effortlessly moved toward me.

"You still have the opportunity to join us. Think of what it could be—what the world will be like." She tried to place her hand on my face, but I slowly recoiled, backing away. I commenced to read her thoughts and felt sincerity in her heart. It was shocking to realize she was actually quite truthful about her claims.

"Demetre was not so stubborn," she affirmed with a cold expression. She frowned in a sign of disapproval.

Upon examining the memories, right now was not the best time to recall thoughts of Demetre. I could only focus my attention on my friend being so far away and separated by the darkness.

"As far as I can remember, Demetre did not have the opportunity to choose," I recalled.

"You are right, he didn't. His parents made that choice for him. We agreed to grant them their greatest desire," she informed me as she inched closer. "They desired a son, so a son was given, and within him dwelled the power of Darkness."

Every time I thought things were beginning to make sense, a new occurrence interrupted my reasoning. I bowed my head, awestruck by what Nephele had just told me. The strangest feeling took place. The rhythm of my heart slowed down as my eyes looked at hers. Rapidly, my vulnerability was succumbing to her provocative manipulation. Even though the room around me was as white as snow, my heart felt as though it was chained within the blackest abyss. To see

Nephele standing in front of me with such beguiling beauty; her relentless power weakened me to the very core of my soul.

"You can still choose to be with us, Isaac. Side with us and end your suffering," she whispered enticingly into my ear.

The very thought that I could be rid of all the excruciating pain I had been forced to endure was a most tempting invitation. I was faced with two destinies; I needed time to reflect, to think, to make the right choice, but at the same time, I knew I could not deviate from the path I had already chosen. Yet, my desire to be relieved of all this suffering was overpowering. Confusion invaded my mind, making it difficult to make the right decision. My eyes fastened onto her gaze.

"How much time do I have to decide?" I asked her as I took a step closer, hoping to stall for more time.

She gave me an uncanny half-smile, indicating her willingness to barter with me.

"Until you wake up again." She rested her hand on my cheek. Slowly she moved her lips closer to mine. Nephele now stood so close to my body that I could feel the breath of her nostrils touching my face, her lips pursed close to mine.

I veiled my eyes; the memories continued to play in my head, my heart slowly beating. Of all the memories, one stood out to me: I would never forget the moment I caught sight of the white lion that killed me and brought me back to life once again, along with the ocean and the landscape that surrounded it; the red eyes that pierced my very soul.

I opened my eyes and smiled as the memories faded.

"So...have you already made a decision?" She anxiously bit her bottom lip.

"My answer to you...is...*no*." Abruptly, I pushed her away from me. I was not accustomed to combating women, but Nephele was not solely a woman; she was an enemy of my soul.

"Not very wise, Isaac! Your end will prove to be far worse than you could ever imagine, you fool. We have the Diary...do not forget that Demetre is host to one of the Generals of Darkness," she roared. "I came here to give you another chance to live, but you have willingly chosen death. There is nothing more I can do now to reverse your decision."

While the words drifted from her mouth, shards fell on the white floor of the room as the glass window shattered. The walls crumbled slowly and cracks appeared like spider webs as they traveled along the foundation. The memories that had formed in the heavens dissolved quickly.

Gasping frantically for air forced me to open my eyes. My body was dripping with sweat. As I looked around to get my bearings I spotted Devin sitting with his head bowed down. Curious, I crawled closer to find that he was only sleeping. My whole body began to shake violently as I tried to grasp what had just happened. Nephele had just appeared to me in my dreams...how was that possible? Was penetrating minds part of her special abilities?

Devin grunted, slowly lifting his head.

"Are you alright, Isaac? You look troubled," he mumbled in a sleepy voice.

I explained to him all that had just happened to me. As I told him the story, his face was transfixed in a complete state of shock.

"So she was able to enter your dreams," Devin said in a reflective tone.

"Yes. She offered it to me again, the power...the choice to side with them...I felt my human nature returning—the vulnerability of my old self returning back to me, Devin," I said, weariness lingering in my voice.

He sighed.

"To have your human will and nature be at its strongest on occasion is inevitable for you, I am afraid. You are human and even if you possessed all of the abilities in the world, you'd still suffer this attack. Nephele wants you, Isaac...the Darkness wants you."

As he continued to speak, my eyes caught sight of Adawnas' sword lying on the ground. With a heavy heart, I bent down, grabbing ahold of the sword.

"What do you think of my decision, Devin? Did I choose wisely?" I asked, somewhat afraid of his answer.

"I believe you were incredibly brave and wise. Even though Nephele's offer may sound very appealing, it will be but a temporary relief. We need to believe this Darkness won't endure for long." As he answered, his eyes never swayed from the sword.

"What about Adawnas? Where did she go?" My biggest fear, I thought, was the possibility that she was in some way connected to Athalas and the others.

"Adawnas has made her choice. Her path from now on is none of our concern," he spoke a bit apprehensively.

His hand reached for the sword within my grasp.

"May I?" he asked. Anguish was explicitly drawn on his face.

I nodded.

"We have to be more alert. The power of the enemy is growing." He gently touched the sword as he spoke. "We must go to Mag Mell and seek aid. Even though I believe many of the inhabitants already know about the Shadows and their attacks—or are even taking part in it all." He sighed. "Now...let us go back to sleep, Isaac. We need all the strength we can get to move on."

He laid himself on the ground, placed the sword next to him, folded his arms behind his head, closed his eyes, and in an instant he resembled a statue in his resting state. *How can he expect me to sleep after what has just happened to me?* I pondered. To my surprise, sleep came to me as the vivid images of the dream played in my mind.

The cold breeze awoke me. Devin was sitting outside our shelter, near the frigid water. As I stepped out, I stopped for a minute to survey the snow-covered landscape.

During the hours of our sleep, the river had frozen over. I was astounded to see how wide it was.

"The River of Abstergo—the widest and longest river in all of Elysium," Devin said as he glanced at the frozen waters. "We are close to Mag Mell. We should arrive there in a few hours." I was relieved by this observation.

"Have you already eaten, Devin?" I asked him. He was straining his eyes across the river, looking into something unseen.

"I am not hungry." He did not bother to look up at me when he answered. Deep in thought, he was focused on one thing: the mission at hand.

"Let us keep moving," he said.

We gathered our belongings from the shelter and were soon on our way. Instead of turning and heading to the forest like I thought we would, Devin followed the trail alongside the river.

"We will have to walk over it. Be very careful as you step onto the icy river," he said, making it sound as though walking atop recently frozen rivers was a very natural activity.

"The river?" I asked, shocked. "Can we try to jump over it?"

He scoffed.

"Do you really think that even with our speed, we could cross this river with a simple leap?" I looked out toward the water again as he spoke. I noticed that my hasty suggestion was impractical. The river was too wide, and I knew he feared the increased possibility of falling through the ice, if we tried to jump. I decided not to complain. He had been around long enough to judge the best course of action in this situation.

"Why not take the forest?" I asked, hopeful that he would agree to my suggestion.

"She came to you…she is probably close. We need to travel the fastest route this time. We are not certain of who has aligned with her," he replied coldly.

A chilling gentle breeze was blowing across the top of the river, scattering the still-soft snow. Slowly we inched along the top of the frozen waters, carefully watching our every step. Devin walked ahead of me. With every step we took, I could feel the ice cracking beneath our feet.

"Is there no other way?" I asked, looking at my feet as they treaded on the ice.

Devin came to a sudden halt.

"Devin?" I called out to him, but he did not answer.

As quickly as the ice would permit me, I hurriedly scuttled to Devin's side, being as careful as possible. The sight I beheld as I reached him left me speechless. A part of the river that had not frozen over stretched out before me, and to my surprise, bodies floated in the water like warped tree logs. Some were missing their limbs while others were missing their eyes or hands. Some of them were still intact.

"They have come," Devin said as his fingers clenched into fists. I heard the echoing of ferocious growling. We both knew instantly what followed those contemptible sounds.

The moment I closed my eyes, I could clearly see what surrounded us. Nephele was closing in on both of us with an army of Shadows. The vision caused me to tremble with fear.

"Isaac, can you see where they are coming from?" Devin asked. He seemed to be very agitated.

"No, but they are close." Instantly, I sensed the presence of Shadows as they resolutely marched in our direction.

"We have to find a way to escape, Devin." The moment I opened my eyes, I caught a glimpse of Nephele laughing with cruel mockery. Though I knew her image was stemming from my mind, her evil presence felt very real.

"I tried to be reasonable with you, but I have wasted my time." The vision gradually faded but it quickly returned. My head burned from the shrillness of her voice pounding in my ears.

The vision vanished.

I gasped for air. Every encounter with Nephele, whether in vision or in a dream, left my body drained of energy and strength.

Shadows were slowly surrounding the riverbank; their desperation and their compulsive thirst to kill attracted my attention. I was awestruck by their numbers.

"They reached it before us," Devin whispered.

"Reached what?"

"Mag Mell! They've destroyed it already...we were too late," he spoke with a tormented voice.

Dead bodies continued flowing down the unfrozen portion of the river, and gradually piled up near the ice.

Four Desert Dragons hovered above us like a pack of vultures over a carcass, slowly plummeting to devour it. Three of them flew to the shore to meet the Shadows while the one remaining descended swiftly toward us.

I recognized who was atop this beast by its malefic presence.

The Desert Dragon carefully landed on the ice, but even with all its care, it could not prevent the frozen river from cracking. Nephele alighted from the creature attired in a long black cloak. Her breast, shoulders and arms were protected by a dark armor. Her soul-piercing eyes landed on me.

At once, silence filled the atmosphere. The Shadows became still, and the beasts stopped growling; even the wind seemed to cease blowing. I saw Athalas, Corbin and Azaziel standing on the riverside accompanied by thousands of Shadows. Their presence together stirred urgency in my heart, especially that of Corbin.

Nephele walked toward us, her face expressing her coldness. "Isaac, dear, did you tell your friend about our encounter last night?" Her smile was evil personified.

"I know what you are here to do, Nephele, but are you incapable of recruiting me on your own?" With every word I uttered, the anger that burned within me refueled my strength.

"I would have been a fool to come by myself." She let out a wicked laugh.

I took out my sword.

Instantly, paralysis attacked my entire body, every limb went numb, and a sharp pain brought me to my knees. My body succumbed to a trancelike state of sleep. Athalas was attacking my mind once again, inflicting unbearable pain upon me.

I faintly heard Devin shout something and suddenly my hearing was gone. The pain seemed to come in waves, beginning with a burning sensation and then ending in agonizing torment. I writhed around trying to contain it, but it was an impossible feat.

My vision was fading, but I knew at this point I could not give into the pain. With my senses slowly failing, I desperately searched within myself for the strength to fight my way out of this agony. With all my might I brought to mind the vision of the white lion that had given me the abilities and reassured me of who I was meant to be. I could not die here, nor could I leave Devin now.

It was then in the midst of this inner battle, Raziel appeared to me. At first, I was not sure if I was seeing an apparition or if he was actually real. I blinked my eyes a couple of times just to be sure I was not dreaming or hallucinating. I realized that he was actually present before me. In his hand he held a dagger adorned with gold and multicolored diamonds. He bored his eyes into mine, smiled and viciously stabbed the right side of my back. I thought I had experienced raw pain before this, but nothing compared to the dreadful sensation I suffered from this blade. I felt the dagger slowly ripping through the sinew of my back. Then, once more, he repeated the act. This time he plunged the dagger into the left side.

The pain immobilized me, pinning me to the ground. Slowly I regained consciousness. My body once again responded to my commands, but my back was burning like hot coals of fire. I could feel something crawling inside of me, as if a creature lurked under my skin, coursing its way through my blood vessels. My body was getting warmer and my hands were trembling. I let out a shout that seemed to come from pure instinct. My eyes opened and I saw Devin and Nephele positioned in the same manner that I had last seen them. I came to realize that time in the realm of the Stars and the Fallen proved to be completely different from my realm. Although I felt time moving at an altered state, it was actually spinning faster.

Two immense wings sprang out of my back, ripping my flesh apart. I felt the rugged tear spreading further between my shoulder blades. I held my breath expecting pain to follow, but I felt nothing. I also noticed that no blood was seeping from the wounds. I tested my wings by flapping them back and forth and was astounded at the way they moved. They simulated the movements of an eagle's wings. The feathers were white and minutely synchronized. I reached behind my back and felt the wings' coverts aligned between my shoulders.

"Impossible," Nephele stammered. The Shadows howled and growled defiantly. At once I picked up Corbin's thoughts; he was confused and even more determined to eliminate Devin and me.

Nephele quickly mounted her Desert Dragon and glared at Devin.

"You truly are a disgrace to us all, Devin—the only Nephilin to ever deny his own kin. You do not deserve the privilege of immortality. This mess could have been avoided if you and Adawnas had been loyal to your people and brought us his body," she said in a somber voice.

It was at that moment that Devin swiftly took out his sword and catapulted it in Nephele's direction. Without the slightest effort, she dodged it, and in the blink of an eye she was standing right in front of Devin.

Instantly, I flew in her direction. The wings maneuvered with rapid speed, moving with accelerated precision. With all my strength I pushed her away from him, thrusting her into the cold river. I knew this would not detain her for long; in fact, I did not think it would detain her at all. I quickly turned around and flew awkwardly in Devin's direction. I clamped my hands around him with a tight grip and ascended as high as I could fly into the clouds. This felt so unnatural and unusual given I had never flown before. Despite the discomfort, in a matter of seconds, it was as if flying was second nature to me, as if I had done it for many years. I looked down to see everything getting smaller as we ascended.

"What has happened to you?" Devin shouted as we soared.

"Raziel…he came to me again. He gave me these." I kept my eyes on the clouds, aiming to soar higher.

"Have you ever done this before?" he shouted as we soared.

I glanced down at him.

"What do you think?" I smiled.

The atmosphere grew colder as we soared. The strength in my arms was slowly giving out on me and my breathing became more and more labored.

"You are not accustomed to this altitude, Isaac. We need to land somewhere," Devin yelled.

A mighty shout of war issued from beneath us, followed by a spontaneous growl coming from behind us. I glanced back and saw Nephele on her beast flying straight at us. Three more beasts sped in our direction. I didn't need any special discernment to identify them.

Hopelessness struck me. I knew we had to find a way out quickly, but I could think of no immediate solution. If we were to fall, the Shadows would devour us completely; if we stayed here, Athalas, Corbin, Azaziel and Nephele would surely eliminate us.

"Isaac, we have no choice," Devin shouted. I saw whisks of gray clouds quickly moving in our direction. I noticed that the beasts suddenly halted and growled viciously in midair the moment their eyes met these clouds. It was then that I realized that Nephele and the others were retreating as fast as they could. I heard the commotion of the Shadows underneath us, their growls clamoring loudly. I could sense the Shadows feared that which approached us. My body could no longer withstand the altitude and my strength was beginning to wane. Both of us were now plummeting through the dark sky. My wings failed me. I felt them shrinking in size until they folded under my skin, hidden in my back.

"Isaac, *try to keep going...*" Devin shouted as we fell. I was struggling to muster some strength, but it was gone. It was in that moment I felt someone holding me. I looked up and saw Raziel. Above him, a multitude of Underwarriors were riding alongside Aquilas and flying in the direction of the Shadows.

XI

Raziel smiled down at me as he firmly held on to both of us. At an amazing speed, he flew us to nearby ruins hidden deep in the forest. His attire was unlike any I had remembered from my visions of him. He wore the dark boots that were common for men to wear out to the fields, and black pants that were worn out. He revealed a bare chest and I saw a black leather bracelet on his right wrist.

"Stay here. I won't be long," he said and then took flight.

Devin was in awe. A joyful look lighted his countenance, but at the same time he stood speechless and in shock by Raziel's arrival.

"Can you perceive their thoughts, Isaac? What is happening? Are they fighting?" Devin asked anxiously.

Even though we were now far from the army, I was able to faintly see both the Underwarriors and the Shadows.

"Their fighting is merciless," I stammered as I tried to concentrate. "The Underwarriors are attacking them in full force, but the Shadows aren't giving up easily."

With much straining, I was able to get a dim view of the Underwarriors fighting. Many Shadows vanished, but many Underwarriors were being destroyed as well. Due to the massive armies gathered in one place, it was difficult for me to depict how the battle was playing out. To watch this vivid enactment in my mind brought me anguish.

"We need to trust that all will be well," I said as I canceled the images from my mind. "I don't want to keep watching this battle. It will not change its outcome and it will only cause greater pain," I said as I walked away from Devin.

"So..." Devin took a few steps closer to me. "Wings, huh?"

"Yeah, it surprised me too. I never imagined I'd ever have these," I responded as I continued to walk away.

Not long after, I heard wings flapping behind me. As I turned around I saw that Raziel had returned.

"They are all taken care of," he said. His very presence emanated great peace, which had overflowed my soul like a refreshing drink from a cool spring of water. His skin radiated with such brightness that it made the snow pale in contrast to Raziel's beauty. I glanced at Devin again and his eyes were wide open, gazing at the Star.

"What happened to the Shadows, Raziel?" I asked him as I made my way to him.

"They were sent back to the Abyss. In the Fourth Dimension dying is worse than living, for if one of us dies, we live in pain forever," he said, almost as if whispering a secret.

"But those Shadows were the lost souls of people. It is not their fault that they were lied to," I exclaimed.

Even though I was glad to be alive I did not agree with his doings.

"It had to be done, Isaac," he replied. His eyes were then set on Devin. "Nephilin, you sure seem to be surprised to see me. Has it been long since you have seen one of us?"

"Yes...I mean...*I*..." Devin stuttered, unable to communicate intelligibly.

Raziel approached him and tenderly placed his right hand on his shoulder with a fatherly pat. "Don't worry, Devin, I know you better than you think." He smiled.

"How d...d...do...how do you know me?" he asked in surprise.

"Well, first I am a Star, servant of the Creator."

Devin frowned, displeased with the answer. Raziel's composure changed; the look on his face took on a very mysterious frown

"I knew your father, Devin," he answered abrasively.

Not a word escaped from any of us for a time. All was quiet. Only the wind rustled softly through the trees.

"My...father?"

"Yes, your father," he affirmed.

"Where is my father, Raziel? What happened to him? Who is he?" He was desperate for the answer. In an instant his hands were around Raziel's throat, trying to force the answer out of him.

"Few of your kind have the privilege of knowing even their father's name," he answered, grasping Devin's hands with a firm grip. "Your father's name is Azael. He fell along with the others when Lucifer betrayed us." Devin slowly released Raziel.

"Unfortunately, my brother did not choose the path of righteousness," Raziel added.

"Your...brother?" Devin stammered.

I did not know what to say. I felt as if I was eavesdropping on an intimate family fight.

Devin sat down in the snow.

"Where are the rest of your fellow warriors?" I asked.

"They are all here, scattered around us in the forest. They will only show themselves if I give them the signal." He turned around. "Warriors, come forth!" he shouted.

Quickly they all appeared out of the trees, out of the ground and even out of the snow.

"It is nice to see you all again," Alexander said from amidst the crowd.

"You...you came," I said, surprised to see him.

"Why did your kind not come to our aid before we lost Demetre and Adawnas?" Devin asked Raziel.

"Our primary duty is to protect Elysium, not to solve your problems and fix your mistakes," Raziel replied in a cold voice. I could see that Devin was greatly displeased at his response, but he knew Raziel was right.

"What happened in Mag Mell?" I asked.

Raziel and the others instantaneously bowed their heads in unison. From what I could guess it was a sign of respect for those who had lost their lives there.

"The Shadows reached the city last night and wiped out its citizens." Raziel cringed as he answered my question. His voice implied great sorrow.

"Did any of the humans willingly ally with them?" Devin asked.

"Not that we were able to witness. When we arrived at the city, many had already been ravaged." Raziel turned his gaze to me. "Even though they were unsuccessful in Isaac to open the Diary, they are still willing to destroy the kingdoms of Elysium to expand their Shadow army even more."

"The expansion of this army should not be difficult now that the Council has fallen and Athalas—the master of Death—is now one of them," Devin contested.

"Not only that, but the gate between Elysium and the Fourth Dimension now lies unguarded. Many creatures have already entered—and will continue entering," Raziel confirmed.

"Is there any hope for Mag Mell? Can we still seek out survivors?" I asked, expecting a hopeful answer.

"Of that I am not sure," Alexander said. "The kingdom appeared to be deserted when we left it."

Those around me had great sorrow expressed on their faces. The marks of battle were visible all over the Underwarriors' bodies. Their silver armors were broken, and their shields were shattered. Cuts and bruises covered their arms and faces.

"Why do you mourn?" I asked. "Why do you mourn the loss of Shadows? Yes, they were humans at one time, but you yourselves said it had to be done." The conversation was broken by a long, eerie silence. We were too distraught to speak.

"Were others killed?" I asked, afraid of an unfavorable response.

Raziel and Alexander looked at each other. "Corbin, Nephele, Azaziel and Athalas fled before we could catch them. I am afraid only Shadows were lost here this morning," Alexander responded.

I knew Demetre...Corbin...was no longer the friend I once knew, but I still desired to see him somehow redeemed from the destiny that was forcefully predestined for him. If I was given the choice to follow the Darkness or the Creator, shouldn't he?

"What must we do now?" Devin asked. "They will keep on destroying the kingdoms of Elysium, and one by one, they will fall into darkness."

The Underwarriors were all silent. I could sense that all tried to think of ways to destroy the Shadows and the Nephilins, but no one uttered a word.

"We must lead the kingdoms to war against them," Alexander boldly proclaimed.

"But how?" I asked, bewildered. Even if a Star was able to defeat Shadows here, it would only be a matter of time before more creatures were released out of the Gate of the Fourth Dimension.

"We have to try...I know it will be a difficult task to convince the kingdoms to believe that Lucifer's army is rising; that the Fallen Stars roam unhindered around us, trying to destroy their people," Raziel affirmed as he paced about.

"We can watch the Gate of the Fourth Dimension for any activity, giving you and Devin time to reach out to the people," Alexander advised; the Underwarriors nodded in agreement.

"Who will we go to? Which kingdom would most likely fight alongside us? Who would have the greatest influence on the other humans?" Devin asked anxiously. Even though the task ahead of us seemed arduous, I saw a dim light of hope in the midst of this chaos.

"Go to the Kingdom of Aloisio. It is home to the beast tamers and skilled fighters," Raziel answered. "Seek to speak with the king. He will know what to do."

Devin rebuked Raziel with a sneer. "We would be wasting our time trying to convince them to go to war against the Darkness. They have been the ones proclaiming that Lucifer is a myth. They raise their children to believe that humans are the only force in this universe, and that everything else is but a tale." Devin walked around apprehensively. "Why would we go to them?"

Raziel slowly walked toward Devin; his expression was undecipherable.

"Where is this kingdom located?" I asked Raziel.

"Your friend knows the way well, Isaac." Raziel turned his eyes to me.

"Azael was not wise in his choice—don't be like him." Raziel looked at Devin. "Don't forget you have the Creator on your side."

"Then he should be the one destroying these creatures...he should be sending out his most powerful warriors to fight this war," Devin replied, placing his hands on his face. He nodded in disbelief at Raziel's statement.

Raziel smirked.

"It was not he who chose the doom of Elysium, it was its inhabitants. Live for the greater good, Devin, I am sure you will not regret it," Raziel replied, clearly enunciating each word.

Raziel walked back to the others. Alexander followed him.

"Can we count on you?" Alexander asked us. I was reluctant to be the first one to answer, because I was not the one who knew the way to Aloisio. It was obvious that Devin was entangled in an internal battle, and trying to contemplate another solution, but we both knew there was no other way.

"It would be selfish of us to let so many perish because we doubted," I told him.

Devin stared up at the sky for a few moments, closed his eyes and took in a deep breath. His mind was set as he declared, "As impossible as this feat sounds, you can count on us."

"Your story of redemption starts now, Nephilin. Do not waste your chance," Raziel said with a smile.

"We will head to the Gates now, and will do our very best to protect it and prevent more Shadows and beasts from breaking in. We are all united in this fight," Alexander announced with courage and boldness.

"Underwarriors! Fly!" Raziel shouted. They took flight. Their flying was beautifully synchronized; they all flew in formation, and their movements were precisely coordinated. Shortly after they had taken flight, they all vanished.

"We must be on our way, Devin," I said.

"Your body isn't strong enough to fly for long periods of time yet," Devin said. "It is best if we travel by horse." Devin closed his eyes; he was in deep concentration and not long after, I heard the neighing of horses emerging from the woods. I had completely forgotten about his abilities to manipulate some animals.

He was pensive as he watched the wild horses galloping in our direction.

XII

We rode quietly through the white forest. The only sounds we encountered were those of the wind and some wildlife. These were moments when my mind drifted away relentlessly trying to understand the tumultuous disaster my life had become. I wondered where Adawnas was, and why she had left us so suddenly. I attempted to ignore the intense pain and sorrow that lingered in my heart whenever I remembered my parents had died at the hands of the Nephilins; the overwhelming distress of having to witness my best friend defect to Nephele's side and the others. I was becoming a master at ignoring these haunting emotions, continuing on as if the only challenge I faced was to reach Aloisio.

As we traveled on, I noticed the scarcity of the vegetation. The air was still frigid and the wind was picking up with increased velocity.

"How far are we from Aloisio?" I shivered.

"Another day's ride," he replied. Ever since our encounter with the Underwarriors three days ago, Devin had been quiet and in deep thought.

"What is on your mind?" I asked him, trembling as the freezing wind began to blow with a blizzard-like ferocity, making visibility almost blinding.

He chuckled. "Like you can't read my mind?"

"Well, I'd rather not read your mind. I would only resort to that if my life depended upon it, and even then I would feel as if I had violated you. I believe you trust me enough to not withhold any relevant information from me," I affirmed.

He tilted his head upward, and scanned the length of the firmament, as though his answer would be found up there. Devin took a deep breath and was silent as he pondered his options.

"Raziel mentioned that this was the start of my redemption." He sighed. "Throughout my long years of existence, I have perpetually wondered if being redeemed was ever possible for me. I left my hiding place to live with the Council for many years, hoping that my efforts would somehow free my soul from the innate darkness always present within me."

It must have been exceedingly difficult for my companion to grasp the concept of receiving a chance for redemption. Having lived many lifetimes believing wholeheartedly that there was no hope for him, and then to discover the possibility of being redeemed from this fate must be undoubtedly confusing.

"I do not think that the Creator would damn you for the previous actions of your kind," I affirmed. I was trying to summon words of encouragement to build his hopes up, but my knowledge was in the infant state of development in reference to this subject. "I just can not remotely imagine you damned, Devin. It is too impossible to fathom."

"What do you mean?" he asked, disconcerted by my allegation.

"You willingly chose to go on this journey with me and Demetre, disavowing your own fallen nature. You have been living these many years struggling to be free from the darkness within yourself. I don't see how someone that is willing to go through such peril could be damned."

He nodded his head, affirming that my assumption was correct.

"Adawnas left..." He inhaled a deep breath. "What makes you think I won't betray you as well, Isaac? Do you know me well enough to make those assumptions?" he continued. "My nature is wicked. Do you believe I am truly able to change what I am? My father fell and bore children with your kind, damning you as well. We are nothing but an aberration destined for damnation."

I was shocked by his reply. What could I say to him that would make him see beyond the past? I thought about how Devin's trials reflected the struggles that afflicted Elysium. How would humankind ever believe in what was thought to be legend? Yes, they would see the destruction, but many were stubborn or too afraid to take a stand. With the driving passion that humans had for power, they might just choose to succumb to the Darkness instead of pressing on toward knowing the hidden source within the Darkness.

"Why do you go on then? Why are you still here in the middle of a frozen wasteland, heading to one of the most powerful kingdoms in Elysium, trying to bring truth to their minds?" I questioned in a blatant voice.

He tightened his grasp on the reins. He did not answer.

"I can imagine you are fighting inside of yourself, wanting to believe that your soul does not have to be damned forever," I comforted him.

"Not only wanting to believe, Isaac...I *must* believe. I have seen so much in this world. Pain, war and deception have always followed the citizens of this land. Still—I want to believe in redemption. It means *life* to me!"

We continued riding. I gazed at the many hills ahead of us, which were all covered in a white blanket of snow; they were radiant under a canopy of gray sky. Small houses appeared scattered throughout many of the hills. For once, we viewed no evidence of destruction before of us.

Although the quaint little village appeared to be quite placid, I kept my guard up.

"Is this Aloisio?" I asked, carefully glancing at the houses in the distance.

"No. Aloisio is surrounded by many small villages. The actual kingdom lies on the other side of the sea," Devin affirmed.

The houses were invitations of a warm welcome. I envisioned a picture of a home-cooked meal, children bustling to and fro cheerily, and the adults reclining lazily around the cozy hearth. They had been built around the trees and the rocks that covered the hills. Smoke rose from the chimneys and the smell of baked pastries drifted through the air.

When the citizens caught sight of us, their curiosity drove them closer. The women with their children and husbands surrounded Devin and me. The people were joyless. Their hearts were weighed down, burdened with great distress.

"Are you from the other side of the forest?" one asked frantically.

"Do you know what is going on? Do you know why the sun has vanished?" another asked as he grabbed my leg.

"We have been under the shadows for too long," said an old woman. "If you have any information, please tell us."

They all spoke at once, asking questions and babbling amongst themselves. Confusion permeated the group of inquisitors. Questions were flying from every direction, but they were not willing to wait for answers.

A man mounted on a gray horse galloped through the crowd. He was clothed in silver armor that was tarnished and covered with cracks and rust. A long, dirty cape woven with the fur of a bear was attached to his back.

"The guard...he is coming..." the old lady muttered.

"What is this commotion about?" he shouted in a loud voice. Immediately the crowd broke up, leaving us stranded out in the open. Devin remained still; his breathing was soft and constrained.

The guard scrutinized both of us, and turning away, he scratched his head.

"Follow me," he said bluntly.

"Should we follow him?" Devin asked.

I did not feel threatened by his gruff appearance, nor did he seem eager to destroy us. The crowd stood aloof, gawking at us with wide-eyed wonder while the three of us conversed. They watched us in a state of terror.

"I see no reason why not," I said, even though I was reluctant to follow him.

As we rode on, I could clearly hear the people muttering amongst themselves.

"The blond one looks suspicious," a man exclaimed in a heavy accent. "Are you going to question him?" he shouted. They were skeptical and it was apparent that they wanted answers quickly.

As the marble streets narrowed, the houses were situated closer to each other. It almost seemed as though they were mounted on top of one another. The trees were barren, void of life, and the lake that we passed by had frozen over.

"Shouldn't be long now," the guard exclaimed as he continued on, looking straight ahead.

As we rode by the last house, we came into a clearing. The foliage was dense. The gigantic trees and small thorny shrubs made it hard to navigate. Puddles of mud and fallen pine trees were scattered along the rugged terrain. In the midst of this gloomy landscape, an old shack appeared.

"You can tie your horses there." He pointed to a wooden pole that sat on the right side of the shack. He unsaddled his horse and quickly headed inside.

"Please, do not hesitate to come in," he yelled out, beckoning with his hand to enter. We tied our horses to the pole and followed him inside of the shack.

The roof and the walls were old and cracked. As I walked up the two creaking wooden steps and onto the porch, I was surprised to see a massive conglomeration of cobwebs hanging from the ceiling.

Once inside, I noticed the fireplace was lit and the aroma of newly brewed barley tea reached my nostrils, tantalizing my senses.

"You caused a great commotion back at the village," the guard said. "Where are you two from?"

"We did not mean to cause any problems," Devin answered. "We are travelers, just passing by."

"That doesn't really answer my question," the guard snapped in a rough voice. He paced back and forth suspiciously, his eyes fixed on us.

I quickly surveyed the shack. There were many wine bottles and lit candles placed on an old shelf. I remained attentive. I did not know what to expect here.

"What is your name?" I asked.

"Abhel. I guard this wee village of Adhelina. What may yours be?" he asked, staring at the fireplace.

"Isaac, and this is Devin. If you don't mind my asking, why did you bring us here?" I approached him, suspicious of his behavior.

Abhel smiled.

"There has been talk abroad of a great shadow that has come." His hands intertwined. "Twenty of our soldiers went to Mag Mell the day before yesterday, but they never returned. We sent out two more of our men yesterday to bring us news of the latest developments, but they did not return either." Abhel sat down on his chair. His left hand began to rub his chin. I could sense he felt very nervous in our presence. "You are outside travelers." He was silent for a while. "Where are you headed to?"

Devin sighed as he clasped his fingers together and bowed his head.

"That is a story we do not have time to tell. The darkness you speak of is true—the Fallen are multiplying," Devin proclaimed hastily.

"Well, I can surely see that you...with the deep blue eyes...you aren't as common as the rest of us..." His voice trailed off as he studied Devin's features closely.

Abhel stood to his feet. "I need you to understand that I lost twenty-two men to this darkness. Forgive me if for insisting, but I need to know if you have more information about all that is happening. Some bodies were found today near the river. The women are not aware of it yet, but I saw the way the bodies were mutilated. I do not take death lightly. Do you know what the reason is for this disappearance and the vast mutilations?"

"Because the Diary of Lucifer has been found," I quickly informed our interrogator.

Slowly, he sat back on his chair and cupped his face with his hands.

"The dark book is then a reality?" he said, mesmerized.

"We need safe passage through your village. We must convince the kingdoms to come together and fight against this turbulent force," Devin affirmed.

I looked out the window behind him and I observed movement in some of the tree branches. I caught sight of a Shadow slowly crawling along the ground on his hands and feet. It headed toward the shack.

"Devin!" I alerted him, pointing at the dark figure. "They are here!" I sprang to my feet.

All of a sudden, the roof of the shack was broken through and Shadows mounted on Desert Dragons descended upon us, growling ferociously. One of them brutally attacked Abhel. They decimated his body. It was torn in half, and his innards were smeared all over the floor of the shack. Blood splattered onto my face.

Devin and I quickly headed outside and mounted our horses. We hurriedly galloped away from the village. I looked up and noticed the clouds were moving in a circular motion like a tornado of darkness. From everywhere, Shadows were springing forth, attacking every house, and killing every woman, infant and child. The screams were deafening.

Fear unleashed its deadly tentacles within me. I looked around in despair. There were too many of them; too many Shadows for us to defeat. They filled the air with their roars.

Above us, three Shadows appeared out of the clouds mounted on Desert Dragons and chased after us with incessant fury.

"You cannot run. There is no hiding…I will never cease to search for you…" The sound of many voices whispered to me, heckling me and pounding my eardrums. I could tell by Devin's reaction that he could hear them as well. The beasts growled fiercely, but they did not attack us.

"Flee…flee…you can run but you can't hide from me…" The whispers continued.

The moment we crossed the border of the village, the Shadows came to a rapid halt. The whispers faded into the atmosphere.

My heart beat at rapid speed the moment we stopped. I alighted from my horse. My knees began to knock together; my feet would not support my weight, as I was unable to stand upright.

"Why did they stop hunting us?" I asked, enraged. "*No!*" I yelled at the Shadows. "Leave them alone, come after *us*." Sweat drifted down my forehead as I shouted with all the strength in me. I did not know if the trembling of my body was because of my rage or my fear.

"Why aren't they coming after us?" I stammered. "*It is me you want…I am here!*"

"Isaac, please calm down. They stopped—"

"If we hadn't come this way they would not have died," I snapped as I shook Devin's shoulders.

Devin shrugged with a sigh of resignation.

"Do you really think the Shadows would not have killed them either way, Isaac?"

I was frustrated. We could've kept on going. We could have ignored Abhel and continued on. Maybe he and all the others would have survived. Maybe the Shadows would have followed us outside of the village. These thoughts raced through my mind.

"We shouldn't have followed Abhel. We should have kept our pace when we first encountered those people..." I felt as worthless as a scummy rat. Guilt swirled inside of me. I felt rage. At that moment, I sensed that I had made a devastating mistake that cost untold lives and misery.

"I made a mistake. I should have taken Nephele up on her offer. All of these lives would have been spared if I had. Why do they have to die like this?" I declared with uncontrolled fury.

Devin walked closer to me. I could see black smoke rising up from the direction of the village. In a flash, I averted my eyes from the scene.

"You are not making sense, Isaac. Please stop this rambling."

I was still for a moment.

"Devin, maybe if I just surrender they will stop these massacres," I said between low sobs, tears descending down my cheeks.

Devin was silent. I could still hear faint screams coming from the village. He placed both of his hands on his forehead and closed his eyes.

"Isaac." His voice was low. "Read my soul."

I was reluctant to concentrate my energy on his thoughts. For some reason, I always evaded reading Devin. Maybe I was fearful of the things I would discover about him.

"I'd rather not," I quipped in a broken voice.

"Please..."

As I slowly closed my eyes to read him I felt my heartbeat slow down, my sight and hearing becoming dim, and I felt as though I was being sucked up into his mind. Faintly, the sound of numerous voices bellowed in my ear. Through a mist, I saw a war taking place at the base of a mountain. The Fallen and the Stars were engaged in battle, warring against each other. Both armies were skillful warriors dressed in their magnificent armors. There was a stark contrast between both armies; a black, rusty armor clothed the Fallen Stars, but the Stars were covered in glistening silver. Amidst the battle, I heard the distinct sound of a lion roaring. Everything stopped and all eyes were fixed on the glorious ray of light that hovered above them. The light cast down flames of fire upon all, but only the Fallen Stars burned. They shrieked and yelled as they were consumed by fire. Darkness began to spread until it covered the entire sky.

The thought shifted. I saw one of the villages of Elysium under the night sky. Men and women joyfully talked around a fire as their children played. Eerie shouts echoed in the background as the dark sky began to shine as bright as day. Out of the illuminated sky, the Fallen Stars descended onto Elysium, falling like shooting stars. When their bodies touched the ground, it caused massive explosions to take place. The village turned into ruins; its inhabitants dissolved into ash as the explosion mushroomed.

The striking image of a child appeared. Due to the facial traits of the baby, I recognized the child was Devin when he was younger. I entered into a green pasture filled with many infants who were lying next to their mothers. They all had similar characteristics to Devin such as the shape of their eyes, their skin and their flawless beauty.

His mind then directed my eyes to look to the sky. Dark shapes appeared from the clouds, heading toward them. I could hear the women's terrified screams as they tried to escape. They each held on to their babies, making their way to the shelter of the trees. The dark beings mercilessly attacked the women, killing them one by one, leaving only the babies behind.

A flaming black being appeared. My body weakened as I looked upon it. The dark being was surrounded by lightning and fire. Its deathlike glare would have caused even the bravest soul to quiver in fear.

When the vision had vanished, I noticed sweat was dripping in rivulets down my forehead.

"Do you still think there is a possibility that if you give your blood you will spare these people?" asked Devin in a low, somber voice.

My breathing was heavy. I was not expecting to see the images I had just experienced.

"The darkness surrounded…by…lightning and fire…was…that…Lucifer?" I was panting.

He lowered his head. "Yes. The other dark shapes were Fallen Stars…our fathers." His eyes widened. "After the fall, Lucifer would not tolerate his servants cohabitating with the women. Thus all our mothers died...and became Shadows. This was a surety that the Fallen Stars could have their 'lovers' closer to them."

I was speechless. There was so much I did not know about Elysium's history. I felt worthless. I had no right to question if I had made the right choice. I had to remain strong and continue to pursue the goal of uniting the kingdoms to fight against the Darkness. Though now I feared that the Darkness had already gotten to the kingdoms and bribed them to fight against the Creator.

"You may find this statement surprising, but have faith that we will honor our allegiance to Raziel and the other Underwarriors," Devin addressed me, resting his hand on my shoulder.

More than ever, I felt in my heart the urgency to reach Aloisio. I was uncertain as to what we would find, or what would happen to us there, but if trusting my instinct that this was the right path to take, I had to be willing to follow it.

XIII

We rode away from the village of Adhelina and ventured into the forest. After traveling some distance, we reached the sea. I had never seen anything like it. Gigantic mountain ranges touched the sky. The mountains surrounded the shoreline as far as the eye could see.

Situated at the crest of the mountains were ruins, which looked majestic, covered in the glistening white snow. In the middle of the sea stood an enormous statue resembling a Star with a spear in its hand. Though I was too far away to make out the details of the statue, I noticed it had six wings.

"Now this is a sight to behold," Devin remarked, mesmerized by the view.

As soon as Devin said those words, the ground trembled rhythmically as the sound of beating drums filled the air. Immediately, I glanced around, hoping to spot the location the beats emerged from, but all seemed normal.

The beating grew louder. I became fearful of what could be happening.

Then I heard them again—voices whispering to me through the gentle breeze. The same voices I had heard back at the village of Adhelina.

"I have seen your heart...I have seen who you are...you are ours..." they said in a perfect melody.

I placed my hands over my ears, trying to drown out the voices of the whispers, but they were unrelenting.

As I tried to stifle the voices in my head, I was surprised to see small red glowing flakes descending from the sky. I turned my gaze upward and saw many falling upon us. They were shaped like snowflakes, pulsating with a soft golden glow.

"Do you hear them, Isaac?" Devin asked with wide eyes and a fearful expression.

"You can hear them as well?" I asked. "Do you hear what they are saying to me?" The whispers grew to a low roar and flowed in unison with the beat of the drums.

Devin's breathing grew heavier as his eyes became dark and hollow.

"What are they saying to you, Devin?" I inquired as I watched him.

"They…say…that we are doomed," he said weakly. "They…say…you will…perish…" His voice trailed off as a blank stare overtook his face.

"Devin, please. What is happening to you?"

The horses neighed loudly, making a ruckus. My horse's breathing increased in intensity; the pigment of its pupils changed from ebony into an iridescent white. I quickly got down from my horse. It let out a low grunting noise and fled to the woods.

I heard a loud thud of something fall to the ground. I looked down, bewildered, to find Devin lying on the ground, immobile; his horse also fled in the direction of the trees. I could hear the drumming sounds and the whispers growing louder.

The small glowing lights strategically positioned themselves around us. I peered cautiously into one that floated next to me. To my grim surprise I was looking at a face, one that struck my heart with terror. It was Corbin.

The beating of the drums ceased; the whispers faded.

A feeling of isolation crept inside of me. I did not know what was happening; neither did I know what was to come.

The silence was chilling, making me very uncomfortable. I glanced at Devin still lying on the ground. His eyes were wide open and he muttered random words I could not decipher the meaning of. With my powers, I tried to read Devin and my surroundings, but I was unable to see anything.

"Why won't you answer me?" I said in a loud voice as I shook Devin's unresponsive body.

The whispers started their repeated chants once more.

"I have seen your heart...I have seen who you are...you are ours..." they continued.

Slowly, I bent down and picked Devin up. The whispers incessantly repeated the same haunting sentence over and over again. I closed my eyes, took in a deep breath, and expanded my wings. I anticipated my body being struck by unbearable pain, but my flight was uninterrupted.

The red lights followed me. I veered from right to left eagerly trying to evade them, but they seemed to know my every move.

My wings fluttered violently as I tried to gain more speed.

"I have seen your heart..." they exclaimed loudly.

"Devin..." I softly mumbled his name.

I could feel something buzzing in my ear. Before I was able to react, one of the small lights entered my head. Its chanting voices howled within me, drowning out every other sound.

"Devin!" I shouted with the strength I had left within me. I looked down, but he was still out cold.

Wake up! Please..." I screamed in terror. The voice inside my head was causing torturous throbbing. Another light made its way into my head, causing the noises from the voices to sound more like a loud roar. The pain was so sharp that I accidentally released Devin's body. I placed my hands over my ears and screamed.

"You are ours...ours...ours..." the voices repeated. I soon realized that I was falling, plunging rapidly toward the water. I felt someone grab my arm, pulling me upward. The voices were still blaring inside of my head. It felt almost as if they were devouring part of my brain.

I was being carried upward at an amazing speed, but just as suddenly as a heartbeat, I began to fall again. I tried to open my eyes, but I was not able to. My senses faded as the voices grew even louder.

My body splashed into the bitter-cold water. I struggled to try to get my arms to respond. I needed them to function so that I could swim to the surface, but despite my frantic efforts, they were unresponsive. My body was quickly sinking.

As my mind came to the realization that I was drowning, something grabbed ahold of me again and pulled me out of the frigid water. As I inhaled, the voices and the throbbing disappeared. When I opened my eyes, the small red lights were gone. I glanced up at the astonishing sight of Devin flying above me. He flapped his wings graciously. They gleamed as they maneuvered expertly; his dark feathers resembled those of a crow. My wings dangled idly at my back. I tried to move them, but they did not respond to my body's command.

The details of the statue became more visible as we approached it. Its grayish color and the corrosion were hidden under the fallen snow.

We landed swiftly at the foot of the statue. I rubbed my shoulders with my hands in an attempt to warm myself up, but my efforts were in vain. My clothes were drenched. I looked around and wondered where the small red lights had gone.

I looked at Devin, eagerly waiting for him to speak.

"How…Um…When were you planning to tell me you could fly?" I asked, my curiosity piqued.

He lowered his head and spoke.

"Never," he affirmed without hesitation. He scrutinized his wings; his face emanated sorrow.

I stared at him, confused.

"What happened… Wh-why d-d-did you pass out?" I asked him.

"The lights loosed voices inside of my head… They spoke very loudly to me. It was unbearable. I have never felt anything quite like it," Devin said, his right hand caressing the dark feathers of his left wing.

"I-I-I-looked inside one of the small red lights," I said, shivering. "I saw Corbin's face."

Both of his wings retracted, shrinking back and folding under his skin. His eyes never met mine.

"Why did you not want to tell me about your wings?" I asked. "How did you get them? Do all Nephilins fly?"

"It is an inherited trait like that of a human having blue eyes. If your parents possess the trait, you will most likely possess it also. Some of us carry very distinctive features from our Star fathers," Devin explained in a low voice.

"What else have you hidden from me, Devin? Are there any other secrets you've been holding back that you would like to share with me?" I asked, taking a few steps back. "I thought I could trust you enough to not have to resort to reading you."

"I wonder why the whispering lights disappeared the moment we approached the statue," Devin answered, diverting from the subject of his undisclosed secrets. I pretended not to notice.

I looked to my right and caught sight of dark muddy walls that protruded upward on the far side of the sea.

"Aloisio?" I asked.

"Yes, there it lies," he said.

To my surprise, Devin clasped his hands together and he softly chanted words I couldn't understand. When he opened his hands, there were small flames in his palms. He walked toward me and placed the flames on my right shoulder.

"This should help your coldness," he said. My body warmed up instantaneously. My clothes were dry, and even my hair was no longer damp.

"We will rest for a while and then we fly," I said. Devin grunted. I knew he was not fond of the idea of flying again, but we had no other choice.

"Would you rather go on foot?" I asked as he walked away from me. He didn't answer.

I wanted to arrive at Aloisio without much delay so that we could unite as many people as possible to fight against the Darkness, but my heart felt troubled and restless. I had not been able to read Devin when I needed information during the appearance of the red lights. Were my powers failing me? What were those red lights? Despite all the rushing thoughts in my mind, I knew I needed to rest for what was to come.

I slowly reclined my head against the statue and closed my eyes.

I saw myself walking through a forest. The vegetation was dense. My feet sank into the muddy floor. There were no sounds of the wind blowing nor of any animals. I used my sword to cut the branches and the foliage that blocked my path. An unexpected mist enveloped me. Distant whispering voices spoke undecipherable words into the air. As I journeyed through the mist, I caught a glimpse of a castle. Three colossal towers stood on their own, surrounding the front of the castle. I was surprised when I saw a lion statue in the middle tower. I looked intensely to be certain I wasn't hallucinating. The closer I walked to the castle, the more visible the details of the castle became. This was the castle of Justicia.

The place looked abandoned. There was no light coming from the windows; the white walls were cracked and the moat had been reduced to piles of rubble. I flew toward the entrance, slowly stepping inside. The white marble floors and huge columns were still intact, along with the captivating staircase. All was quiet and ostensibly calm.

From behind me I heard footsteps. I glanced over my shoulder; my hand grasped onto my sword's handle. Demetre appeared from the darkness, holding the Diary, slowly walking in my direction. My body froze; I stood speechless.

"You cannot escape, Isaac." Once again, I heard voices whispering around me. In a flash, Demetre's body melted like ice under heat and from the remains of his decomposed body, his fallen form, Corbin, arose. His piercing red gaze struck me with fear. I saw Nephele walking out from the shadows. Her blue eyes were fixated on me. Her skin was as pale as snow.

"I will always find you, Isaac." Her voice was deep and ominous. "Your blood is ours. The Dark One owns your mind." The images in my mind dissipated instantly.

"Isaac...Isaac..." I could hear a voice faintly calling my name. I opened my eyes to see Devin shaking me roughly. I leaped out of his grip and reached for my sword; he retreated.

"What is wrong?" he asked, shocked at my recent action.

I shook my head.

"Um...nothing...just a bad dream," I replied, letting go of my sword. "Been having a lot of those lately." I thought it best for me not to mention my dreams to him. Even though my heart was greatly troubled by them, I did not want him to worry any more than he already was.

"Should we take off now?" I asked him.

He stood to his feet. "Can you handle it?"

I nodded my head. We both took flight, leaving behind the gigantic statue. I felt an increase in my speed since my last ascent.

As we flew, images of the vivid dream seemed to be engraved on my mind. My heart was troubled by Nephele's words. Devin was silent as he flew; his eyes were focused on Aloisio. The sky grew increasingly darker as we approached the Kingdom; the air around us felt colder. Without using my powers, I could sense that something dark was at work in the atmosphere.

Devin changed course, heading toward one of the hills; I followed behind him. Shortly thereafter, I noticed Devin descending in the direction of a valley located on the right side of the Kingdom's wall. Again, I followed.

"Why are we landing here? The kingdom is still far ahead of us," I asked him, bewildered.

He paced through the woods hastily, heading in the direction of Aloisio. "You don't want to get near those walls with wings on your back, Isaac. Guards are positioned on top of them, watching day and night. This kingdom has always been known for its amazing skills in battle. They might think we are enemies."

Because we were unaware of the situation here in Aloisio, I had no other choice but to agree with him. I trusted him. He had been around for some time and had extensive knowledge of these lands

After some time trekking through the woods, we found ourselves standing at the foot of the wall. Before us stood a massive corroded iron gate. Wooden spikes extended above the top of the gate about six feet. As I gazed up I saw two heavily armed guards chatting.

"Look there!" one of them exclaimed to the other. "Walkers…"

"What brings you here?" one of them shouted with a heavy accent, bending down to get a better look at us.

"We are simply travelers passing by. We would like to come in to buy some food and find a place to rest so we can be on our way," Devin shouted.

"Wait there!" the other shouted.

Soon enough the gate opened and two other guards headed our way. Their armor was made of silver and underneath their chest plate they wore a red cape that covered most of their body. Their arms were heavily armored, and strapped around their waist was a beautiful silver sword. Both guards had blond hair and deep green eyes.

"Follow us," they commanded. "Don't ask any questions now."

I hesitated. I could see Devin was also doubtful.

"Why should we follow you?" I asked. I looked up and noticed two more guards looking down at us.

"*Hey!*" a guard shouted from atop the gate. "Is ev'rything alright?" His accent was also heavy.

"Yes...yes, everything is alright. We are just taking them in for quick questioning," one of the guards with us replied. The guard turned around and continued to stand watch of the gate. Right away, I heard commotion coming from the wall above.

"Denali...they killed Denali and Fridverd. They are impostors!" he alleged.

Devin and I looked at the two guards standing next to us. "You will want to come with us now." The one to my right gestured for us to follow them.

Quickly they led us through the gates. I caught a glimpse of a vast marketplace located at the entrance of the city. My attention was captured by the high towers of the colossal cathedrals and other grand monuments scattered throughout the kingdom. All the houses had golden roofs with etchings and designs on their walls. Every door and window frame possessed golden patterns that shone with great intensity.

We were walking amongst a crowd, trying to make our way through the busy market. After we moved past the crowded streets, we came to a graveyard that had been built near an abandoned cathedral. The graveyard was meticulously landscaped with many trees and beautiful statues that were erected near the old graves. The cathedral appeared old, unkempt and discolored; the stone walls were covered with mildew. The high tattered ceiling had become a dwelling place for birds and other night creatures.

"In there." One of the guards pointed in the direction of an abandoned house located next to the cathedral.

I looked at him.

"Are you...do you really expect us to follow you in there?" I asked, looking at the state of the house. Half of the roof was missing; the walls had holes covered in cobwebs.

"If you want to know what Raziel has to say about the Gates you will want to follow us," one of the guards alleged emphatically.

My eyes widened. Devin gasped. Without any resistance we followed the guards. I was eager to find out the secrets that Raziel and the Underwarriors had uncovered at the Gates of the Fourth Dimension.

The wooden floor creaked as we stepped inside the living room. Broken canvases hung on the remnants of the colorless walls. The floor was covered with shards of glass and broken pieces of wood. A massive hole stood where the fireplace had once been.

We continued to venture further into the house. Once we passed the living room, to our surprise, we faced an old, double iron door that to our surprise was wide open; the lock had been destroyed. We continued through the iron door and followed a dark stairway that led underground. The floor was no longer constructed of creaky wood, but of cobblestone. I felt water dripping down onto my head from the roof and looked up.

One of the guards lit a torch, but the darkness was still intense.

"Before we proceed, could you tell us your names?" Devin asked them.

"Danathaniel," the one to my right responded. "Cresta," the one to my left replied. I sensed distress in their voices.

"The Nephilin?" Cresta asked scornfully. "Why is he with you?"

"I believe I can speak for myself," Devin contested before I could even think of an answer.

There was an unnerving pause.

"Why should we believe anything uttered by a Nephilin?" Cresta asked in an aggressive tone.

"Please, this is not the place, Cresta," Danathaniel interrupted. "We are almost there. We need to discuss more urgent matters. Raziel already told me about Devin. Let us say that he is...different." His voice was calm, but weary.

"Light them up!" Cresta shouted. Many torches ignited around us, bringing clarity to the room. It was an underground prison. Skeletons were scattered around us and beside me, standing in the shadows between the torches were many dark human figures.

"I apologize for our choice of meeting space," someone from the crowd of dark figures said aloud. "Please understand that in the current state of things, we must be extra careful, especially with your kind, Devin." Devin shot the man a cold look. "My name is Tonma, I am one of the commanders of the Underwarriors. Raziel has sent us here to inform you of the things we have seen."

Curious, Devin looked around. "Well then, please tell us. Let us not waste any more time." Devin's voice inferred agitation.

"The situation is much worse than we imagined. Since the fall of Justicia and the Council, creatures of the Darkness, Shadows, Beasts and Fallen Stars have infiltrated Elysium. They are now living amongst the people, pretending to be ordinary men and women. Some citizens claim to have seen strange creatures roaming the forests," Tonma exclaimed with concern in his voice.

After a brief silence, he continued, "The red lights you saw are called Whispering Lights. We can sense their presence when they are near. They were sent out by Corbin and possess the power to torture the mind."

Tonma walked out of the shadows and approached us. He circled the room with his gaze fixed directly on us. His blond hair cascaded down his shoulders; his thick brown cape dragged along the floor, covering most of his body. "Aloisio has been taken over by the Darkness. Men were called by the king from surrounding villages to destroy all of the kingdoms of Elysium. The men were instructed to kill every person in sight, in order to create a greater army of Shadows."

"Please tell us something we don't already know, Tonma," Devin replied.

Tonma continued talking, ignoring Devin's sarcastic request.

"The reason why your powers are decreasing is because the Nephilins have taken over this territory and have found a way to cancel your abilities in this region. We are not yet sure how they managed to do it, but it has been happening to some of us also."

I was struck with fear; this information caught me completely by surprise. Cancel my abilities? But the Creator himself gave them to me.

"But how…"

"Marco, king of Aloisio, willingly surrendered his life to serve Lucifer," Tonma continued. "He now serves the Darkness."

"Where is Raziel?" I asked.

"He is at the Gates of the Fourth Dimension, fighting and defeating as many Shadows and Beasts as he can alongside the rest of the Underwarriors, but the Fallen Stars are not wasting any time. They are infiltrating Elysium, preparing for a swift attack designed to annihilate all of the kingdoms and exterminate the human race."

"But I decided not to shed my blood; I decided not to accept Nephele's offer. Even if all of the kingdoms fall, the Diary cannot be opened," I said.

Tonma chuckled softly.

"Isaac, you are not the only one of your kind, my friend. There are other bearers…others of the bloodline. There are four more that have been chosen."

"Other…chosen…ones?" I mumbled, astonished at this newfound revelation.

The storm of emotions that stirred within me was almost impossible to contain. All this time I thought I stood alone on this quest to overcome evil. Loneliness was a strong enemy I had to unceasingly combat inside of myself daily.

"How will we find the others who were sent here?" I asked, hopeful.

"Unfortunately, that I do not know." He sighed. "This war is just starting, and you will need all of the strength you can muster to redeem the kingdoms of Elysium."

Silence filled the room.

We were all in deep thought, trying to think of ways to defeat or delay the Darkness.

"What must we do, Tonma?" Devin asked.

"You know," he chuckled. "It is still shocking to me that you are able to deny your dark nature so easily, Devin. I suppose redemption can be found in the most unexpected places." He peered deeply into Devin's eyes. "Unfortunately, I don't have an answer to your question."

"These other chosen ones, are they on their way to Aloisio?" I asked him as I still attempted to grasp everything I had just been told.

"Yes, they are all being led to this place," Tonma answered.

"How? Who is leading them here? How do they know about us?" I asked.

Tonma set his gaze on me. "Just know that they are heading this way as we speak for the same reason you are here."

"We must head back to the Gates," Cresta announced. Tonma nodded in agreement.

"I stand by what I said before. The Creator should send an army from the sky and destroy all of our enemies!" Devin implied with an angry voice.

"Devin," Tonma said in a soft voice. "The humans were the ones that chose to fall, and they brought this upon themselves. Free will was given to all, even to your kind. The Creator will never intervene to finish something before its end has come. You must understand that every choice will lead to a consequence. Today Elysium suffers the consequence of choices that were made in the distant past." Tonma turned around, placing his hands on a massive boulder. Using all his strength, he rolled the heavy rock away, revealing a tunnel that sat hidden behind it.

"We must carry on," he continued. The others nodded in agreement. "Let us find the other ones. We will join with them. Lucifer cannot win." Tonma handed me one of his torches.

"We will meet again, I promise. Do not let your guard down," Danathaniel said in an encouraging voice. As I watched them disappear into the dark tunnel, I tried to collect all the information I had just been given. Joy filled my heart with excitement just knowing there were others that carried the same burden as me.

"What should we do now?" I asked Devin.

"We look for the others. The question is where will we find—"

His sentence was cut off by the sound of footsteps coming down the stairs. I heard the sound of metal hitting the hard cold floor.

"Get ready to attack," I whispered, afraid of what might be approaching.

I saw the walls begin to brighten and then from the darkness someone appeared. All three of us stood there, motionless, staring at each other, contemplating our next move.

"Isaac," the young man called out. I noticed that his clothes were worn out and dirty. Around his neck he wore a scarf, and to cover his hands, he had on an old ragged pair of gray gloves.

"Yes," I replied. "How do you know my name?" I approached him.

He took a deep breath.

"Raziel..." he barely whispered as he took short quick breaths. It was quite obvious to us that he was exhausted.

"Raziel?" My eyes widened in surprise. "You know him? How?"

"He told me to come to this place. He introduced me to the lion with wings. I was told I would find you here in Aloisio." Even in the dim light I noticed the trembling of his hands.

"What does he mean by lion with wings?" Devin asked, doubtful. I knew exactly what he was referring to.

222

"You mean the Creator? Is that the lion you speak of?" I asked.

He smiled. "Yes, that is the one. While I was in the sea, Raziel appeared to me and said that I would find you here."

I could not believe what I had just heard. There really were others that had gone through the same experience as I had. This revelation was a great comfort to me.

"Who are you and why are you here?" Devin asked with suspicion.

"My name is Petra. I come from the Kingdom of Swordsmouth, near the Great River. I have come here to warn King Marco of the Darkness—"

"Well, you are too late," Devin cut him off.

"Late? How so?" he asked, shocked.

"Nephele and the Fallen Stars have already reached Aloisio and King Marco has joined forces with them. Right now, they are probably lurking somewhere in Aloisio with the Diary in their possession."

His facial expression changed immediately; he looked surprised. He slowly reached inside of his tattered brown bag and took out what appeared to be a book. It was covered with old pieces of cloth. As soon as he uncovered it, whispers echoed throughout the prison. I had not forgotten the last time I had heard such sounds. The cover of the book bore the identical symbol I had seen on the Diary. The only difference I saw was a second vertical line present inside of the circle.

"What is that?" I asked, intrigued.

223

"The Book of the Light-Bearer," he stated as he reached out his hand to let me get a closer look at the book. His eyes were firmly fixed on mine.

We were all silent.

"You mean to tell me that there are more books?" Devin inquired as he approached Petra.

I marveled at the book, analyzing each small detail.

"Where did you get this, Petra?" I asked, puzzled.

From the shadows we heard the mutters of numerous men.

"The men that killed them probably headed this way," one of the men shouted.

I knew they were referring to Danathaniel and Cresta, but little did they know that they were long gone. Petra quickly placed the book back into his bag.

"We need to get out of here now," I whispered.

To our benefit, Tonma and the other Underwarriors had not rolled the stone back over the tunnel.

"Are you sure we will be safe going through there?" Petra asked, staring into the darkness.

"It will be a lot safer than remaining in this prison," Devin replied, walking inside the tunnel. Without hesitating, I followed him; Petra was at my heels.

It was dark; humidity was ever present in the air. There was no sign of any light source as we felt our way deeper into the tunnel. In the distance I could faintly hear the voices of the soldiers in the prison. They were arguing among themselves. As we quickened our pace, I heard terrifying screams coming from behind us, followed by the sound of bones breaking. The echoes resounded loudly throughout the tunnel; fear struck the very core of my soul.

"What is happening to them?" Devin asked under strong breaths.

If my abilities had not been cut off here I would be able to read them, but I was still powerless.

"Whatever it is, it is killing those men," I said. My eyes narrowed in an attempt to better see my surroundings.

Silence fell over us as we continued forging ahead to make our way through the pitch-black tunnel.

I was startled when I heard a strong roar coming from behind us, followed by the sound of beating drums, which caused the ground beneath our feet to tremble.

"What in the name of Elysium is that?" Petra whispered as he walked.

"Whatever it is, it is coming after us," Devin replied, fearfully.

"Come on!" I shouted. With all my might I was trying to run in this dark tunnel. Unexpectedly, as I scurried forward, my foot was no longer touching the ground. I plunged in the unknown darkness. I heard Petra and Devin scream as they fell. Despite my lack of abilities in Alosio, my body flexed its wings as I plummeted downward; I felt a sharp pain throughout my back as they expanded to their full width.

Below me I could hear splashes. I flew down as fast as I could in search of Devin and Petra. My body shook violently when I plunged into the icy water.

"Devin! Petra!" I called out to them as I made my way through the freezing water.

"We are here!" I heard their muffled voices.

I could not see them through the darkness. Once again, the roars resounded. They were coming from above us, probably from where we had just fallen. I heard someone or something make a loud splash right next to me. I shivered when I felt the ripples of water touching me. Whatever had followed us was now lurking in the water not far from us.

The smell of putrid decay infiltrated the air.

There was silence. I could hear Devin and Petra gasping for air.

"No. Who are...no..." Petra shouted from the darkness. Following the direction of his voice, I heard Devin grunting. Terrifying screams reverberated on all sides; then dead silence. I heard the water crashing around me. The strong stench of whatever had come filled the air. My heart was beating incredibly fast.

"I see you," a voice whispered.

"Show yourself, creature!" I commanded.

"Look harder." The voice came from behind me. I felt the pressure of two cold hands against my face. Its palms felt like sharp knives cutting through my scalp, penetrating my head and crushing my brain. I closed my eyes; the pain was unbearable.

XIV

I opened my eyes to find my arms and legs completely immobile, without feeling. An intolerable piercing draft of cold air hung in the air as my senses returned to me.

I turned my head and a sharp pain in my back caused me to wince. *My wings,* I thought. My speculation was correct. Someone had chopped them off.

As I checked myself, I realized my wrists had been chained along with my legs. The chains that bound me were old and corroded. I was standing on the balcony of what seemed to be an enormous cathedral. The floor was constructed of perfectly inlaid black and white squared tiles. I was alone. The grayness of the sky was so dense it was almost black. I looked out from the balcony and saw many houses, and beyond the houses, the statue of the Star that stood alone in the middle of the sea. Undoubtedly, I was still in Aloisio.

Multiple bruises covered my whole body. Every piece of clothing but my black pants had been ripped off of me, leaving me without any protection from the bitter cold. My teeth chattered violently as I inhaled the frigid air.

"Devin! Petra!" I shouted to the top of my lungs, but there was no answer. I was discouraged, but not ready to believe the worse had happened. I tried to jog my memory, to retrace the steps to remember what took place after I blacked out, but my memory was blocked. I could only recall vague impressions.

A throbbing headache pounded in my forehead. The pain made me nauseous. I caught a glimpse of Nephele; she appeared before me, her eyes peering hauntingly into mine.

"I see our Capios have done a terrific job in capturing you three."

"Capios?" I asked in a hoarse voice.

"Yes...creatures from the Abyss. Apparently, the Gate of the Fourth Dimension is not being watched so vigilantly," she said with a snarl, hoping to see my reaction, but I was not about to entertain her depraved humor.

I moaned.

"Capios are shapeless creatures, invisible to the naked eye. The only evidence of their presence is their growling, which serves as a warning to their prey that they are about to be taken. Once they latch onto you they automatically take possession of your senses. Quite useful and interesting beings they are."

There was silence after her explanation. Because of the pounding headache, I was too weak to even lift up my head.

"Will you continue to believe the lying fools that surround you, Isaac?" she queried. Her cunning voice became soft and almost soothing.

"Where are they?" My lips mumbled the words feebly.

"They are safe, that is all you need to know." She approached me. "Why are you being so difficult? You must know that aligning yourself with us is the wisest choice. Do not be fooled by the words of others. We have cut off your special 'gifts' so that you could see that we are stronger than any other entities you know."

I chuckled. "When you say it like that, it sounds almost believable," I retorted with a sarcastic smirk.

There was silence.

"Now tell me," I said weakly. "Do you not need my blood anymore to open the Diary? You have been pursuing me with such relentless obsession that I thought your life was now driven by the ruthless desire to have me shed my blood for the Diary."

"I am learning how to be patient with your kind, Isaac."

I allowed my eyes to look deeply into hers.

"You lied to me. You said I was the only one that could give you blood to open the Diary; not that I expected anything different from you."

She chuckled.

"Well, I must admit, it was not easy to believe Athalas when he informed me that there were four more like you, especially when we discovered that four more books existed. Since Petra has also been captured, I suppose it is true. Your value to us is vitally important—only you can shed blood to open the Diary, but opening the book isn't enough. You have to read the words written on its pages. Every book-bearer can only open the book that lies in their possession. Demetre, however, was meant to be a host." She paced around the balcony as a soft breeze blew her hair. "All he was ever meant to do was to be a dwelling place for Corbin."

"Are they related to me?" I asked. Even with the slightest movement the pain throughout my body intensified.

"That I do not know," she answered.

I gasped for air. I could feel the muscles on my face begin to twitch.

"You know, it is baffling to me that you are able to invade a person's mind, make them dream what you want them to and inflict much pain upon them, but you cannot force them to choose what you desire for them."

She viciously glared at me, but this time with a different expression in her eyes; eyes that seemed eager to destroy me. She leaned her face in close to mine and spat at my right cheek. Anger rose up inside of me.

"Then why do you think you are chained here?" She turned her back to me, facing the kingdom. "Besides, it is only through him that I can enter your mind," she chimed.

"Him?" I asked, revelation dawning on me.

"The Dark One." She sighed resolutely. "There is a very special connection between you two—something that the

Nephilins and the Fallen Stars are to also discover. Your minds are connected in some mysterious way."

My breathing grew faint. "Bastards," I said angrily, clinching my teeth.

"The citizens of this kingdom are all ignorant of the present danger—the motive for this darkness is under their very noses," she declared, ignoring my comment. "They think we have recruited their men simply to train for a war. Yet they are completely blind as to what this war is about, or where it will take place. They are all scared, running to and fro trying to create a solution, some theory to explain all of this darkness. Also, having Athalas—the commander of Death— on our side is something very beneficial to the cause."

"Why are you holding me here, Nephele? You know I will not shed my blood willingly."

She paused a moment.

"There is someone that I want you to see before your special treat," she said.

Nephele opened the massive wooden door that was to my left and on the other side, I caught a glimpse of a very long hallway. She closed the door behind her upon leaving.

Frantically, I shook my arms, hoping to find a way to break free from the chains, but my efforts were for naught. I stared up at the gray sky and my mind drifted away. I wondered, questioning Raziel's whereabouts, and what had happened to Tonma, Devin and Petra. Did they all share the same fate?

I began to doubt the reality of all that I had experienced: the memories of the white lion, the sea. They all seemed more like a distant dream to me. All of the people I had encountered, even the Underwarriors, were like a myth in my mind at this moment. Everything seemed to be so surreal.

A flash of lightning dashed across the sky; rumbles of thunder followed. I was hungry; my body had been beaten and was in a weakened state. The door flew open and two Nephilins walked in my direction. They unchained my hands and dragged me down the hallway. The floors followed the same black and white pattern from the balcony. There was writing all over the walls and statues throughout the hallway that made the space feel somber. Even with my dulled senses, I was able to decipher some of the words. One of the phrases caught my eye.

"Judgment Comes Swiftly When Least Expected."

Another door opened to my view. It was a throne room. Two guards were positioned at the entrance as we entered, both armored from head to toe in silver. Their helmets were shaped like human skulls with two horns on each side. A red cape was draped behind their backs, touching the floor. The room was decorated with beautiful white stones; ornate statues and mosaics surrounded us. The ceiling was painted with depictions of human torture. In front of me was a throne, which exuded with royalty and majesty. The golden allure of the throne which was erected in the center, stood out above all of the white accessories in the room. A man sat upon it his left arm reposed on the armrest with his head resting on his hand. The two Nephilins that accompanied me left.

"Leave us," the man on the throne ordered; both guards that were positioned at the door's entrance retreated. To discover that these guards were human was a big surprise.

Silence dominated the room as I stood before his presence in awe.

"I will not pretend that I do not know who you are, Isaac. Neither will I hide what it is I want from you," he said with a kind voice.

My body continued to grow weaker.

"What is…your name?" I stammered.

"King Marco." He raised his head up and his dark eyes were now looking directly at me. His black shoulder-length hair cascaded in front of his face, covering his left side. "I will not say I am sorry for what has happened to you. It was the only way I could get you here to show you what I must do. Consider your presence here to be a…favor from me."

I was speechless, and honestly too weak to even make an attempt to reply.

"Your weakness displays the fallibility at which the Creator is capable of taking care of you. If you are meant to be this book-bearer, why are you still here in this room, weak on your knees, and at my disposal?"

I closed my eyes and realized that the weight I felt within me was a lot heavier in this room.

"Why have you brought me here?" The pain that coursed through my body was markedly intensified with every word I spoke.

King Marco stood to his feet and walked down two short staircases positioned in front of his throne.

He deliberated momentarily. "I do hope my timing is right." Measuring the moment, he painstakingly drew back the white curtains that draped onto the right side of the throne. As I peeked through the frosted windows I caught a glimpse of the sea. From a distance, I could still see the statue of the Star. Lightning ripped from one end of the horizon to the other.

"I want to show you something real—something tangible," he said, walking away from the windows.

"I know you are not in the best condition, but you do need to see this," he said ominously. He gruffly pulled my right arm and placed it over his shoulders.

He led me in the direction of a painting that hung on the far left wall of the room. It was a depiction of a masterfully painted field of flowers, a breathtaking sunset and many Stars flying. In the painting, one of the Stars was seated on a rock, holding a harp in his hand.

My blood rushed through my veins at every step. The remnants of my amputated wings moved as if they wanted to expand. I could not understand why my body reacted this way.

Instantaneously, my senses came back to me. I felt invigorated. A boost of energy flooded my body, empowering every member.

"What happened?" I asked, shocked.

King Marco looked at the painting and laid his right hand over the Star sitting with the harp.

"This painting is special. Your body is reacting to the power that Lucifer still has while his body sleeps. Even though he still slumbers, your body can sense its vibrations," he countered as his hand traced the canvas.

My eyes were fixed on him, anticipating an unequivocal answer to my question. Surprisingly, my ability returned and I was able to pick up my surroundings, and without delay I could read his thoughts. There was a vacuum within him, an empty shell. Incoherent thoughts and memories scattered without rhyme or reason in his mind. Amid the collection of illogical thoughts, I recalled the image of a dark being I had seen when I had read Devin's soul. It was the Dark One.

"You sold your soul to Lucifer, didn't you? You are no longer a mere human, are you?" I charged as I returned from the vision.

King Marco belted out a frenzied roar.

"I see you are no fool. I know of your gifts, Isaac, but I don't think you are yet able to capture all that is in this room," he said menacingly.

"Why do you say that?" I asked; my fists tightened as rage arose inside of me.

"Because the Star you see playing the harp in this painting is a manifestation of Lucifer."

My heart skipped a beat as I heard his affirmation.

I concentrated my attention on the Star portrayed on the canvas. I was hesitant about using my powers in the room again. Whenever Lucifer appeared in my mind, a feeling of loss and desperation overcame me.

I felt as if fire burned inside of me. My hands trembled, and to my surprise the painting began to move. This image of Lucifer played the harp beautifully while the other Stars flew against the beautiful sunset. Sudden flames circulated throughout his body, burning everything, including the six wings that were marvelously pinioned to his back. A low screech came from him as his body was incinerated. He resembled nothing like the apparition I had encountered before in Valley Hills.

"Why is my body responding to the painting like this?" I asked, panting, gasping for air, eyes transfixed on the canvas.

"It is because you approached this painting that your powers came back to you. Even as he sleeps he has been gracious enough to give you back your strength, but if you walk away from his presence, your body will return to its ordinary human state," he affirmed with a gentle, yet malefic voice.

From behind us the door burst wide open; Nephele, Athalas and Azaziel made their entrance.

"The Shadows are quickly approaching the city, Marco. They are on the opposite side of the sea, swimming to shore as we speak," Nephele informed him with a smile stamped on her face. Athalas remained at her side. "Many Whispering Lights are accompanying them."

"Who sends the Lights?" the king asked.

"Corbin," Nephele replied.

I turned to face the king.

"You would destroy your own people...for them?" I asked in disgust.

The veins on his neck became visible as he scowled at me. He punched the brick wall, wounding his right hand.

"Do you still not understand the magnitude of power that is at play here?" he shouted as he removed his bloody hand from the wall. "Do you believe you have the ability to withstand the vast army rising from the Darkness? Many kings are very much aware of the Dark One ascending again. This is the power of Lucifer. In the same way he decided to return your abilities to you, he has the power to take them away in an instant." He moved his hands in a flagrant way as he spoke. It was apparent that he was tormented.

"Isaac, you are smarter than this, aren't you?" Athalas asked with a sneer. "Please do not be a fool. We are giving you another opportunity to join us."

"Where are..." My voice trailed off. I was not able to finish my question when I saw Adawnas appear from behind them.

"Stop being so insolent, Isaac," she said in her lovely, caressing voice.

"What an unexpected way to meet you again, Adawnas," I said, shocked. My mind was flooded with the vivid images of our journey together.

"It is amazing to watch how stubborn you can be, Isaac, and your fortitude is commendable. These are qualities I desire to have on those that are with me," a mellow voice bantered from behind me. I turned around to see the impossible happening. The painting had completely come to life. The Stars flew on the painted sky, the beautiful sunset emanated heat, and Lucifer, in the form of a Star, looked at me with penetrating, inviting eyes.

"Adawnas is right," he said with a smirk. "You mustn't be so resilient in your choice now."

"This cannot be real," I whispered to myself, dazed.

"I did warn you, didn't I?" Lucifer said with a cunning smile. "The voices in the little village of Adhelina, I was speaking to you. I warned you. You cannot hide."

Lucifer started to play a somber melody with his harp. "You said this could not be real? Well, let me prove to you how real I am, my dear Isaac."

My body returned to its apathetical state and my strength diminished as the strings played their melody. At the sound of every note, the bruises reappeared on my skin, my legs could no longer support the weight of my body, and my heart seemed crushed with a heavy-laden burden. King Marco laughed deliriously.

"Remarkable...this never gets old." He clapped his hands in amusement as he watched the scene.

I gasped for air incessantly.

"Never gets old? Why? Have you tortured others this way before?" I asked in a broken voice. In caution, he stepped toward me, knelt down and whispered in my ear.

"How do you think I persuaded all of those men from the villages to join us?" he balked. "They have been sent out to go throughout Elysium and kill as many men and women as possible. It is obvious that no man with a sound mind would agree to that. I had to torture every single one of them."

My eyes met his. They were empty, dead and hollow. Even in my weakness, I could feel rage growing inside of me. From outside, I heard chants and perverted growls.

Lucifer laughed. "Yes. They are finally coming! My army is urgently in need of new soldiers," he said as the Stars in the painting melted away like snow under the sun

"So you mean to kill these people before they discover the truth, so that they can all become Shadows in your army?" I asked, breathing heavily.

He clicked his tongue quickly three times. "Don't look at it that way, Isaac. Look at it as redemption. They will not have to share the same doom as humanity," King Marco responded.

"Marco," Lucifer said sharply. "I have ordered the Shadows to destroy everything in this city. Aside from Isaac and Petra, there are three other young ones that have been bitten by the white lion that are also carrying my other books. Find them and take them to Corbin, alive. I will be in the Dark Woods Forest, waiting. Pay attention to my manifestations there."

At that moment, the beautiful painting melted away; its contents poured onto the marble floor like water. I noticed that Nephele was holding something in her hands. It was covered with a black cloth.

"What is it that you are holding, Nephele?" I asked.

She chuckled.

"The Diary of Lucifer and the Book of the Light-Bearer," she replied with a smirk.

"The books?" I scoffed.

"We will have plenty of time to discuss this matter, Nephele. Now, let us proceed to meet the Shadows," King Marco broke in with a smile. He turned to face Adawnas. "Are our other guests ready to leave?"

She nodded and then looked at me.

"How many other books are missing?" King Marco asked Nephele.

"Three," she replied, keeping her eyes locked onto mine.

Through the doorway, I caught sight of Devin and Petra being brought in by two heavily armored guards. Wearing spike-clustered helmets, the guards' faces were void of expression, lost in the darkness. Devin's body was completely covered with bruises and wounds. They had stripped him to his waist and left him with only a pair of ragged torn pants, his bare feet dragging on the floor. He was barely conscious. Petra was also hurt, but was still lucid, his eyes glistening with fear. Seeing them in this state caused my heart to sink into the deepest pit of despair.

"The other three have been spotted near the Court of Many Meetings," one of the human guards reported.

The chants grew louder, and were accompanied by the piercing screams of people in the streets.

"Hold him down," King Marco ordered the guards that stood by the door. Adawnas and Athalas remained unmoved; their eyes were watchful and attentive to the guards' actions. The guards came in my direction and pressed down on me, holding me against the floor. I could not muster any strength to fight back or even move.

"You see...he has rescinded your abilities again, Isaac," King Marco said as he approached me. "And now you lay here, a pathetic species, without any strength left to fight." He stretched his hand forth toward Athalas. Deep inside I knew what he desired, what they all desired. They wanted my blood to open the Diary.

King Marco took a dagger out of his cloak and without hesitation he cut my wrist. "Bring Petra closer!" he shouted as the blade opened my skin.

His eyes glistened as blood spurted from my wrist. Quickly, Nephele brought in the Diary and placed it on the puddle of blood that had formed. After he was finished with me, he proceeded to also cut Petra's wrist; his blood streamed out onto the black and white marble floor.

"This ought to do the trick..." King Marco decreed as his eyes savagely gaped at my open wound.

"Take him out of here," Athalas ordered the guards as he pointed at Devin.

"The Soul Exchange," Nephele said in a joyful tone. "Perform the Soul Exchange. If he isn't willing to shed his blood for the Diary, let us call on a Fallen Star to come dwell inside of his body. We have another innocent boy here. The mixture of their blood will be enough to perform the Exchange."

As strength ebbed from my body, it grew weaker and weaker. Where was the power of the white lion? As I bled, my mind filled with thoughts and questions. Why was I not able to stop these attacks now? Hadn't the white lion given me power? With every stroke of my heart, I could feel my soul succumbing to the darkness.

Lucifer had been triumphant in purging me of my powers. I could not receive visions, or interpret anything, move anything, or even discern anything with clarity. My strength had rapidly declined. I struggled to remain conscious. I bowed my head and closed my eyes. I felt the disintegration of my soul corrupt the very essence of my life as I surrendered to the darkness within.

NEPHELE

XV

I watched as Athalas performed the Soul Exchange on Isaac's frail body. The Soul Exchange was a dark power that could only be performed in Lucifer's presence and with the mixture of innocent blood. Even against one's will, the weakness of the mortal body allowed a Fallen Star to come and take possession.

The snarled grunts of the Shadows increased. They were quickly approaching.

"We must leave at once. The Shadows are almost upon us and we have clear orders to meet Lucifer in the Dark Woods Forest," Adawnas said urgently. "Will he die if we do not complete the Soul Exchange now?" she asked.

"No. He will not," I responded, disappointed. I eagerly wanted to see the Fallen Star that was soon to dwell inside of him.

"Very well, let us leave then."

I nodded in agreement. Athalas ripped the white curtains from the wall and wrapped Isaac's bloody body.

"Guards!" Marco yelled. "Take Petra and Devin and lock them in the Prison of Despair."

"The Prison of Despair?" I repeated in shock. "Do you really think you are making the right decision? We will need Petra."

He let out a disgusted sigh.

"The Prison will keep him from escaping," he scoffed. "I don't need you to judge every decision I make."

His repugnant attitude enraged me. "I want to make sure that your human mind is capable of executing the tasks that the Dark One is requiring of you," I yelled, ready to attack him with my powers.

"As much as it would delight me to watch the two of you fight, we have to go to the forest and meet the Dark One. Do you not hear the Shadows?" Athalas said.

There was an uncomfortable pause as the distant shouts of the Shadows echoed.

"Can we put our differences aside?" Athalas pleaded, laying his hand on my shoulder.

I disdainfully nodded in agreement. Even though he had sold his soul to Lucifer, I still despised him.

The guards entered the chamber and covered Petra's head with a black sack, tied his bloody hands and legs with ropes and dragged him to the dungeons. Many were unaware that the main entrance to the Prison of Despair was situated below the substructures of the cathedral, located here, in the Kingdom of Aloisio.

"Let's go," I said, leading the way down the somber hall.

Athalas swooped up Isaac's body and placed it over his shoulder.

"Be careful with him," Marco said as they both followed. Adawnas walked next to me.

We contained our words as we made our way down the hall, heading to the doors in the lower level of the cathedral. Our footsteps reverberated like echoes as we walked. The stairs were made out of wood with golden patterns etched along the handrails. The iron doors were located at the bottom of the stairs.

"Is the chariot ready?" I asked Marco as we approached the double-chained doors.

"The chariot is right in front of the cathedral," he quickly replied.

I opened the door to find the black chariot standing right in front of us. A blast of cold air blew across our faces.

The chants and shouts of the Shadows were intensifying. The sky darkened as panic settled in. The citizens were confused, chattering among themselves and wondering at the meaning of the roars.

Marco opened the door to the chariot.

"In here." He smiled as he pointed to the red cushioned seats lining the chariot.

Athalas gently laid out Isaac's body.

I stepped inside the chariot and took my seat. Athalas and Adawnas sat next to me.

"The humans...so unaware of the danger," I muttered under my breath as Marco took a seat next to Isaac's body and closed the chariot's door.

"You may proceed," I ordered the guard that drove the chariot.

As the horse pulling the chariot trotted along the thoroughfare, I gazed at the beautiful monuments the humans had built; pity they were all going to be destroyed soon. The ornamental cathedrals and the beautiful houses built alongside the cobblestone roads were soon to be nothing but ashes.

"What is on your mind?" Marco asked intently.

I chuckled.

"I suppose I have been silent for quite a while now."

He nodded.

"I know Lucifer will send us back to look for the others. He will want them captured alive...along with their books."

"Do you think the books are in this location?" Athalas asked, hoping for a positive affirmation.

"I know that they are," I responded. I knew it would not be long before they were found.

Adawnas was unusually quiet. I pretended not to notice, but her silence concerned me. I read her mind and knew that she was feeling insecure; she still had doubts about her decision to side with us again, even after my benevolence to her in all I had shown her.

"You have chosen wisely, Adawnas. Have no doubt about that. The Creator needs a dose of his own medicine. He damned our kind to an eternity of darkness before some of us were even born," I said as I gave her a deep, penetrating look into her eyes.

Her eyes shied away from mine. She kept her gaze upon the thundering sky.

"Having lived all of my years in the shadows, I wanted—I hoped the light could actually touch me, even if briefly—when I was with Isaac and Devin." She sighed deeply.

"Please understand. We are *not* made for the light. Evil runs in our veins. We are wicked by nature...and birth," I reminded her, revolted at the words that drifted from her mouth.

I understood very well what I spoke of. The memories of the day I became a Nephilin would never leave my mind. The agony and the pain my body went through, the day when I had lain with Mordred and given birth to the first Nephilin, Duane. Out of all the women that had lain with the Fallen Stars, I was the only one that Lucifer extended mercy upon to survive. All the other women were killed after their transformation.

The howls of the Shadows were getting louder. The ground trembled as they marched in our direction. Murmurs filled the atmosphere. As we crossed a bridge that connected the far side of Aloisio to the road, I saw Shadows climbing out of the water, yearning insatiably for the lives of the people that lived here.

Adawnas' eyes widened when she saw them. Their numbers had increased dramatically. Like ants they marched toward the kingdom; their voracious howls and their heinous growls struck terror.

"There they go...the wild savages," Marco mumbled as he turned to observe Aloisio being overtaken by the Shadows. It wasn't long before screams were heard and black smoke billowed upward above the houses and buildings. Soon the entire kingdom was in flames. The shrieks and cries of the people were like music to my ears.

The hatred in my heart for humans was something that burned within me every moment of every day. Their fragile bodies and torpid minds were not worthy of life. I much despised the days where I was human. Mortality was unfitted for me.

"How does it feel, King?" I asked him. "I know you have offered your life to Lucifer, but there must be some humanity left in you."

King Marco turned his gaze to me; his eyes brightened with a luminous glow.

"When I sold my soul to Lucifer, I chose to die to everything human in me, Nephele. Humans are weak, thus the reason why humanity has reached this chaotic state."

"Leave him alone, Nephele," Athalas ordered with his eyes fixed on me.

How dared he speak to me in such a humiliating manner. With a simple twitch of my right eye, pain overtook him. He belted out a bloodcurdling scream; a pool of blood spurted from his nostrils.

"Nephele!" Adawnas yelled. "Stop it!"

With the power of my thoughts, I cast him out of the moving carriage and onto the muddy road; the black horse that pulled the carriage was quickly agitated by the sight, coming to an abrupt halt. The human guard that drove the carriage was silent, immobile.

"How dare you give me orders? It amuses me that you, out of everyone, believe you have the authority to give *me* orders. I should end your lowly existence right now...take you out of your misery."

With a quick blink, I removed his pain. He held his throat in his hands, gasping desperately for air. As he lay on the road, I caught sight of a smoke cloud circling throughout the dimly lit sky. I glanced behind us to see Aloisio burning.

"Why would you inflict pain upon him?" Adawnas asked. "We are all on the same side."

I scoffed.

"I side with no one but the Dark One. All the long years of my life I have walked this earth alone. We may be working for the same goal, but my heart is bound to only one master." My eyes twitched again and Adawnas was hurled violently out of the carriage, landing onto the ground, shrieking and writhing in pain.

"Let this be a reminder to you; do not regret the choice you have made, Adawnas. Know which side you are on. Do not waver in serving the Dark One wholeheartedly. If you do, I will know."

I overpowered her mind. I transported her to a dark forest. The trees around her were incinerated, the branches dry and stripped of any sign of life. The forest floor was covered in ash and the air she breathed was filled with intoxicating fumes. She screamed with a desolate hopelessness at the sight.

From behind her, Death appeared in its grotesque form. Its golden eyes and yellowed teeth gave a menacing glow in the dark. It coiled about her with its snakelike tail, tightening its grip.

"Do you not think that is enough?" I heard Marco's muffled voice. "We are wasting time. Lucifer is waiting for us in the Dark Woods Forest."

I was aghast to have to release her mind, but he was right. I withdrew from Adawnas' mind and climbed back inside the carriage.

"Adawnas and Athalas, please come aboard. We don't want to be late now, do we?" I said as I made myself comfortable in my seat.

They both climbed aboard, their eyes staring down at me with great disdain. It disgusted me.

We journeyed down the road in silence. The weather was changing. Flurries of snow drifted from a sky that was being split apart by lightning.

"You took longer than expected," the unmistakable voice whispered in my ear. "I suppose I should be very understanding during these times, am I correct?" the voice suggested with a ring of sarcasm.

"Master, I apologize for the delay," Athalas said with a stammering voice.

As the snow flurries descended, some of them began to pulsate with a dim red light. The light slowly transmitted to other flurries. Sounds of beating drums resounded. The small glares of deep red light conjugated with the others, only to form the shape of the Dark One. They merged into a body, giving shape to a pale narrow face, black hollow eyes and skeletal hands. He was clothed in old rags that flowed down to the forest floor, covering his feet.

"It is dreadful to have to appear in such a way before you, but I had no other choice," Lucifer said in a hoarse and broken voice. Sweat dripped from his dark wavy hair onto his forehead.

"This disparaging state of yours won't last long, master," I encouraged. "We have the body inside the carriage. We were not able to finish the Soul Exchange in time. We had to leave the cathedral to meet you here before the Shadows arrived."

Lucifer smiled.

"Not finished yet, darling?"

I detected a contemptuous note in his voice as he uttered the last word. His weakly manifestation moved swiftly toward the carriage. With a single movement from his finger, he removed the body from the carriage and laid it down on the snow-covered ground.

"Why is this not finished yet?" he asked. Fear seized my body. The white curtains that wrapped Isaac's body disintegrated. I knew out of all those living and dead, he was one of the few that could destroy me.

"King Marco, perhaps you could give me an answer?" The sarcasm in his voice was noticeable. "Or…perhaps you, Athalas? Can you tell me why?"

Athalas shook his head as a sign of defeat.

"Maybe you?" He pointed to Adawnas. "Why is my bidding not done?"

She did not speak a word.

A sharp pain attacked my head. My skin and my flesh turned a grayish shade of death as pain coursed through every nerve in my body.

"I know you can tell me, Nephele," Lucifer said as my feet were lifted off of the forest floor. "There is no time to waste and you, out of all the others, know that very well."

The moment the pain took me over, I felt as if I was the most helpless being. I was tossed against a tree with such force the tree splintered and crumbled to the ground.

"Enough of this nonsense!" Lucifer demanded as he moved around us. "I hope in the future your actions will reflect that you understand the urgency of the moment."

Slowly I rose to my feet.

"Please, dear," he said with a sweet tone. "Finish what you have started. Do not forget that though old age and disease cannot touch your kind, swords and spears can indeed put an end to your long life."

I looked down at Isaac's bloody body. Judging by the color of his skin, life was subsiding from his lifeless form.

"Athalas…the dagger," I said.

Athalas vigilantly walked toward me, laying the dagger next to Isaac. I carefully removed the pieces of cloth that were bound around his wrists. As I did, I heard the sound of a rattlesnake moving from above me.

As I lifted my head, I saw a gigantic black snake positioned next to the Master's manifestation. Its glowing yellow eyes shone distinctly against the darkness of its skin.

"Kill him now," the snake hissed with each word. "You must not fear, child."

I held Isaac's wrist and stared at their open wounds oozing with blood. A moment of exhilaration flooded me to know that, even though he did not shed his blood willingly, we were still able to perform the Soul Exchange.

"Beautiful, is it not?" Lucifer whispered excitedly. "To see my new dwelling place being fashioned. This body will be of great use to us."

I inflicted another cut on both of Isaac's wrists with the dagger. As the blood flowed to the ground, my heart leapt with joy. I noticed Athalas', Adawnas' and Marco's hearts had quickly accelerated.

"Ah, this one will be a spectacular trophy." Lucifer slowly moved closer to me. "His face shall not change, only his spirit. Isaac's soul will linger on in the Wastelands as a Fallen Star makes his abode inside his body." A whimsical smile beamed across Lucifer's face.

"Do you choose, my lord?" Adawnas asked. "The Star that will dwell in his body?"

"No, child. That I leave up to the Fallen Rulers to decide. They command my armies and train them for battle. Even if I wanted to choose, my body lies in a place where I simply do not have the luxury of making the selection myself."

Isaac's body had grown cold; his skin had a purple hue and his lips darkened.

"He is gone," I affirmed, touching his cold body.

Lucifer gave a sigh of relief.

"There are others...others that will do what he was not able to...the other four will read their books," he said as he folded his hands. "Now, we wait."

Our wait wasn't long. In a matter of seconds, Isaac's body regained its color; his eyes opened and they were crimson. His hands trembled; his teeth clenched. I watched in awe. Beads of sweat flowed from his brow down to his neck.

A thunderous growl escaped him as his body landed with a thud against the forest floor.

"Mordred," Lucifer mumbled.

Mordred stood to his feet. "My lord, it is such irony to return to Elysium in human form. It has been a while since I've had a body of my own," he said with a frightening voice. His crimson eyes would cause even the bravest men to cower in fear.

"Finally, you stand before me in human form," I said as the aching memories returned to me. Memories I tried so hard to forget but they had been deeply ingrained in me. I was displeased that Mordred had been the one chosen to dwell inside Isaac's body. "We have been fighting for the blood of this young man for a long time, but he refused to shed it voluntarily."

Mordred scoffed. "Not to worry, Nephilin, there are others out there that will read their books and lay down their lives for the Dark One. It is only a matter of deciding the most effective move to persuade them."

The way he uttered the word *Nephilin* stirred up rage inside of me. I knew that he was one of the creators of our kind. I wondered if he had already forgotten our past together; I surely had not. It was strange to see him inside Isaac's body. My memory still held on to his former appearance quite vividly.

"Mordred, it really is delightful to have you standing here...your presence brings me great joy," Lucifer said with coldness.

"What would you have us do now, my lord?" Marco asked.

Lucifer held up his right hand.

"Touch it, Marco," he said with an enticing voice. King Marco stood there, frozen and in shock. I knew little about Marco, but I was aware of his great longing for the privilege to touch the Dark One's hand.

"Yes, my lord," he delightfully spoke as he stretched forth his hand. The moment their hands met, Marco let out a deafening scream, and with a brutal force he fell to the ground.

"Even with all of your authority and power, with all the knowledge you possess"—Lucifer's voice deepened—"you are of no use to me, but only to host the one I truly desire to see here."

Marco crawled pitifully from one side of the ground to the other.

"But I aided you. I sided with you, my lord. Why are you doing this to me?" His voice was breaking; the veins in his hands were visible through his paling skin.

"You are a mere host, Marco. The kingdoms will be destroyed not only by swords and spears, but also by the allegiance of their kings. Aloisio and Billyth were mere examples to others of what we are capable of doing." Lucifer knelt next to Marco.

"But I gave up my life for you," Marco stuttered.

Lucifer grinned maliciously.

"Exactly, and to give up is to lose something you hold dear...*king*."

All of us present in the forest were shrouded with fear. Adawnas stood paralyzed. Athalas kept a vigil on the snake.

"Erebos, come to me, my darling."

The snake swiftly slithered its body over the forest floor to encounter Lucifer. Slowly, he knelt down, his body quivering. "We have been waiting for this day since the War, but now your time has come." He took a deep breath and smiled. "Are you hungry?" His hand gently caressed the snake's long, dark body.

"No, please!" Marco screamed in fear and torment.

"It must be done!" Lucifer shouted. Marcos' deafening screams intensified as he trembled. I could hear his heart beat; it pounded as the snake approached him. I heard the snake's heart beating at a normal pace. Erebos' body tightened its grasp around Marco.

As soon as its body had taken Marcos', the snake's yellow eyes met its victim's horrified gaze. Erebos' mouth opened and released small flickers of ghoulish light. The lights floated around Marco's head and entered his skull through his ears and nose.

"My lord, no! Please." These were Marco's last words before Erebos viciously sunk its vile fangs deep into his neck.

"Drink," Lucifer ordered Erebos.

Blood dripped from its mouth as Erebos sucked out Marco's blood. He was unconscious; his arms and head dangled unrestrained.

"This was much unexpected, my lord," Athalas uttered in a faltering tone.

Lucifer let out a hideous laugh.

"I do not doubt your heart, Athalas, but your concern is superfluous. One's servant should not tell his master what is right and wrong."

When my gaze returned to Marco, Erebos was no longer gripping him. I searched around but he was nowhere to be seen.

"Erebos is no longer here, Nephele," Mordred whispered in my ear. I turned to face him. "It has taken over Marco's body."

To my surprise, Marco's body slowly regained its color, changing from pale to an olive tint. Even the garments he wore brightened. His teeth clattered against one another; his chin trembled.

Marco's body movements came to an abrupt stop. Lucifer gazed at the stilled body, waiting for a sign of movement.

"Nephele, long have I waited for this moment," Marco said in a sharp voice. There was a low hiss at the end of every word he spoke.

"I beg your pardon," I said.

"To see you through human eyes is mesmerizing. The beauty you carry is truly breathtaking," he said as he lifted himself from the ground with his hands. His gaze was tender and beguiling.

"Erebos, we have much to do," Lucifer said in a broken voice.

I looked at the others and realized that they seemed as surprised as I was.

"You have been away for far too long. There is much to be done!" Lucifer added.

"Welcome, Erebos," Mordred said with a sly grin.

"How rude of me...introductions..." Lucifer slowly stretched forth his skeletal hands, pointing at each one of us. "This is Athalas, Adawnas, and this is Nephele."

Erebos nodded.

Why had Lucifer kept us in the dark about Erebos? I had been so faithful and loyal to him. Why would he choose not to mention his plans to me?

"My lord, why did you not mention your intentions with Marco? Having knowledge of your plans would have meant a great deal to us all," I said, fearful of his reaction.

Lucifer moved in my direction, his disfigured face set on me. When he reached arm's-length, he gave me a kind smile.

"Tell me, Nephele...Am I not kind to you?" His eyes pierced me to the core.

"Yes, my lord," I said as I lowered my head in respect.

"Do you believe I am a good master to you and your kind?" The breeze caused his garments to move gently.

"Yes...my lord..." Deep inside, I regretted questioning him, but a part of me felt slighted. It seemed as though I was not worthy of his trust.

"Very well, if I believe that it is necessary for you to know any of my plans or strategies—I will be kind enough to tell you. Otherwise, simply obey and do not waste time concerning yourself with an empty soul."

With his hand, he reached for my face, gently touching it. My heart discerned not if it should fear him, or embrace the attention he was now giving me.

"I must go back now...my spirit cannot be out of my body for this long. Until the books are opened and read, my powers will still be limited. I have called you five to carry out my will." He looked intently at every one of us. "Of all the servants that I have that roam this earth, I have chosen you to carry out my bidding." Lucifer gave a halfhearted smile. My heart throbbed with joy. To serve the Dark One in his time of need was an honor, my life's purpose.

"Adawnas, assist Nephele—help her in battle." Adawnas bowed her head slowly. "Much rests on the both of you."

"Athalas, Death is still at your command, correct?"

"Yes, my lord," Athalas responded.

"Use this gift wisely. Do not be foolish with your authority. Even though your soul belongs to me, you still have a human body. Humans are prone to act foolishly, even frivolously," Lucifer said as he moved promptly toward Erebos.

"Now you, Erebos..." he said in a low, ominous voice. "Infiltrate the kingdoms of this world. Deceive all the kings and the rulers...make them blind to all truth." Lucifer stretched forth his right hand.

"Now you, Mordred, you are special, the father of the first Nephilin." As Lucifer spoke, his eyes widened. "You already know what to do: hunt down the other three. Bring them to me alive and unspoiled." His face closed in on Mordred. "It would have been a delight to have Isaac shed his blood willingly, but to see his body in your possession brings me great satisfaction."

Mordred smiled.

"It is my pleasure to seek out the remaining three chosen ones. I will do whatever it takes to persuade them to offer up their blood for your cause, my lord."

Like dust scattered by the wind, Lucifer's body slowly disintegrated; swiftly turning into a mere shadow.

"None of you have the luxury of failing. The kingdoms must all be ready when the armies move in from the Abyss. The humans must become demoralized, even more inept than they already are. Keep them away from the truth of the Creator. Do not underestimate our enemies...I have known them since the dawn of the universe and I have seen their battle tactics. The Creator is no fool when it comes to war." His voice was breaking up as his disengaged body vanished. "Now, I go back to my resting place until I am strong enough to visit you again. I will return when you least expect me."

As soon as he was finished speaking, Lucifer disappeared into thin air.

XVI

Dark Woods Forest was silent. I glanced behind me to see that my four traveling companions were quiet, deep in thought. For a while, I gazed at the snow-covered trees as I breathed in the crisp air that lingered in the atmosphere.

"I must be off," Athalas stated. "I must go to Justicia and speak to the other Council members there."

Without a sound, Erebos came alongside Athalas. "I will accompany you," he said malevolently.

Athalas looked at him with apparent disapproval of the idea.

"Why is it you feel the need to join me?" he asked curiously.

"Given you are the commander of Death and I was called to deceive the kings, it seems befitting that we work together," he responded with a beguiling grin on his face.

"That is not a bad idea," Mordred added. "As a matter of fact, I think we should keep a close eye on this one, Erebos. One never knows what plans may be lurking inside his head. He sold his soul to Lucifer, but he still has a human body."

Athalas jumped up immediately and stood face to face with Mordred.

"I can guarantee that my loyalty lies with the Dark One." Athalas reacted in defiance. His face was flushed with blood, and the bluish-purple veins on his neck had stiffened, giving him a disfigured appearance.

"Enough!" I yelled as my eyes met Athalas'. With my powers, I flung his body against a tree. I inflicted pain on his body.

"Need I remind you of what I am capable of, Athalas?" My patience had grown short.

"No…please…the pain…stop…" he begged.

"The moment I release you from my grip, you and Erebos will take off to Justicia and you will both find a way to work together. Agreed?" He nodded in compliance with my painful suggestion.

My cravings were satisfied to see Athalas in this feeble state; it always energized my depravity to watch this groveling swine brought to his knees. Despite his claims of loyalty to the Dark One, I could never imagine myself being fond of a human, let alone to trust one.

His body wracked with pain, Athalas slowly raised himself and stood upright, his face looking completely distraught.

"Are we ready?" Erebos asked, looking smug with a deceptive smile on his face.

Athalas shamefully acquiesced.

"Erebos, send messengers with reports of all of the plans you devise," Mordred commanded. Erebos gave a nod of affirmation, then he and Athalas disappeared, vanishing into thin air.

Silence lingered. Adawnas remained motionless.

"Where is Corbin?" Mordred asked me.

My breath faltered at the sound of his voice. I tried to remain strong in his presence but our past was still too vivid for me. The fact he behaved as if nothing had ever happened between us enraged me; I was livid.

"He…he is taking care of some affairs…" I gasped.

"I want him to go along with me to track down one of the missing book-bearers—Ballard Radley," he said as he turned back to look in the direction of Aloisio.

"He…he is in Justicia with the other Council—"

"Insolent fool," he cut me off. "Do not think the fact you became a Nephilin gives you knowledge of the extent of the powers and abilities of the Fallen," he said sharply. As he spoke, he placed his right hand over his chest and breathed in deeply. The moment he exhaled, shining lights came out of his mouth along with sounds of drums playing that moved in sync with the lights. Like fireflies, the lights danced in midair.

"Whispering Lights," I mumbled.

"Lights, I order you to call upon Corbin. Tell him we must search for the book-bearer, Ballard Radley," he commanded the lights, which dispersed at the sound of his final words. A gentle breeze followed.

"You are becoming a loyal servant to me, aren't you? I remember when you were still a human girl. I could not take my eyes off you as you pranced around the forest on that day," he said as he walked around me. "You looked at me, not knowing I was a Fallen Star. I had to have you.... You took me to your village to care for me, thinking I was ill. I watched you as your gut expanded abnormally in a matter of hours. Your reaction to the damage you had brought upon humanity was gratifying to me. You do know it was because you fell that we were able to get the other women, right? You were the one that opened the door to us all."

I stared at him in disgust.

"I wonder why the Dark One allowed you to live and ordered all the other Fallen Stars to kill the other women they had slept with after they had their baby Nephilins. Who knows...maybe you would've made a great Shadow," he wondered aloud with a sadistic twist. "All the other women did a great job as Nephilins. I wonder if the memories of their days as humans still linger in their minds even after they became Shadows."

I was at a loss for words when I heard him say this. I felt a cold chill run through me, the memory of my vivid past haunting me.

"How dare you?" I said, repulsed by his arrogance. "Do you think just because the Fallen Rulers appointed you to take over Isaac's body that you can say whatever you want? I wasn't destroyed because I found favor before the Dark One's eyes. I was spared because he saw courage in me."

He let out a malefic cackle.

"Oh, please. Nephele, you are a mere puppet. Do you really think he has a spot in his so-called 'heart' for Nephilins? The Dark One only cares about his servants as long as they are of use to him. Make him rely on you to do all he wants and he will surely never be rid of you. Can he without doubt rely on you?"

To have my weaknesses exposed and to be in the presence of one that knew me so well caused me to feel vulnerable. I turned my back on him so his eyes couldn't meet mine.

"You know, it is a pleasure to be by your side again, Mordred. The strategy of the Dark One placing the three of us to work together is ingenious," I said. I felt as if a knife was thrust into my throat as these words flowed from my mouth. I knew that somehow I was going to have to overcome my painful memories and find a way to work peacefully alongside Mordred, even if it meant the death of me. I needed to prove to the Dark One that I was worthy of his full trust.

Adawnas approached us. "I do find our alliance to be one of our strengths. Like Erebos said, we must be united in order to fulfill the Dark One's wishes."

"And this coming from the one that not too long ago believed in a redemption for her kind from the Creator...so insightful," Mordred replied with a flippant sarcasm.

Adawnas remained quiet. She turned her gaze to me.

"Where are the book-bearers?" she asked.

"Last we heard they were spotted close to the Court of Many Meetings—near the cathedral in Aloisio," I responded.

"It is time to head back to Aloisio. We must find all of them. We need to capture them and convince them to shed their blood and read the books. Lucifer's body needs to be awakened." Mordred's voice faded into whispers along with his body. He returned to a shapeless dark shadow. At an amazing speed, the shadow surrounded us and in a matter of seconds we were transported to Aloisio, standing in front of the walls. The gates were destroyed and lay flat on the muddy ground. Screams of torment were a delight to my senses as we walked through Aloisio's streets. The Shadows were destroying everything in their path; some cast their bodies in the burning flames that had overtaken homes and buildings, causing massive explosions.

Mordred, Adawnas and I walked in the midst of the massacre fearlessly.

"Where are the other Nephilins?" Mordred shouted.

"They are probably waiting for our arrival at the Prison of Despair," I called back.

"Let us head to the entrance of the Prison in the dungeons of the cathedral. We need to find Azaziel and the others and inform them of the bidding the Dark One has commanded us to do. We need to spread out and find them," Mordred affirmed.

"How are we supposed to identify the book-bearers?" Adawnas asked.

Mordred scoffed. "You will know who they are, Adawnas. Once they set eyes on you, they will tremble with fear—*that* is how you will know who they are. They know we are here."

The Shadows attacked the women and the children in massive numbers throughout the kingdom. Desert Dragons soared above Aloisio. They descended on the monuments, completely decimating them with their flames. There were children frantically running, calling out for their parents.

The cathedral stood in front of us, shining in full majesty. We entered the monumental structure and found that everything was left untouched. The oil paintings were still hanging on the walls, precisely positioned. The massive windows were intact, but hazy due to the rising dust and smoke. Even the candles were still lit.

"Take us to the entrance, Nephele," Mordred urged.

Inside the cathedral, on the left side of the wall, there hung a canvas that depicted a warrior smothering a dragon. The warrior sat upon a winged lion and held a sword in his hand. Next to the canvas was the secret door that led to the Prison of Despair. The door was invisible to the human eye and even to some immortals.

"The humans were completely unaware that we built the connection between the Prison and the cathedral," I remarked as I touched the stone wall. Only one with the power to enter one's soul in dreams and visions could open the door.

With my inner vision, I was able to see beyond the wall. With a simple thought, I saw the lock that stood on the other side. I focused on the old rusty lock until it moved, opening the door from inside. The moment I unlocked it, the stones began to shift violently.

A sudden glare of red light stenciled a pattern on the stones: three straight lines surrounded by a perfect circle. Never had these lights appeared before.

"Intriguing," Mordred said in a low voice. "What is this symbol?" He approached the wall.

Stunned, I gazed at the symbol, trying to figure out what it meant. "I have never seen such a thing," I confessed, a bit confused.

We all studied the symbol, bewildered. The glare of red light vanished from the moving stones. As soon as the door was wide open, the symbol disappeared.

Though the symbol was a surprise to me, it did not impede my insatiable desire to find the book-bearers.

In haste I charged down the dark passageway. Our footsteps were loud as we sped down the stairs. Gargoyles were scattered throughout the place. The smell of mold fumigated the atmosphere. There were no windows on the walls and no other light, only the burning torches. All were silent.

"Where are the other Nephilins?" Mordred's voice was broken and agitated. "Why here? Why did they have to hide here?"

"Do I sense fear, Mordred?" Adawnas chuckled in amusement. "The brave Fallen Star fears the entrance of the Prison of Despair?"

Faint voices sounded around us.

"I see Isaac has come to us," Azaziel implied, unaware that Mordred had taken over Isaac's body. Azaziel's hair was so blond that it glowed, even in the dark. His eyes absorbed the soft light of the flames, making them lighter than usual.

Mordred grunted and rushed toward him.

"I am not Isaac," he said with a robust grin. "I am Mordred—a Fallen Star."

"Is he the one, Nephele? Is he Duane's father? Is he the one you spoke of in the past?" Azaziel asked. From behind him, the other Nephilins appeared.

"The...one? I am not..." I muttered in confusion.

"One of our makers?" The weight the words carried was undeniable. It forced me to relive the memories of Mordred and myself in my mind once again.

My breathing faltered. "Yes, he is one of them," I said in a somber tone.

Mordred's eyes gazed upon every Nephilin with a commanding presence. Slowly, one by one, they knelt before him. A huge smile spread across his face.

"It is an honor," Azaziel whispered. "We have only heard the vague tales of our makers, but to actually be in your presence..."

My heart was used to pain and betrayal, but it was not accustomed to the surrender of a vulnerable and weak nature. I felt as if Mordred's presence uncovered my nakedness to all.

"It is *my* honor to be here to do the bidding of the Dark One," he said as he paced about the darkness fuming with hostility, searching the loyalty of every Nephilin. "I must say I am truly proud to be one of the creators. Of course glory must also be given to Nephele. She chose me on that day and I chose her…" His voice trailed off.

"Can we move on to the task at hand?" I said in a loud voice. "We need to find the remaining three book-bearers!"

Their attention was immediately drawn to me.

"It was said by the guards that the three were spotted near the Court of Many Meetings earlier today. We must find them," Adawnas alleged.

"Easy for you to say. There is a massacre waging outside. We may live forever but our bodies can still die by the sword," Duane said as he stepped forward. After all these years, it was still an awkward moment to lay eyes on him. I could never forget the day I gave birth to him; the day my human body changed and I became what I was—a Nephilin.

His words caused me to become possessed with repulsion. How could he be this meek and insecure? Pain would be the only way to bring him back to the reality of what needed to be accomplished. He fell with a loud thump onto the cold floor; his teeth were clenched and his whole body contorted.

"The time to hide in the shadows of this world is long gone. The time has come for what humans believe to be a myth to become a tangible reality. The Nephilins will come out of hiding and the Dark One will reign," I challenged, hostility ringing in my voice. "If we are to achieve this goal, we must all band together. Nephilins, we are brave and made for greatness. Let our courage not be crushed." I released Duane. The dark leather vest he wore had bloodstains on it.

Blood ran out of his nose and his eyes changed to crimson. He stood to his feet and shot me a piercing look. His eyes were moist with tears.

"Your lack of courage is dishonoring, Duane. Refrain from speaking if you are not encouraging any of us," I said coldly.

He retreated back into the shadows, hiding from my sight.

"Very nicely done. I think we are all on the same page now?" Mordred bantered with a sneer. Silence overtook the prison.

"Nephilins, the time has come for the dominion of the Fallen. Let us go and kill as many humans as we can," Mordred's voice exclaimed mightily. I looked at him only to see his lips were not moving. His voice had penetrated our thoughts. "But remember, our main focus is to find the book-bearers. Be not mistaken, they will know who you are. Once they see you, they will either fight or try to flee from you. Be ready to capture every one of them. *Do not kill them.*"

Loud shouts and shrieks sounded. Some of us expanded our dark wings and flew while others took their shadowed shapes and made their way out. The gargoyles were crumbled to pieces as they floundered about.

"Victory!" we alleged repeatedly.

We departed from the cathedral with great fury, destroying any object in our path.

"Since we will not be returning, what say we destroy this cursed place? There is no need for this cathedral anymore," Duncan shouted the moment we were out of the cathedral. "Justicia has already been taken and we can enter the Prison through there!"

Others that had the same ability followed. From the sky, they expelled fire from their wings while the remaining Nephilins on the ground used their powers to aid in destroying the massive monument.

Around us, bodies lay scattered, and Shadows infiltrated everywhere, fulfilling all of Lucifer's requests.

"The war against Elysium begins!" Mordred shouted.

I killed every child, woman and living creature that stood in my way. I hunted them with all the power I had fueled by my hatred for the humans. I eagerly inspected every crook and cranny of every corner, in every house, and every small room to find them. Bodies were being tossed all around; screams of terror intensified with every moment.

I felt my body being thrown with such a powerful thrust, I landed on top of one of the destroyed homes. Disoriented, I picked myself up.

"Who dares?" I hollered.

"Your kind has done much damage already. Did you think your deeds would go about unnoticed?" a voice spoke, but I could not see through the dust that rose from the roof I had fallen upon.

"This is just the start of what is to come!" I warned.

"It is folly for you to believe that you and your kind could roam these lands, searching for the book-bearers and we would do nothing to stop you." The voice sounded closer. Out of the rising dust, he appeared. I could see the silver armor shimmering with golden stripes. Slowly, the dust dissipated from his face.

"Alexander," I moaned.

"We will not forsake Elysium to be taken over by Lucifer's torment." His blue eyes gleamed.

As I rose from the ground, my eyes were pinned on his.

"So the Underwarriors have come? I am afraid your arrival here is a bit too late. What happened? Did you forget the Gate of the Fourth Dimension?"

"We have not forgotten anything, Nephele. Do not be so foolish and presumptuous to believe that you know our strategy." Wings sprang out from his back, with feathered plumes of the purest white.

I did not hesitate; I hurled myself upon him with fury. I feverishly attempted to punch and kick him, but he was amazingly fast. With a firm grip, he grabbed my shoulder and flung me with great force; my body bounced against a column. With my powers I concentrated my fury and cast paralysis upon him. Unexpectedly, he was able to elude my attack.

"I can see your attack, Nephele!" he yelled.

"Bastard. Dodge this!" I shouted as I released a sphere of pain in every direction. I did not care who or what it struck, I wanted him to suffer. I heard screams coming from somewhere close. It was apparent the attack hit some of the humans that ran.

It was silent. I checked my surroundings.

"You really believed that we were going to forsake the other book-bearers? We have come to rescue them, even if it means death." Alexander's voice was a simple gesture that broke through the silence.

277

"I hope you are ready to die!" I would not allow them to take the book-bearers.

Faint voices could be heard in the distance; red lights reappeared followed by the beating drums.

"Whispering Lights," I mumbled as I watched them approach one another and take the shape of the one we had been waiting for.

It was Corbin. His hair was tied back and he was clothed in battle garments that resembled a snake's body. Dark silver metal covered both of his arms and chest. There were small spikes protruding throughout his armor.

Out of the dust, Alexander stepped forward. "You," he said. "You may be hiding inside Demetre's body, but I would not have easily forgotten how oppressive your presence has become"

"I do recall our last encounter. I believe it was on the day the Creator doomed us all for simply discovering our true potential," Corbin related as he approached Alexander.

"You got what you deserved—you all did." As Alexander spoke, a light shone around his wrist, moving over his hand. From out of the brilliant light appeared a shining sword. In an instant, the light disappeared.

The blade was made of pure silver. The golden handle had the face of a lion engraved right in the middle. Red rubies were inlaid around, shimmering as the sword moved.

"You took them away, didn't you?" Mordred's voice deepened. "Where are they?"

Alexander was quiet. He did not move a muscle. Beyond him, I counted four shadows. They made their way through the rubble. Could it be that Petra escaped the Prison of Despair? That was impossible.

"There they are!" I shouted as I shot in their direction. Corbin vanished, his body transformed into a shapeless shadow that floated in the air. Battle cries were heard from the sky, followed by an ambush of more Underwarriors. As they headed toward us, Nephilins appeared and attacked them. There was a clash in midair. Grunts and groans of pain arose from the battle. I maneuvered away from the fight trying my best to keep a sharp eye on the four shadows as they fled.

I heard the clinking of swords and the clamor of bodies being struck down. In a matter of seconds, Shadows arrived to the scene. There was no way they could have gone far—of that I was certain. There were too many Nephilins and Shadows for them to escape unnoticed.

"Death to all the Underwarriors!" Mordred's cries were deafening. The Shadows swarmed around the Underwarriors, making it all the more difficult for them to see us.

Ahead of me stood the Over Hall of Aloisio, engulfed in flames. Part of the ceiling had crumbled and two of the five front columns had fallen. I hurried inside.

"Are you here?" I yelled out. My voice was loud enough to be heard from afar. "You cannot hide from us. We will find you—all four of you." The fire seemed to be dancing as it consumed the curtains and the furniture in the room.

I waited but there was no response. I heard the screeching of Desert Dragons close by. They were probably hiding outside, waiting to feast on the putrid flesh of the human remains. *They cannot outrun me—not alone at least,* I thought.

I closed my eyes and sent out a field of pain in the area. If they were in here, at least one of them would be inflicted with agony. To my right sounded a bloodcurdling scream. I headed in the direction of the scream, and when I reached the burning curtain I discovered a girl. Her flaming red hair covered half of her face. Her skin was pale and her lips colorless. Her clothes were worn out, along with her boots. She had an old leather bag hanging from her shoulder.

"You are one of them, aren't you?" I said as I penetrated her mind, inflicting excruciating pain. She screamed.

"Answer me and I will make the pain go away."

She dragged herself on the floor, wriggling about in circles, shrieking; her hands were firmly pressed against her head as her body contorted from the pain.

"Alright," she yelled. I stopped her pain; she breathed heavily, sweat dripping from her forehead.

"What is your name?" I asked, kneeling down next to her. Her eyes were steadily fixed on me as she crouched back in fear.

"Xylia...Xylia Justine," she responded in a hoarse tone.

"Xylia, do you happen to have what I am looking for?" Blood dripped from her blouse sleeve. "You know, if you tell me what I want to know, I might be able to help you."

"What is it that you seek?" She was panting.

I shook my head. "No, no! Please, let us not waste any time pretending we don't know what I want to know. Are you one of the book-bearers?"

"Nephele!" Alexander's voice boomed loudly from the flames as he headed toward me. His ragged garments were stained with blood.

"It seems like I have found another one, Alexander!" I shouted. Xylia let out terrifying screams. "I have her in my grasp and I will only spare her life if you convince her to come with me."

"Release her..." My heart skipped a beat when Devin appeared behind Alexander; three other shadowed figures appeared with him.

"Um...A little friendly reunion, I would assume?" I suggested with a sneer. I knew this time I was outnumbered. Desperation overtook me realizing that I was so close to the books, yet unable to attain them.

"Let her go," a boy with long brown hair and green eyes spat out. "You are outnumbered!"

"What is your next move, Nephele?" another voice spoke up from behind me. As I turned, I could not believe who was speaking. It was Ely. I had locked him away in the dungeons of the Prison of Despair right after the Council discovered he had warned Devin about Cyro coming for Isaac.

"How did...how did you all escape?" In my mind, I retraced every detail of the Prison, trying to think of any way they could have escaped.

"I bet your lord never told you that one of the books can open and close the Prison," Ely touted.

"The symbol on the wall..." I was stunned.

"It is a shame that your master has been keeping secrets from you," the brown-haired boy once again shouted.

The world around me seemed to cave in. I looked and saw all of them standing before me. *It would be foolish of me to fight them all.* As quick as a breath, I fled. I knew where I had to go in order to find answers. I was no fool to think I could flee with no one chasing after me. Flashes of golden light were being cast in my direction. A foul voice echoed.

"Do not run, Nephele." Alexander's voice was deafening.

The smoke and the haunting screams of war faded behind me. Alexander was hot on my trail, determined to catch me. I headed toward the mountains. I felt a weight pulling on my legs; my body was thrashed onto the icy floor of the valley that sat at the foot of the mountain. One of the flashes of light Alexander cast in my direction had hit me. Pain stung my foot relentlessly, and then shot all the way up my thighs.

"You coward! All the lives you've taken, all the children you have killed…" With sword in hand, he grabbed ahold of me by the neck and tossed me around like a mere doll. "I should make you suffer for all of the evil you have committed."

I tried to run, but he held my neck in a tight grip. He pressed my body hard against the snow-covered ground as he choked the life out of me. In all of my years, my powers had never failed me. To be confronted by one that was not only able to see my attack, but also flee from it, was frightening. I closed my eyes as he raised his sword. I heard a loud thud and then I felt something warm dripping onto my face. When I opened my eyes, I saw Alexander's bloody body fallen next to mine; the blade was still inside of him, sticking out of his gut.

"It is dangerous to roam around without protection, Nephele," Corbin's voice bellowed from behind me. "Even someone as powerful as you must be careful."

Quickly I stood to my feet. "There was no need for you to come searching for me, Corbin. You are needed in Aloisio."

He smiled. "Not anymore. All of the humans were killed and the kingdom was destroyed."

"Did you find any of the book-bearers? Any at all?" I asked expectantly.

He sighed. "The book-bearers were nowhere to be found."

I scoffed. To think how close I came to acquire that which we eagerly longed for brought me great disappointment.

"Ely, Devin, and Petra escaped the Prison of Despair and found the other three…"

"How do you know this?"

"I saw them, but I was surrounded…they mentioned that one of the books has the power to open the Prison of Despair. I am afraid we are not aware of all of the abilities these books possess." Fury possessed my whole being.

"Where are the Underwarriors?" I wanted to know.

"Dead," he replied without emotion.

Corbin peered up into the dark sky; light snow flurries cascaded lazily upon us. "Worry not. They will be found." His hand gently caressed my face. "Let us go to Justicia. I need to show you what is stirring in the heart of darkness." My body turned into a shadow as my eyes gazed into his. We moved toward the borderline used to cross between Justicia and Elysium. I was eager to see what lay waiting for us in Justicia.

XVII

Little did he know about my true desire. I wanted to go to Justicia not only to know what stirred there, but I longed for answers. Rage ignited in me the moment our feet touched the grounds. A thick fog enveloped the landscape. Lightning and thunder ripped the sky. Corbin and I walked silently. After a short while, the silhouette of the castle emerged from the fog.

"You first," Corbin said, gesturing a sign for me to walk ahead of him.

At every step, I couldn't refrain from thinking if the Council members were aware of the other powers the books possessed. Were they traitors? Did they hide this information from us?

"You are awfully quiet, Nephele," Corbin alleged as we crossed the moat in front of the castle.

"My mind is at war, Corbin," I replied with eyes still set on the castle.

"Against what?" he asked curiously.

"Even though the Council members claim to have sold their souls to Lucifer, I find it hard to believe they aren't plotting something against us all," I answered with a bitter voice.

"You believe they knew about the powers the books possess?"

I didn't answer his question. The moment we were in front of the massive wooden doors, I violently brought them down. The halls inside were dark except for the few lit candles sitting on top of the scattered furniture. Rubble and dust were everywhere; the statues destroyed.

"Where are they?" I asked Corbin angrily. "I need to see them!"

"Nephele, they will answer your every question…"

"Are we sure about that? Are we sure they are not hiding anything from us? Have they turned on us?" I heard faint voices coming from the dining hall.

I walked in and found Mordred, Athalas and the other Council members seated at a table. The table looked rugged and old, as if it was built out of the remnants of wood that remained after the attack of the Aquilas.

"Would you care to explain to me how is it that you did not inform us about the abilities of the books?" I yelled impatiently as I released pain all around the room. Many of them were taken by my attack.

"Nephele, stay this madness!" Mordred yelled.

"I will stop when one of them speaks the truth," I retorted angrily.

Mordred turned to Corbin. "Would you care to enlighten us on what she is talking about?"

"One of the books has the ability to open and close the Prison of Despair. Ely, Devin and Petra escaped the prison and were seen in Aloisio."

Clamorous chatter spread throughout the room. Athalas stood to his feet, striking the wooden table in rage.

"How can this be? You mean to say that now we have none of the book-bearers in our possession?"

"Please, Athalas, do not act surprised. You knew...you all knew..." As these words spewed from my mouth, the pain escalated—tormenting everyone it touched.

"We did not know!" a man with a gray beard and light gray hair screamed out. "We did not know of the book's ability...ple-please...you must be-be-lieve us..."

"I *have* believed you enough!" The pain rushed out of me with an uncontrollable and fatal fervor. I felt my strength increasing to heights it had never reached before.

"You must believe us." Athalas fell to his knees. "We knew not..." Beads of sweat fell from his brow.

Corbin approached me. "He may be telling the truth." My breathing was heavy. My body trembled as anger coursed through my veins. "If you kill them, we will never know the truth," he added.

I ceased my attack.

"May this be a reminder to all those who hide or have hidden information that may help us retrieve the book-bearers. I have grown weary of dealing with the lack of willingness to fulfill the task the Dark One has asked from you all."

I walked toward the man with the gray beard and hair; he trembled.

"What is your name?" I whispered as I gazed at him.

"Hor-Horace…Horace Dublin…"

My eyes did not fail to see the wounds on his right arm. Perfect shapes of claws that had tried to rip his flesh apart.

"Are you in pain?" I asked the man. His frightful eyes bored into mine.

"Yes," he choked. "Once the Aquilas attacked, one of them tried to kill me."

I sneered, my tongue slowly caressing my lips.

"Do you have family, Horace?" My hands rested on top of his.

Frightened, he stared at me. "No…we…you know we were not allowed a family…. The Creator did not allow the Council members to have one," he spoke with a quivering stammer.

"I see." I gently touched his arms. "So, does that mean that you have spent all of your life living here in this castle, caged in the Fourth Dimension?"

"Yes my lady, the Creator chose us during the dawn of days to stay here in Justicia and guard the Diary…. We were not allowed to leave. The other humans, those created to dwell in Elysium, they were the only ones allowed to have families…" His voice trailed off.

"When the Creator appointed the Council to guard the Diary, he never mentioned the existence of the other books or the powers they possess?"

Silence lingered for a while.

"No…"

I chuckled.

"Now that you no longer protect the Diary—or anything else—what is your purpose?"

"To ser-serve y-you and the Dark One…" Tears rolled down his face.

"Indeed you do…"

His eyes turned red, the veins around his neck protruded. He violently screamed as I imparted pain, but the magnified intensity of it was fueled by my rage. I wanted to kill him, here in front of the Council members. I wanted this to be a foretaste of what would happen if any of them turned on us or had undisclosed information about the books or the book-bearers.

"No, please…I live to serve you…" His voice faded as his body melted like ice.

"Indeed, you did…" I mumbled as his body changed into a water-like substance. Shortly after, the floor was wet, his body coursing like water spilled on top of a table.

When I turned to inspect the reactions from the others, they were all awestruck. I walked up to Corbin.

"If you say we should believe the Council members, then believe them we shall." I sat down in the chair Horace was originally sitting in.

"Please, Corbin, you said you wanted to show me what was brewing in the heart of darkness," I said as my fingers impatiently squeezed the arms of the chair.

"Yes, of course." He stretched his hand and signaled the remaining Council members to take a seat.

They all quietly returned to their chairs around the table.

"In the heart of the Abyss, the Fallen Stars are breeding an army more powerful than any we could conjure up in Elysium. A curse was created by the Fallen Stars to enhance the strength of arms of our servants."

"A curse?" I asked inquisitively.

"We have given the serpents that inhabit the Abyss the ability to battle. They have grown human features from their scaly bodies and can now walk, run, and some can even fly. We call them Lessers."

"So they drag themselves on the ground or..." one of the Councilmen interjected.

"No. They have grown limbs, and a torso. The only thing that distinguishes them from humans are their bright yellow eyes, Ahmos. When the Creator sent us to the Abyss, these serpents were already there. After studying them for many years, we came to the conclusion that they could be used for such a curse," Corbin said.

"What curse?" I asked him curiously.

"We have studied the power since the day we fell but now, it has been perfected to fit our needs. We call it the Dark Exchange. Ever since the Creator banished us from Tristar, we studied ways to fight back. We gathered our forces in the Abyss and looked for ways to strengthen our powers."

"It simply means that we are able to incubate a part of our being into another living creature, causing their emotions to be aligned with ours," Mordred added.

"Will you not grow weaker if a part of you is inside another being?" I asked.

"No," Corbin responded as he paced around the room. "We are duplicating ourselves into them. They will have similarities to those who give them their new mind, but we choose which senses or powers to give them."

There was silence in the room.

"Is there living proof of this curse?" My hands clasped together as they both rested upon the table.

"The Fallen Stars have brought one, my lady," Ahmos said from across the table. "It is here in Justicia."

"Where is it?" My curiosity ignited.

Mordred gave one last glance at Athalas; he stood to his feet and headed out of the room.

"When Athalas returns you will see for yourself," Ahmos answered with a grin. Shortly after he had finished speaking, I heard a hiss coming from the hallway. Athalas walked in with a serpent wrapped around his neck; its head dangled on his right shoulder. The snake lay still, its eyes looking down. The snake's dark scaly body had scratch marks stamped around it, probable signs of resistance against its capture. Under its head was a design pattern that traveled throughout the entire torso.

"I thought you brought one of the Lessers, not a simple snake..." I mumbled.

"Be patient, Nephele," Corbin replied as he laid the snake on the floor. He closed his eyes and stood next to the snake, motionless. I saw the snake slithering, its eyes wide open. The animal lifted its body from the floor and shot a dark stare at Corbin.

Corbin mumbled words that I could not make out; his face displayed a great deal of agony. The snake's mouth moved, lisping unintelligible words.

I shot a surprised look at Corbin.

"Watch closely," Mordred whispered into my ear as we both watched the scene unfold before us.

"Can the curse be performed on humans?" I asked pensively. My mind was already drifting away, pondering about other ways this curse could be used.

Limbs grew forth from the snake's body. The round-shaped head of the creature expanded into a human-shaped skull. Before long, it stood in front of us in its full stature. The body looked human except for the small faded scales that were still attached. The face had yellow eyes, a nose and an abnormally long mouth. Ahmos ran and covered the Lesser's nakedness with a ripped curtain that was lying in the corner of the room.

"Can it speak?" I asked, amazed at the sight I beheld. I looked at the creature standing in front of me and saw possibilities for the usage of this curse.

"A Lesser is controlled in portion by the mind of those that give them a part of themselves," Corbin said as he paced around the creature. "A part of my mind is inside him. I can control it from wherever I am."

"Well, please let us see your power at work," I said.

Corbin glanced at the Lesser quickly and it turned toward me.

"I will give it the ability to speak," Corbin said excitedly.

"I serve you...no fear." The hoarse voice that came from the creature was petrifying.

"What about its speech? Can it use words coherently?" I asked.

"Their brains are partially like a snake's, therefore they are unable to develop full sentences."

The Councilmen approached and bowed their heads in reverence to what they saw. Ahmos was on his knees with his eyes fixed on the creature.

"The Lessers will help us take over Elysium and hunt down the book-bearers. We must figure out a way to use the Dark Exchange to enter their minds and force them to open the books and read their pages," Ahmos stated joyfully. His ashen eyes widened expressively.

"How come we were not informed of this curse before?" I asked Corbin. "This would have made our jobs easier. We had Isaac and Petra in our possession. We could have entered their minds and forced them—"

"The curse was just now perfected." I was cut off. "We did not want to risk using this curse on the book-bearers," Corbin replied as he paced around the Lesser.

"We do not yet know the extent of the hidden powers of those books. One is to wonder, what else they are capable of other than accessing the Prison?" I questioned.

No one spoke.

"Councilmen, you are all dismissed. Go now and rest," Corbin instructed as he turned to Mordred. "Mordred, see that they all go to their rooms quietly."

"Come, we must be off," Mordred ordered with a grin on his face as he clapped his hands. "Your master, Mordred, will make sure you are all tucked in for the night," he said in a snide tone.

I noticed the Lesser exiting out of the room with soft, slow movements.

"Where is it going?" I asked Corbin.

"To the garden, right behind the castle. I have ordered it to sleep there," he replied as he approached me.

As the Councilmen marched out of the dining hall, I sauntered over toward what was left of the balcony from the attack. The balcony faced the garden that was right behind the castle. Even in the darkness, I could see glimpses of red-colored flowers and statues scattered around the landscape. I could faintly hear the flowing waterfall located near the riverbank.

"Is everything well with you, my lady?" Corbin asked as he walked up behind me.

I took in a deep breath of air and the faint smell of roses that lingered.

"So many possibilities.... My mind is trying to decide which direction we should go with this that would most benefit us."

Corbin grunted. "That direction has already been taken care of."

I turned to face him. "By whom?" I asked sharply.

"Me, of course. There is a greater plan that is yet to unfold."

I was silent, waiting for him to elaborate. "You see, beyond this garden, there is an invisible wall that protects this part of Justicia from interfering with Tristar, where all the Stars and the Creator reside. This wall was built by the Stars after the fall of Lucifer. Since Justicia is the only part of Tristar that is accessible through Elysium, the Creator wanted to make sure the Councilmen would stay here in the castle. We have been thoroughly studying its defenses and..." There was an uncomfortable pause.

"And what, Corbin?"

"The day the Dark One ascends to power, we will attack Tristar through its invisible defense wall. By then, Elysium will be taken by the Darkness and our army will be numerous. We will overtake Tristar and dethrone the Creator."

My eyes looked out at the never-ending darkness that stretched beyond the garden as my hands clasped together. "They will be ready for us. The Stars will know. The Creator knew of the day the Dark One betrayed him. His all-seeing eyes are always open," I affirmed.

"He will never expect an attack from inside of his kingdom. All those that have approached the wall thus far have perished, but we have an advantage that he is unaware of. There is one inside Tristar that has sided with us."

"Do not be a fool. How can he side with us without the Creator knowing? He knew about those that had taken Lucifer's side. He knows of the one that will betray him…"

"Not this time," he said, enraged. "We have covered our tracks well. I cannot divulge the secret of how we kept our source hidden, but know this—we will destroy the Creator." A soft grin stretched upon his face.

"Once they hear of the destruction that has come upon Aloisio and the other kingdoms and villages, they will wonder who was responsible for such doing. When they discover that we were the ones that brought such destruction, they will give in to their fears and will surrender to us," I affirmed.

"Nephele, they will fall. We have powers that no one can stop. We will gather the five books and we will defeat the Creator." He placed one of his hands on my shoulder reassuringly. "His body is beyond the invisible wall. The Dark One sleeps in the Wastelands of Tristar," Corbin said.

I saw the Lesser taking a stroll in the garden. It roamed around, stopping to admire all that surrounded it. The creature crawled onto the dirt and curled up into a ball, falling sleep.

"Not a very comfortable way for one to rest, do you agree, Corbin?"

"Not to us, but he doesn't mind sleeping out," Corbin said, staring at the Lesser. "I best be off," he declared, walking back inside the dining hall.

Thoughts rushed through my mind faster than I could bear. I needed to know more about the powers of the creature that slept in the garden. I looked up into the moonless sky; stars were hidden behind the gray clouds that hovered above me. *Endless...endless possibilities,* I kept on thinking.

"I see that you are still awake." I glanced over my shoulder and caught sight of Adawnas walking in my direction.

"And I see you are not yet in bed." My face turned away from her.

"I apologize for my absence during tonight's meeting. I heard it was most eventful." She walked over to where I was standing.

"Where were you during the meeting?" I questioned.

"I had some errands to run," she responded coldly. I ignored her insolent response completely. My mind was occupied, thinking about the Lesser.

"Do you know about them?" My heart beat faster at the mention or even the thought of these creatures.

"The Lessers?" she asked as she looked up into the sky. "Indeed I do. I have not yet seen one though."

"They could change our fortune in this war. Imagine the Lessers and the Shadows fighting together." I pointed to the Lesser that slept in the garden. The creature seemed to have some sort of blending ability, causing it to be almost invisible.

Adawnas gasped; her eyes widened, captivated with amazement.

As quick as shadows, we drifted from the balcony down to the garden. The Lesser was curled up, sleeping near one of the water fountains. I admired him, intrigued by every detail of the wondrous creature's body. To know that it was a part of Corbin's mind inside of it, causing it to breathe and roam about, was mesmerizing.

Without warning, the Lesser coiled itself upward and let out a ferocious growl. It stood on all fours and focused its bright yellow eyes on Adawnas and me. I noticed the remaining scales that were on its skin raised throughout its entire body as it growled.

"I suppose despite having human features, you are still a mere animal," Adawnas said, approaching the Lesser.

"I watching." There was a low hiss behind the words that proceeded from its mouth. "I watch this." It pointed to the castle.

"Watch it?" I asked the creature.

It walked toward the darkness ahead of us. "Enemies there. Many strong." Its neck twitched and its legs wobbled as it walked about, pointing in the direction of the invisible wall.

"Do you know what lies beyond the darkness?" Adawnas tried to touch the Lesser, but it deviated its head from her hands.

"Yes. Desert places...sleeping ones." It continued to make its way toward the obscure landscape. I heard water splatter when its feet touched the riverbank.

"Where are you going?" I asked it. "Are you unaware that we must stay here in the castle for now?"

"Enemies approaching." It screeched loudly. "Approaching from the darkness."

"Enemies," Adawnas muttered. "But beyond the darkness, there is only one enemy that could be coming."

I heard faint voices in the air; the wind's chill grew colder. From the darkness, small dim lights appeared. They shone bright in many different colors, flying around like a flock of birds in the sky. They gathered together as one and then exploded into thousands of smaller particles, scattering themselves in the air, and then they rejoined each other and took the shape of a phoenix.

In all my years of existence, I had never seen a sight so...unexplainable.

From behind the phoenix, a shadow rapidly approached. As it drew closer, the illuminated creature gazed at me with inviting eyes.

"Who are you?" I asked the enlightened being.

"Eldon—one of the gatekeepers from Tristar." At the sound of every word, the light particles glistened, exuding many colors.

Suddenly the unexpected: a loud explosion took place. The shadow collided with Eldon, causing a great cloud of smoke to rise. Growls and roars resounded like clanging cymbals. The Lesser was agitated; it stumbled around the garden, howling loudly. The battle between the shadow and the lights was intense. The illuminated cloud of smoke formed by their ongoing collision continued to fall into the river and out again several times.

"I shall leave this place," said a voice from inside of the shadow.

"Return to your resting place. You shall never be permitted to cross this border." Eldon flew around the shadowed being, scattering small particles of light. From the moving shadow, a face appeared. It was Lucifer.

"My lord," I muttered in shock.

"What is taking you so long for my awakening?" he shouted as he combated against Eldon.

"Away with you, Lucifer. Go back to slumbering in the Wastelands. Your spirit may move about freely but your body will remain imprisoned forever," Eldon shouted.

"Let him through," I yelled as I released pain. I was tossed with brutal force against the water fountain. Adawnas ran in my direction.

"I won't be locked in the Wastelands for long, Eldon. Nephele, where are the book-bearers?" His voice was echoed in the atmosphere. "My spirit cannot endure transporting itself like this much longer, I need a body of my own!"

"Be gone, Lucifer," Eldon shouted as the light particles turned into flames.

Lucifer's face vanished and the shadow receded. The clouds moved above, forming a circular funnel as a storm raged. Lightning and thunder ripped through the sky and the wind gained strength.

Flashes of light came out of Eldon. The glares from the phoenix-shaped lighted form dissipated like mist on an early morning. All that remained of him was the flicker of a dying flame that hovered above us. Shortly after, the flame diffused itself and the storm ceased. The Lesser calmed down and crawled back to its resting place.

"He suffers...Lucifer is suffering," I said bitterly. "Adawnas, we must act fast. The book-bearers need to be found."

"We will find them all," Adawnas affirmed. "They are vulnerable and weak."

Silence settled. The quietness of the garden made it seem as though nothing of great importance had taken place. Amidst the silence, I heard the sound of branches snapping. I used my mind to read my surroundings and I felt another's presence.

"Someone is here," I whispered, diligently searching around. I stood motionless, surveying every corner of the garden.

Breaking the silence, Adawnas yelled aloud, "We know you are here! You cannot hide."

The sound of crackling twigs and footsteps drew nearer to us. I focused my mind on the direction from which the noises and energy were coming from and released pain. There was a loud scream followed by a hard thud.

"He is one of them," I alleged as I laid my eyes on the young boy. He was dressed in rugged clothes, his boots ripped, and he was engulfed with dust. As he writhed in pain, I thoroughly analyzed his features. His eyes were as light as honey; his hair was a light chestnut brown. Cuts and bruises marred his face.

"Where have you come from?" Adawnas yelled. I increased the pain, injecting it inside his body, striking every organ. Blood seeped through his nostrils.

"Stop," he yelled. "Please."

"Not until you tell me where you have come from and how you got here," I said.

He tossed himself about in torment.

"Are you ready to tell me now?" I inquired.

The screams ended abruptly. Though his body twitched and turned, there was a lack of expression on his face. Sweat dripped like water down his face.

"Let us take him inside of the castle. He could not have come this way on his own. He will eventually give in and tell us how it is he got here," Adawnas remarked.

I halted the attack. With my mind, I tried to search his mind and see if I could find any answers. To my surprise, I was not able to uncover anything. There was a shield protecting his thoughts from my view.

"What do you have with you?" My patience was waning quickly. I could tell he was fighting with every ounce of willpower he could muster to keep his eyes open. I slapped him.

"I...carry...nothing," he mumbled faintly.

"Liar!" I tossed him into the waters of the river. "What do you carry with you?"

"It is no longer with him," Adawnas said as she hurriedly scrambled to the place he had fallen. "It is here." She lifted his bag from the ground and began searching inside of it.

"Well? Anything?" I asked eagerly.

Her eyes glistened. "Indeed." She took out what seemed to be a book wrapped in old black pieces of cloth from inside of the bag.

Slowly, she removed the old black cloth, exposing the coveted book within the wrappings.

"The Third Book of the Destroyer." She dropped the bag as she embraced the object.

"Let's take him inside," I declared.

XVIII

The boy did not dare try to escape our grasp. Adawnas walked beside him as I walked in front of him, making our way back to the castle.

"Where should we take him?" she asked as we walked inside the dining hall.

"We need answers." I looked over my shoulder; his gaze encountered mine. "I will take him to the interrogation room, inside the Prison of Despair. Call Mordred and Athalas. Do not take long," I commanded.

Adawnas nodded and walked up the staircase, heading in the direction of the rooms. The boy looked distraught. His drooping eyes showed signs of weariness; his heavy breathing denoted that the pain inflicted upon his innards from my attack had subdued his body.

"How are you able to shield your mind from my powers but you cannot protect your body from my attack?" I asked as we marched along the dark alley that led to the Prison's entrance. He remained silent as we crossed the iron gates, entering the prison.

"I could make it more painful inside of you until you answer me." He remained silent so I applied more pressure until I could hear his pitiful grunts and moans.

"Stop..." he managed to squeal through his clenched teeth.

I anxiously hurried inside the cold prison. His heartbeat accelerated as his eyes beheld the concealed chambers of torture. My footsteps echoed through the prison, in unison with the sound of the continuous dripping of water from the ceiling. Soon, all sounds merged with that of the river that flowed inside the prison.

"Are you ready to talk now?" I prodded him. "We don't have to walk all the way to the interrogation room." He shot me a cold look.

"Very well," I acquiesced. "Have it your way."

I took him inside one of the rooms. The subzero temperature caused his body to shake. An opening in the ground disclosed another set of stairs leading downward.

"You see, after we walk down these stairs, your real questioning begins. I can save you from suffering great pain if you only tell me who sent you, and how it is that you can shield your mind from mine."

He dazedly stared at me with weary eyes. He took in a long deep breath and bowed his head.

I maliciously grabbed his arm. "Let's go, sweetheart. We have much work to do," I avowed impatiently, as we grappled our way down the stairs.

As we descended, the gargoyle statues that stood in the corners of the somber room were lit with torches. The room had been built to recognize the presence of anyone who entered it. As the light increased its strength, I caught a glimpse of an old wooden table and two chairs.

I released my hold from him as I strolled my way to one of the chairs.

"Please, do sit," I gestured, taking my seat.

He tossed his debilitated body into the chair; weakness had overtaken him so that he was barely able to keep his head up.

"I know you are suffering. I know you do not wish to go through this pain any longer, but there is a way out." He let out a low groan. "All you have to do is answer my questions. Can you do that?"

The boy glanced back at me with weary eyes.

"Yes," he shuddered.

A soft smile spread across my face. "Very well, what is your name?"

"Ba...Ballard...Ballard Radley," he stammered with great difficulty.

"Ballard, who has sent you and how did you find this place?"

He coughed. "I was not sent by anyone. I was told of this place by Raziel and Devin." He coughed again. Blood squirted from the corner of his lips.

I slapped him. "Do not toy with me, boy. I could kill you right now with my bare hands." I approached him, stopping inches away from his face. "I think I understand your plan now. You did come on your own, didn't you? You wanted to be brave..."

"I don't have the need to prove bravery to anyone. The only things I care about are the books you have in your possession," Ballard disclosed with a broken voice.

"I care not about what it is that concerns you, boy. How did you get here?"

"My...my book...showed me the way to Justicia..."

"Your book led you to Justicia. How?" These meaningless answers angered me.

Silence!

"Stupid boy. Do you really believe that I won't kill you right now?" He squealed like a pig as I inflicted more pain into his inner organs. "I could easily slaughter you like an animal and toss your remains to the Desert Dragons."

A blaring screech permeated the walls throughout the Prison. It sounded like an animal being tortured. I was highly alarmed. The sound was unfamiliar to me. I felt my heart beat pounding in my chest.

"Who is there?" I hollered, while making sure to keep my eyes on Ballard. The screeches grew louder; I felt the temperature rise.

"You's may not do this...I isn't lettin' you," a voice whispered.

Adawnas, Mordred and Athalas stepped inside the interrogation room the moment the voice spoke.

"What is that voice?" Mordred questioned.

"Death," Athalas replied with a raspy voice.

Inside the room, a grotesque creature sprang up from the ground. It came as a shadow. Its golden yellow eyes gazed at me. A snakelike tail was exposed as it moved swiftly across the room. Its arms were disproportionately long.

Athalas frowned as he set eyes on the creature.

"Go back to the bottom of the Prison, Death. You have no business here," he ordered.

"Immortals think theys can cheat me, heh? No...immortals wrong, yes." Its voice was thunderous.

"Your master has ordered you to go away," I shouted in a loud voice. My patience was already growing scarce.

Its laugh was eerie and dark; there was a soft glow emitting from its body. "I no master any longer."

"How dare you?" Athalas' voice implied rage. "I have graciously ruled over you since the dawn of days and this is how you repay me?"

Its body was fading. "You lost authority the day ones greater than yous took me."

"I am ordering you to *return* to the bottom of the prison," Athalas declared. His hands tightened into fists.

"I belongs to you no longer..." Its voice trailed off as its body vanished into thin air.

"How dare—" Athalas did not get the chance to finish his sentence. Death reappeared engulfed in flames and smoke. Like a blanket, it wrapped itself around Athalas. He yelled in desperation.

"Long you owned me...long you tell me what to do. Not now...no more," it growled furiously. "One came and conquered me to him. I belongs to you no longer."

"Do you hear that?" Mordred asked me. Sounds of human screams filled the room. The walls of the room trembled. I looked to my right and caught sight of a doorway contoured by a dim glow slowly being outlined on the wall.

"You come with me now. My master awaits." Death's chilling voice reverberated as the doorway opened.

Death brusquely grabbed Athalas' body, dragging him in the direction of the doorway. He screamed vehemently. Even though he was chosen to serve the Dark One, I could not deny that I felt relieved to see him being taken. The fact he was still human didn't allow me to trust him wholeheartedly.

"Please, don't let me go where Death takes me," he screamed as he clawed at the floor, fighting so he wouldn't be taken. Fingernails and bloodstains dripped on the cold floor, trailing back to the direction of the doorway.

"Come away, come away to world of shadows...here you dwell," Death whispered as it dragged Athalas through the doorway.

There was silence among Adawnas, Mordred and me. None of us dared look upon one another's face. As the doorway disappeared, I wondered who had conquered Death.

The Creator himself had given Athalas authority to rule over it and now this authority had been taken from him.

A bright light shone upon me. I looked at Mordred and was shocked to see that his body was illuminating the light.

"What is happening to you?" I asked in despair. He pressed his hands against his head, falling to his knees. He rolled around the floor; torrents of blood gushed from his nostrils and ears. The light had taken him over, enveloping his body, shining out from his eyes and mouth.

"Adawnas, where was Corbin when you called Athalas and Mordred?" I asked, frightened that my suspicions might be correct.

"He wasn't in his room. Once I arrived at his room, I did not have the chance to—"

"Go find him." I clenched my hands together tightly. "This is impossible," I whispered, fearing the worst.

The flashes of light coming from Mordred's body ceased. His still body lay on the floor.

"What is going on?" I asked Ballard. "Do you know what is happening?"

He gave me an innocent smile. "You are never going to achieve what you so desire. The conqueror of Death has come."

Where is Corbin? I kept asking myself as I tried to make sense of all the chaos.

"He-he has indeed returned," Mordred stated as he stood to his feet.

"Mordred," I said dazedly. "Are you alright?"

"Mordred?" I looked into his eyes and I knew Mordred was no longer inside this body.

"Isaac?" I said fearfully. My question was answered with a snide grin.

I was awestruck. This was impossible. I was the one who performed the Soul Exchange; I was the one who poured his blood over the book. His soul could never return. It lingered on in the Wastelands.

"Leave this body now," I commanded, gritting my teeth.

"No," he responded, his eyes coldly staring deep into mine.

My attack was released from me with fury. I concealed my attack to strike him directly. White wings sprang from his back as he took flight. He swerved away from my attack, flying to his left.

"So the red flashes that streak out of you are your attack?" he asked as he lingered in the room.

"Isaac, how is this even possible?" I shouted, confused. "You have ruined all our plans," I lamented. Anger boiled inside of me.

He retracted his wings, his feet touching the floor. "Nephele, there are questions that you will never know the answer to," he alleged with an assertive tone. "If you want to know what fate awaits you all, follow me." He let out a smile as he darted out of the interrogation room, quickly pacing up the staircase. I followed him. From this moment on, I no longer cared about Ballard or Corbin. I wanted to destroy Isaac. I wanted to find out how it was possible for his soul to return to his body.

"You are still human, Isaac. Eventually your human desires will get the best out of you," I shouted as we both flew around the prison, coursing our way toward the stairway that led to the exit.

Once we exited the prison, Isaac flew through the immense glass window located above the entrance to the castle, making his way out. I maneuvered my way through the darting shards of glass. I came to a halt when I saw the other Nephilins standing motionless on the moat as war cries resounded. As I plunged my way downward, I saw Adawnas standing in front of the castle, her eyes fervently looking ahead.

"What is going on?" I asked as I landed on the moat.

"Corbin is no more." She bit her bottom lip as she nodded her head toward the darkness. Out of the shadows, a man appeared. He slowly moved across the garden located in front of us. His dark hair moved with the blowing breeze.

"He is no more..." I repeated. "Where is he?"

The war chants grew louder; the ground trembled. I failed to see what was heading toward us.

From the darkness, many men appeared, marching in perfect formation, making a long straight line behind the man that stood as their leader. Isaac flew down from the sky, positioning himself next to the man.

"The Exchange is over." The voice sounded just like Corbin's. "Death now belongs to the one that is greater than its previous master. Our souls are no longer slaves to your desire," the man next to Isaac bellowed loudly.

I could not believe my eyes; the man standing next to Isaac was Demetre. His spirit had returned from the Wastelands.

"Die, die, die," the men accompanying Isaac and Demetre chanted together. As they shouted, lightning broke through the dark sky. I could not believe what I saw. Underwarriors, many of them appearing like a cloud of locusts, were converging from the dark clouds. To my knowledge, they had all perished in Aloisio. They joined Isaac and Demetre, making a perfect straight line ahead of the men. The chanting and shouting ceased. A chilly breeze blew as silence began to settle.

"If it is a war you want, it is a war you shall get!" I shouted at the top of my lungs.

"We do not want a war, Nephele," Isaac answered in a loud voice. "We want justice!"

"Attack!" I yelled. A mighty roar arose from Isaac and those that stood with him. The ground trembled as the men catapulted in our direction. The whooshing sounds of wings violently flapping joined the battle march as the Underwarriors and Nephilins darted toward the sky. Explosions of light colored the dark sky as both Underwarriors and Nephilins released their attacks. The clashing swords could be heard when the men and the Nephilins that remained on the ground collided. While some Underwarriors and Nephilins used their special abilities, others used weapons. I took flight, causing pain all around me, attacking both Underwarriors and men.

I stopped in midair, surprised when I saw the rays of the sun piercing through the dark clouds. The light caused the clouds to turn into vapor. The light touched the garden, the castle and the battle that raged beneath me.

The Underwarriors slammed many Nephilins against the castle as flames engulfed its towers. Some Nephilins turned to ash as swords and spears pierced them; the ashes were scattered throughout the garden by the wind.

"Here, you will meet your doom," I heard one of the Underwarriors shout as he approached my son, Duane. I watched as Duane took flight and headed in the direction of the flaming towers.

I fled toward the castle when I remembered the books were still inside; I had to retrieve them before they were found. I passed through the flames and rubble, dodged the debris and falling stones to get to my bedroom, where both books were under lock and key.

The moment I landed inside my room, I could not believe what I saw; the door had been broken down and the room was ransacked.

"They have been taken," a man spoke from inside. He stood to my right partially hidden in the corner, near the window. "What you seek is no longer here."

"And who must you be?"

"Nathan, one of the Underwarriors," he responded.

"I thought you were all destroyed."

"Nephilins are not the only ones with tricks up their sleeves."

I could no longer control myself. I attacked him with a simple thought, and tossed him against the window. The moment his body broke through the glass, he took flight. I followed him, flying quickly to block him as he headed outside into the battle.

From the ground, dust rose up from the battle. I heard cries and groans coming from the battlefield. Nathan and I collided in the air. The intense impact tossed us both in different directions. I skyrocketed into the river behind the castle. The water was frigid, the air chilly. The blunt impact hurled my body with such force that I sank all the way to the bottom of the river. I swam with haste back up to the surface.

The moment my head was out of the water, I saw lightning and thunder coming from the direction of the invisible wall that protected Tristar. I heard a low hissing noise and observed that the Lesser was still curled up next to the water fountain.

A loud screech bellowed above, followed by a blaze of fire that tore the sky apart.

"Go back to the shadows," Eldon's voice resounded as I swam toward the riverbank. I searched for Eldon but I could not see him.

"I will not be held prisoner here." Lucifer's voice was menacing. The wind picked up and the temperature continued to drop. Out of a blaze of fire, Eldon appeared in the sky.

A dark dust also arose, covering all but Eldon as it approached. Once the dark curtain of dust neared the river, the dust scattered. I looked up into the sky and it was as if the sky itself was being ripped apart by the sunlight as it slowly faded. Gray flocks of ash fell softly from the sky. The ashes burned as they touched my skin.

I took flight. A very thick mist arose and surrounded everything, blinding my visibility. I could still hear the sounds of war coming from far beneath me. I hovered inside the mist, trying to get a better judgment of my bearings.

Lucifer's shouts rose to a loud crescendo. I could see Eldon's figure moving about as the darkness reached to the sky, mixing itself with the thick white mist, blinding me as I frantically tried to grope my way through.

I can still hear them, which means I am still in Justicia, I thought.

"The earth is shaking...the earth is shaking..." I heard the men repeatedly clamoring.

Weariness increased inside of me. My vision grew even dimmer as a flash of light shone brightly, illuminating the mist and the landscape. I squinted, trying to see, but I couldn't. I felt branches brush against my arm and shortly thereafter, I collided against a tree. I plunged down, landing with a thump against the ground.

I was surprised when I felt a sudden chill. I moved my hands and felt snow on the ground.

There is no snow in the garden, I thought as I moved in a daze, crawling on the floor.

As my vision returned to normal, I could see the gray sky above me. The mist had vanished and the Nephilins, Underwarriors and the men still battled. I looked around and there was no sign of Eldon or Lucifer.

The castle was to my left, burning to cinders. I tried to understand what had happened. The vegetation around me, the shape of the trees and the falling snow were certain signs that we were no longer in Justicia. It was then that I realized where we were. Somehow, we had been transported to the borderline that connected Elysium and Justicia. I couldn't understand how all that had happened.

Why have we left? I wondered.

It was in that moment that Shadows sprang up from the ground and attacked the Underwarriors. All the questions I now had must be laid aside for the moment. I had to join the others in battle. I jolted toward the battle and attacked as many men and Underwarriors as I possibly could.

As I fought, I could not ignore the many Nephilins that disintegrated to ash, but I rejoiced to see as many Underwarriors' bodies lifelessly rested on the forest floor. With my mental power I tortured many with immeasurable pain that I released around me. Shadows mounted on top of the men and bit them ferociously on their necks and legs. Scarlet blood spilled onto the white snow.

Another violent tremor shook the place, this time coming from the direction of the castle. The Underwarriors were bringing the castle down with their powers; some shot out rays of light like cutting swords as others destroyed it with their punches and kicks. Dust arose as the castle walls crumbled to the ground, while the ceiling continued to burn.

One of the Underwarriors attacked me from my right, striking me with his sword and tossing me into a puddle of blood that had formed on the snow-covered ground. As he attacked me, a Shadow mounted onto a Desert Dragon descended from the sky and in one swoop bit the man in half and swallowed half of him. The Desert Dragons and the Shadows that rode them had come in countless numbers.

They snatched both Underwarriors and men with their claws and tossed them in the air.

"Where are the five?" I heard a Nephilin named Duncan call out, attacking the men with fire. As he clenched together both of his fists, fire engulfed his hands. "Where are they?" he continued shouting. Since none replied to his frantic screaming, fire issued forth from his hands, engulfing the men in flames.

I was surprised when White Dragons appeared in the sky. They roared and hovered over us, moving in sync with one another. The Dragons were wearing armor on their snouts and horns. A massive plate covered their torsos. From the ground, their wings appeared to be longer than their bodies.

From the woods, an army of many men charged toward us with loud roars. They were fully clothed in golden armor and held spears, swords and shields. Their helmets were shaped like a dragon's skull, adorned with two silver horns on each side.

"Humans?" Duncan asked as he looked at me, surprised.

"Do they not know they will perish if they join this battle?" I said as I watched the lot of them attack the Nephilins. Five men dashed toward me with swords in hand, attempting to wound me. With a single hand gesture, I tossed them all against the trees. The White Dragons spit fire as they flew in the air with their human riders. As the flames shot from their mouths, I saw something that I did not expect to see. The blue flame they released consumed our kind. I became desperate. I was unaware that White Dragons could kill us.

"Fight to the death!" Duncan shouted to all the Nephilins repeatedly as he flew about.

I picked up a sword that was lying on the ground and attacked the Dragons in the sky. The Dragons I had wounded plummeted to the ground, screeching in pain, their riders falling off, their bodies thrown violently to the ground. In the midst of the battle, I wondered how these humans knew of our location.

I quickly returned my attention to my surroundings when I saw Isaac coming in my direction from the sky. With a simple thought, I dragged him away from the battle and tossed him deep into the forest. I followed him as his body plummeted from the sky.

"Despite your great abilities, you should keep a close watch out for your enemies," I said as his body hit the ground with a hard thud. I attacked him with my power, executing pain upon him.

He groaned as he struggled to stand on his feet. "Do not waste my time, Nephele," he murmured.

"Waste…Wasting your time? You are the one that has been wasting *my* time. You have taken the life of one that was dear to me."

"And I will take the lives of many more. You have no idea of the things I saw while my body was possessed by one of Fallen Stars."

I felt my power growing weak. I could see Isaac regaining control of his limbs.

"You must understand. I am no longer the same naive boy from Aloisio, Nephele. When you performed the Soul Exchange, my soul went to the place where all the others are. I died without a choice just like them, but I died knowing the truth about the Creator and Lucifer. The things I have seen have given me a new perspective on this journey. In the Wastelands, Death was conquered by one mightier than Athalas. Demetre and I were released to fulfill the purpose designed for us both."

"That being?" I asked, enraged.

"To be the keepers of the Diary. To never give in to the temptation of reading its pages; to keep it safe from enemy's hands. I may be its bearer, but Demetre will aid me during this journey, no matter what the cost. *That* is my mission...and Demetre's."

I laughed. "You are still human. Nothing that you say or do can change that. Sooner or later, the Diary will get to you and you will open it, willingly. Will you really be able to contain yourself, knowing you hold such an important book?"

"I will fight with all that I have," he affirmed in a strong voice. His speech was bold and full of authority.

"The Fallen Stars and the Nephilins have chosen the wrong time to attack. As the darkness rises, so does the light. There are some humans that have not and will not turn their back on the Creator."

"That explains the futile efforts of the humans that are wasting their lives fighting against us."

He closed his eyes and clenched his fists. "They fight because even Lucifer and his armies aren't strong enough to cause their hope for redemption to grow dim."

"Fools! All of you! Why do you do this to yourself, Isaac? Look at you! Do you not see all the power and the abilities you possess? Think of what you can be if you ally yourself with us!" I declared.

"I wondered where I would find you, Nephele. It is of no surprise that you stand next to Isaac," Erebos said with a smirk, strolling in from the darkness of the woods.

"King Marco?" Isaac asked. He scowled the moment he laid eyes on Erebos.

"Boy, this body is no longer a dwelling place for a king of men. A greater power now lives within this vessel." The kingly robes that once clothed him were now all ragged and torn; blood dripped from his fingers and toes. "Excuse my appearance, but I had to feed."

With the palm of his right hand pointing toward Isaac, he released a flash of red light that was shaped like a whip. With great force it flew toward Isaac, stopping only an inch away from his face.

"Try harder, beast," Isaac mocked.

My mind attacked him viciously; he screamed and the whip wrapped around him, lashing him with great strength. Isaac struggled against the attacks, moving his body about, trying to free himself from the whip. He tried to push us away by using the power of his mind. Small cuts and bruises appeared as the whip tightened around Isaac's body.

"This only proves how human you still are. I am a Fallen Star. I have been alive long before you, boy. And yet you have the gall to defy me." Erebos laughed aloud as he watched Isaac struggle. Immediately, his whip transformed into a snake; its body wrapped around Isaac.

"Where are the other book-bearers?" Erebos demanded, tightening his grip to emphasize his supremacy.

Isaac defiantly looked into Erebos' eyes, but remained mute to his cynical maneuver, and refused to divulge the coveted secret.

"Intensify the pain, Nephele," Erebos commanded as he belted forth a satirical shrill. "Show the boy what we are capable of."

"I am beyond seeing what you all can do, Erebos." Isaac's teeth chattered and sweat flowed from his brow like tears. The snake Erebos held in his hand disappeared into a mist. In a flash, Erebos stood in front of Isaac and held his face in the cup of his hand.

"If you don't tell us where the others are, we will find them anyway. We will lock you all in a dungeon and torture you until you only have the sheer will left to shed your blood for the Dark One and pledge allegiance to him," Erebos promised with a malevolent sneer.

I was thrown against the trees by the force of a loud explosion. Dirt and rock flew about as the explosion intensified. Above me, I saw Nathan leaping over the treetops as he darted flashes of light in our direction. When the light touched the ground, loud explosions ignited. Nathan's face was covered with blood.

I looked at the ground and saw Isaac lying unconscious on the floor. Erebos stood to his feet.

"Is this how you want to fight, Underwarrior?" Erebos shouted as his limbs shriveled, melting into his body, making way for a tail. His skull changed its shape and his eyes inverted to a bright golden glare. He revealed his visage in form—a coiled snake, cunning and lethal.

Nathan did not respond with words but with action. He flew toward Erebos, wielding a flaming sword in his right hand.

"Clever of you to come against me with fire," Erebos remarked as his body stood upright, ready to attack. With one hand, Nathan held his sword and with the other he cast exploding flashes of light at me. Because of the flaming attacks, the floor of the forest was enveloped in flames. The trees became burning torches. Soon the smoke filled the sky. The flames were spreading quickly.

Erebos grabbed ahold of Nathan with his tail. "Fool. Your efforts are in vain. Even if you defeat me, we will find them."

"Destroy him!" My voice was drowned by loud thunder. Lightning flashed across the sky, creating a kaleidoscope of colors. The clouds moved in as a whirlwind and the wind picked up, causing the trees to bow low toward the ground in surrender to its strength.

White Dragons crossed the sky in great haste, howling as they flew. It was as if the clouds were falling upon us, slowly closing in on the ground. The snow on the trees was picked up by the strong winds, creating a curtain of pure white. But even through the snow, I could not miss the massive funnel cloud that touched the ground.

Abrasive shouts rang out from where the battle was being fought. Horses and horsemen appeared from the trees, fleeing into the heart of the forest. Nephilins crossed beyond the clouds, through the sky, flying in the opposite direction of the funnel clouds.

"The earth is in changing." Nathan's voice was alarmed. "Elysium was not created to be under such darkness. Nature itself will revolt against this destructive force." Erebos quickly reverted to his humanlike form.

The flames intensified as the wind blew. With a simple move of his right hand, Nathan transmitted a flash of light, illuminating everything, blinding me to all the action. In a matter of seconds, my vision returned. Nathan was gone, along with Isaac.

"Damn you!" Erebos shouted.

"They cannot have gone too far. Nathan was weak," I retorted as I flew toward the turbulent sky.

The view that appeared before me as I flew was unlike anything I had seen in all the ages past of this world. The funnel clouds were scattered profusely throughout the firmament; the flames had spread, reaching as far as the mountains. I was dumbfounded, not knowing what to call a storm of this magnitude. The snow that was on the forest floor scattered in the air as the wind continued to blow unabated.

"Listen to what I have to say." Lucifer's voice echoed through the atmosphere. "My body may still be asleep, but let me assure you, I shall not delay my attack on this land." Joy filled my heart as his voice reverberated. "To the ignorant humans that are fighting against that which they know nothing about, I now speak to you. I will destroy every man, woman and child in Elysium if the book-bearers are not found by my servants. I can assure every single mortal that the worst evil has yet to be revealed unto you."

The circling clouds merged into the shape of a face. "Once again I warn everyone, your efforts are but folly against my powers. Give your allegiance to me and you will save yourselves from the imminent doom of this world."

I rejoiced with every word as it penetrated my heart. His voice brought me peace and reassurance to our cause.

As my heart filled with joy, my body felt a sharp, stabbing pain and a blinding light obstructed my vision. My arms and legs became numb as I felt my body plunge to the ground.

XIX

With no power to resist, I was forced into a twilight state. After a short slumber, I opened my eyes.

"You are finally awake." I heard Erebos' distant voice as my senses were restored. "That bolt of lightning impacted you quite hard." All around me, I could see smoke rising from the torched brush trees and scattered debris. A putrid smell dominated the atmosphere. The ground was moist and murky.

"What happened?" I asked Erebos, disturbed.

"After you fell, all of the armies fled because of the intensity of the storm," Erebos said as he sat atop an ashen tree trunk.

"Where are the other Nephilins?" I inquired, still in a daze.

"Probably back at Aloisio—hiding at the entrance of the Prison of Despair."

"And the Shadows?"

"They fled toward the woods," Erebos affirmed, not bothering to move a single muscle.

At this point, I was close to the edge of insanity. Every time we were so close to snatching the book-bearers, some unexpected occurrence delayed our capture.

"There is one that I believe can help us." He took in a deep breath. "Come closer." He scanned the forest as he spoke. From behind the trees, a human-shaped creature appeared.

"I found it shortly after you fell," he announced, his steps coming closer to the creature.

"Am I supposed to know what this creature is?" The creature's skin resembled a human's, but it had a greenish tint to it; the texture was as smooth as that of the finest silk. Its skin glistened as it paced in our direction.

"My dear, it is the Lesser you met." Erebos touched the creature's arm with trepidation. The creature had the features of a man, with chestnut brown hair, light hazel eyes and a pointy chin.

"I believe I can speak for myself." The Lesser's voice was deep and ominous. "I do not need you to speak for me."

"I thought it wasn't capable of speaking on its own—at least, not with such eloquence," I mumbled, looking at Erebos.

"He...my lady...not it," the Lesser sharply affirmed; his eyes shot me a dark stare.

"My speech came to me when Justicia was overtaken by the darkness," he exclaimed. "After the light came to us, it was as if my mind was unveiled to all other things." His head twitched and his eyes moved in a rapid motion. "I am still adjusting to having a mind of my own."

"His abilities might have evolved when the castle of Justicia was separated from Tristar," Erebos stated with a curious stare.

In awe, I marveled at him. I had already seen potential in the Lessers but now, my mind could barely fathom all the things that we could do together as an army.

"Now that you have a mind of your own," I said as I approached him, "I must ask you this. Where does your allegiance lie?"

His gaze met mine. "I have not known any other way than that of darkness. I have no knowledge of a choice as to where else my allegiance could lie."

"Do you remember if there are any others like you?" Erebos inquired.

He paced around in circles as he looked up at the trees. "Many more. My mind could never forget those that lie in the darkness of the shadows of the world...my brothers and sisters at arms."

"What is your name?" I curiously asked.

He approached me with heavy breaths. "I do not remember."

"May I give you a name?" I asked.

His eyes widened in surprise. "My lady, it would be an honor," he responded.

Behind this creature's newfound knowledge and speech ability, I could clearly see the lack of confidence inside of him. The best way to have him trust us completely was to give him identity.

"Cahir...you shall be named Cahir," I stated.

He gave me a soft smile. "Why...thank you," he softly mumbled.

"Now that we have given you a name, we must ask you for something in return," I cajoled.

His eyes widened. "Anything you need. I will serve you both," he said, joyful.

"What are you doing?" Erebos asked me, confused.

"Take us to the other Lessers," I prompted, ignoring Erebos' question.

"Nephele..." Erebos shot me a piercing glance as his voice trailed off.

Cahir's eyes were filled with sorrow.

"Is there a problem with my request?" I asked.

"The darkness where the Lessers are hidden in has never been touched by any of this world. The darkness is too deep. Humans would have to dig for years in order to find the place where the Lessers slumber. Besides, these Lessers are not the same as I am. Their minds are still empty. No one has ever given them abilities of their own."

"Nephele, maybe what you are asking of him is not an easy feat to achieve," Erebos added.

"But..." His voice deepened. "There is a path that immortals may be able to enter through."

"Where are the Lessers located?" I asked him. "Tell me where they sleep."

"They sleep under the Ruins of Madbouseux, in a place called The Heart of Elysium. The mystery of the disappearance of Madbouseux's people is hidden in this remote place."

Very few dared to go to Madbouseux. Even immortals feared the Ruins, for none knew what evil lingered in such place. Some feared that the power that dwelled there was even greater than Lucifer's.

"Are you willing to take us there?" Erebos bade him. "We will be sure to reward all of the Lessers if you show us the way. We will give them abilities of their own."

His eyes widened and moistened with tears. "You would reward me?" Cahir asked with simple amazement.

Erebos nodded.

"Do you know where the Ruins are located?" Cahir asked with a hopeful stare.

"Yes, we know where they are," I replied.

"Meet me at the entrance of the Ruins."

To my surprise, the moment the words escaped Cahir's mouth, his limbs disappeared; his facial features diminished back into his body as he transformed himself into a snake. His size was massive; his back expanded to a length that was long and thin. He slithered on the ground, creating a crater with his body. In a matter of seconds, he slid under the forest floor.

"Are you sure you want to go to the Ruins, Nephele?" Erebos asked. "We don't know what we will find there. There must be a reason why not even immortals tread upon those grounds."

"If we are to bring the Dark One back, we can no longer avoid taking risks. I do not fear death or pain. If our armies are failing in the capture of the book-bearers, we must look for alternatives," I conjectured.

Erebos gave me a reassuring smile. "Let it be as you wish."

Erebos and I rushed to the sky. An avalanche of emotions stirred inside of me. Even to my kind, knowing that an entire group of people disappeared from Madbouseux without any trace of war or struggle was bizarre and thought-provoking.

Erebos and I remained quiet throughout the journey. The landscape changed dramatically as we approached the borders of the Ruins. Mountaintops reached the sky, disappearing into the cloudbank. Antique statues of kings and queens were broken, partially mounted on the mountain ledges.

Erebos and I headed toward the ground. We landed in a nearby valley. Ruins of monuments were scattered around the place.

"Let us continue on foot," I said, quickly surveying the surrounding landscape. "The cloudbanks are making it difficult to fly."

Erebos nodded in silence.

A thick mist covered the trees that towered from above the dark, ashy ground.

Silently, we followed the trail up the mountain. The whispers of a soft breeze scattered the ashes that rested on the tree branches, creating a curtain of gray.

Ahead, beyond the gray dust that hovered, I spotted the entrance to the Ruins. Remains of a fortified wall were broken and scattered over the ground. An archway jutted up in the center of the wall. Carvings of men in battle, men seated upon thrones and warriors fully armored were etched throughout the monument.

"Awkward to see something so magnificent sitting here abandoned," Erebos exclaimed as he cautiously walked around, analyzing the surroundings.

"All the more reason for us to be on high alert, we do not know what lies throughout these lands. Very few, if any, have dared to venture here."

Whispering voices echoed in the air. The voices were reminiscent of women and children speaking all at once. "Do you hear the voices?" I asked Erebos.

"How could I not?" he responded in a somber voice. "The voices you hear are of those that lived here on the day of desolation."

I was startled when I saw Cahir walking toward us out of the mist.

"Day of desolation?" I burned with curiosity.

"The day all had vanished to the unknown darkness…the day the Book of Letters arrived," he whispered as he rambled about.

"Were you here when all of this happened?" Erebos inquired.

"I remember now. The day we all disappeared was a result of our king's decision," he whispered.

The whispers stopped; an uncomfortable stillness began to settle in.

"What decision brought about this destruction, Cahir?" I asked.

"The Book of Letters mysteriously appeared in the Kingdom of Madbouseux. A peculiar book it was for it held the power to raise an army that would obey whosoever possessed it." Cahir meandered in the direction of the archway of the Ruins.

Cahir had my full attention. "What is the current location of the book?" I inquired.

"The Stars snatched the book away, for the king of Men that ruled Madbouseux had his heart corrupted, giving in to the dark power of the book. It sought to raise an army to destroy the world. He was consumed by the book's power."

"So the Stars have the book?" Erebos queried.

"I know not if the Stars have the book. I do know that the book lies in Tristar."

Astonished, I looked at Erebos. We had never heard of the Book of Letters or of the power it possessed.

"But we are here for the other Lessers, correct?" Cahir asked, standing beneath the archway. "Shall we go?"

Erebos silently looked at me as we marched in the direction of the archway. I felt a chill run down my spine as I walked under the monument.

We ventured into the ruins. Ancient marble stones sat at the foot of the magnificent temples and houses.

The majority of the remaining houses were without a roof, with only their foundations standing. With every step, my feet crushed the shards of glass that littered the ground.

Cahir approached one of the temples that remained standing.

"In here," he said, walking up a set of stairs. Five statues circled the entrance of the temple. They were statues of women holding the head of an ox. The garments of the statues draped all the way to the ground, covering their feet. Small crowns with a ruby embedded in the center sat on the heads of each statue. The perfection of the oxen's faces left me speechless. *Amidst so much destruction, how could these statues be in near perfect condition?* I wondered.

Upon entering the temple, I was immediately aware that it was empty. There was nothing beside the vast empty space that was built with the purest marble.

"Why are we here?" I asked Cahir, somewhat confused.

"This is the entrance to the Heart of Elysium." His voice was low. Once again, we heard the voices of many children and women echoing inside.

"What are they saying?" Erebos asked.

"The events that happened here were too burdensome to be forgotten. Since none of them abandoned this place by choice, it is as if their souls whisper their desires," Cahir replied, his voice gentle and mellow.

"Will we find those that used to dwell in Madbouseux in the place you are taking us to?" I was anxious to know.

An empty stare was expressed on his face. "Yes. We were all sent to the Heart of Elysium."

Cahir moved to the middle of the temple. He got on his knees, his hands trailing across the cold marble floor. A flash of light illuminated one of the marble tiles, revealing a stairway that led underground.

"We must go down," Cahir affirmed with an assertive tone.

I cautiously approached the stairway.

"Are you sure we want to do this?" Erebos asked me once again.

"The Dark One *needs* a body of his own. Imagine how pleased he will be once he realizes we worked tirelessly, searching every avenue to bring him back," I answered.

"Watch your heads," Cahir warned us as he descended the dimly lit stairway.

The smell of burning sulfur overpowered us, becoming more pungent with every step. At the bottom, a dim red light was shining.

"What is this place?" Erebos inquired, his eyes soaking in every detail of our surroundings

"This tunnel was built in secret as the passageway to the Heart. The people of Madbouseux were ordered by their king to dig until they reached the heart of the world. The king claimed that the Book of Letters revealed to him the location of the Heart," Cahir stipulated as we approached the light that was coming from a doorway located on our left.

"Now we cross the darkness before we reach the Heart," Cahir avowed as he approached the last step, and led our footsteps along the lit pathway

We followed Cahir, trusting his direction. We entered a gigantic grotto; stalactites hung majestically from the ceiling, dripping with water. Every drop echoed loudly. Puddles of burning sulfur were scattered across the ground.

"Where do we go from here?" I asked Cahir. Even though I feared this place, I had to remain strong.

Cahir shot me a glance over his shoulder. "We must journey in the direction of the tunnel." He pointed toward a small opening in the massive wall ahead.

We continued to journey down past the grotto, approaching the tunnel. The voices of the women and children faintly spoke in the air.

When we stood at the entrance to the tunnel, the voices ceased. Once inside, we discovered a small spring of water.

Cahir stepped inside the flowing waters that only touched up to his calves. "We are close, my lady," he confessed, his eyes fixed inside the tunnel.

"I will go first," Erebos stated, walking ahead of me.

A cold shiver shot up my body when my feet touched the water. It was bitter cold. The water level rose with every step, going all the way up to my waist. Visibility grew dim as we moved forward.

"It is a good thing you are immortals. Ordinary humans aren't able to withstand the temperature inside the tunnel," Cahir alleged.

A few moments later, I heard a loud splash coming from up ahead of us.

"I think Cahir disap..." Erebos' voice trailed off as the sound of another loud splash followed.

Something grabbed ahold of my leg, pulling me toward the bottom. I tried to swim back to the surface but the suction was strong. I couldn't see anything but the darkness. The water temperature kept on dropping as my body violently descended. I touched the ground beneath me. I tried to fight against the strength of the water, which kept me pinned down. In a feeble attempt, I tried to move my hands and feet but my body did not respond.

I kept my eyes open, trying to find a way to be free from the water's powerful hold.

Surprisingly, a light began to shine from above the surface. I noticed the water level quickly dropping, reaching my nostrils. I took a deep breath and quickly got to my feet. My clothes were drenched.

I felt the heat of the light that shone above. When I peered up, I was bewildered at the sight. It was the sun, brightly shining in the blue sky.

A carpet of the greenest grass I had ever seen stretched across small hills. In the distance were mountains with altitudes that ascended to the clouds. The humming of birds and the sound of other critters melded together like a well-played melody.

"Do you see this, Nephele?" I heard excitement in Erebos' voice from behind me. As I peeked over my shoulder, I could see him and Cahir standing beside a small hill.

"What happened, Cahir?" I asked furiously. "Is this some sort of trick? You could have warned us!"

"I had no memory of the waters being so violent, my lady. I am glad to say that we have arrived."

"Is this the Fourth Dimension? Where are we exactly?" I demanded an answer from Cahir.

As a canvas burns when set on fire, my surroundings burned away. Ashes and smoke filled the air as all the beauty turned to ash.

Not long after, the smoke faded away, unveiling a shocking landscape. The trees were dead, the hills covered with thick ash. The sky was gray and a path of cobblestone sprung out of the gray ground.

"This is why many cannot return to Elysium. This place can read the strongest heart present and manifest its desires on its landscape. Part of your heart desires peace, but you know that inside of you, darkness lingers," Cahir explained as he strolled down the cobblestone path.

"Where are we?" I demanded to know.

"The Heart of Elysium. This is where the inhabitants of Madbouseux were sent after the king surrendered to the power of the Book of Letters." Cahir's voice was somber. "Now we stand next to the grave where the other Lessers sleep," Cahir informed us.

Silence, almost reverently, lingered about us.

"No other being has ever been here?" Erebos asked.

"The only ones I have seen venturing into this place are the Fallen Stars. They come to the Heart to perform and experiment with the Dark Exchange on the other Lessers," Cahir replied.

I turned to Erebos. He was absolutely astonished. "I cannot help but wonder why I was never told about this place," Erebos bellowed. "I knew of the Dark Exchange and of the Lessers, but I never knew my brothers held them here. They always told me they used the snakes from the Abyss to perfect the Dark Exchange."

"There are secrets here that few are aware of, Erebos," Cahir conceded.

"You mentioned that this place held the secrets to the disappearance of the people of Madbouseux. Where are the people?" I asked.

"You will see..." he whispered.

Cahir climbed a nearby hill. At the top of the hill, Cahir rhythmically stomped both of his feet. With each stomp, a violent shout came forth. I watched as small cracks appeared on the hill's ashy surface. Like glass, it began to shatter. Reaching out from the cracks, hands stretched forth, waving and twirling.

"This hill was a snake pit. The serpents that the Fallen Stars used to perform the Dark Exchange were kept here," Cahir said as he continuously stomped his feet against the cracking hill.

Bodies came out through the cracks. They crawled about, howling and screeching. These were Lessers but these looked different from Cahir. They had bright yellow eyes, an abnormally large mouth and their bodies were covered with small scales.

I read their minds, only to discover that they were empty, void of any thoughts and emotion. A continuous flow of mindless bodies were coming out of the first hill and then other hills began to break open, releasing more Lessers.

"Are the Lessers the secret to the disappearance of the people of Madbouseux?" I asked Cahir.

"Because of the corruption that overtook the king's heart, a curse came to rest upon the people of Madbouseux. Some of the people turned into snakes and were banished to this place. It wasn't long after that the Fallen Stars discovered us and then..." His words failed.

"Cahir, their minds are empty," I retorted.

Cahir scoffed. "Then you must fill them, Nephele."

I was shocked at his unexpected allegation.

"And where are the Fallen? Have they abandoned you here to rot?" Erebos asked.

"Abandoned? No, no. Mordred said that they had to take care of some urgent affairs, and they would return to give us minds of our own," he replied adamantly. "I cannot help but also wonder why you were never informed by the Fallen Stars of this place, Erebos."

I knew Mordred would not be returning to this place for a while, because he no longer had a human body to host himself in. His spirit must recover from being cast out of Isaac's body before he is able to find another host.

The Lessers were scattered over the hills and on the ground. They piled up on top of each other; mindless beings, drooling and waiting to be given a mind of their own. My mind pictured the Shadows and the Lessers banding together to create an army invincible to all. The Lessers' brains were an empty vacuum and the Fallen were too occupied in other realms to come and give them minds of their own. The Nephilins could fill their minds with the thoughts and actions necessary to defeat the Creator and retrieve the books.

"Maybe we should lead them out of here," I queried, not hiding the grin on my face. Erebos smiled.

"My dear, we could create an undefeatable army, but would the Fallen not come for us when they discover we have taken the Lessers out of here without a direct order?"

"I do not care if they do. My allegiance is not to your kind—I care only for the Dark One. We cannot leave such an army abandoned here in this desolate place. You and I both know that Mordred will not be returning for them anytime soon. The other Fallen Stars are probably tending to his weakened spirit in the Abyss. We could do it," I affirmed. "Are our desires to see Lessers and Shadows fighting together as one invincible army not the same?"

"I do desire their union very much," he said, musing. "My allegiance lies with the Dark One also. I am prepared for the consequences that might come with taking this army of Lessers out of the Heart of Elysium."

My hands gently caressed his face; his eyes darkened as he gave me a smile. Dark tears strolled down his pale face; his veins turned black and became visible under his skin. Every single one of the Lessers that were scattered around the hills and on the ground were consumed by his power. Their eyes darkened; tears also slipped down their cheeks. Moans of agony erupted as their cries filled the air while they stood up on their feet.

Erebos' body trembled as the Lessers approached him. They growled and roared, standing in a single line.

"You mentioned that only a part of the inhabitants of Madbouseux became snakes. What happened to the others?" I faced Cahir. "Where are they?"

Cahir smiled; his head twitched. "They became monsters…worse than Shadows if you ask me," he answered.

"What kind of monsters?" I asked curiously.

"In the Book, the king discovered a curse that could give humans eternal life." He eyed the growling Lessers.

"How do you know all this, Cahir?" I wondered how he knew what had happened to the other citizens, given he was a snake not that long ago. *How could an animal retrieve so much information?* I was dumbfounded.

"I was a human once, Nephele. I know it may be hard to see me that way…" he said brokenly. "But the king had a purpose for the other people," he continued.

Erebos was on his knees; the screams of the Lessers grew louder.

"What purpose, Cahir?" I shouted above the screams.

"To breed an army that would overtake Elysium. They found a curse in the Book of Letters called 'The Letters of the Dark Wine'…" Cahir hissed.

"Dark Wine? Why was it named that way?"

"The curse spoke of a drink the humans had to consume in order to live forever," he responded.

"What was it, Cahir? What was the drink?" I asked.

He paused for a second. "Blood," he answered coldly. "They had to drink the king's blood in order to become...immortal. You see, the king offered his life to Lucifer, which tainted his blood with the power of Lucifer's Darkness." He paused briefly. "When a human gives his life to Lucifer willingly, if this human feeds another human with his own blood, they will become blood drinkers—*immortal* blood drinkers, that is."

I was left speechless. I had never imagined that such a curse could exist.

"What happened to the immortal blood-drinkers? Are they here in the Heart of Elysium?" I asked impatiently.

"Yes, they are here. Their bodies are in a never-ending state of decomposition, but their souls continue to rest."

"Are they strong, Cahir?" In my mind, I was already plotting a strategy on how to utilize these beings in our army.

"Indeed. They are fast, agile and skilled in battle," he responded. "That is why the king chose them to become the generals of his army. The lesser skilled became snakes...useless snakes..."

I looked at Erebos. The veins on his neck were no longer visible; his eyes had returned to their normal crimson color. Sweat flowed from his brow.

"Did you hear what Cahir said?" I asked Erebos, not being able to contain my joy at the newfound information Cahir had divulged to me.

He grunted. "Yes. Despite all the pain I went through, I *did* hear what he said."

"I say we find the blood-drinkers," I implored. "Tell the Lessers to wait here while we look for them, Erebos."

Erebos had dark circles under his eyes as a result of the strength drained from him during the process of the Exchange.

"Do you know where the blood-drinkers are?" Erebos asked.

Cahir nodded his head. "They are asleep in a valley not far from here."

"Asleep?" Erebos mumbled.

There was no denying the anxiety that rose within me at the thought of finding the blood-drinkers. We had never heard of the stories about the disappearance of Madbouseux's people. There must be a very good reason why these tales were hidden from our kind. Still, I was insane with the desire for great power and above all else—I wanted to please the Dark One. I wanted to raise an undefeatable army, even if it was a costly price.

"Take us to them," I ordered Cahir.

Erebos turned to the Lessers that stood motionless, waiting for his command.

"Stay here and wait until I return," he declared in a loud voice. The Lessers moaned and grunted, standing perfectly still in a straight line.

"We must follow the cobblestone road that leads us deep into the mountains until we reach the blood-drinkers' resting place," Cahir said as he hastily led us.

I glanced back as the thick gray mist caused me to lose sight of the Lessers.

The landscape around us looked desolate.

"Cahir, you have mentioned so much about the king and his doings, but you never told us what became of him. Where is his body located now?" I inquired. Erebos shot me a piercing glance.

"Well, he is here in the Heart, sleeping with the lot of blood-drinkers," he replied. "Even with all the power bestowed upon him, the king had a desire to become like the blood-drinkers. His own powers were not enough for him. He drank his own blood so that the curse could also alight upon him. He was driven with the desire for immortality, even if it meant being a servant of Lucifer and a blood-drinker."

"But if the blood that coursed through his veins already belonged to Lucifer, why did he have to drink his own?" I asked as we followed the path along the desolate road.

"You really seem interested in these creatures, Nephele," Erebos affirmed with a worried look stamped across his face. I nodded.

"The blood only gives immortality when it touches the lips," Cahir answered. "The king decided to drink his own blood as a precaution, in case something was to ever happen to him."

Cahir kept his eyes attentively on the road as he answered my questions. I read his thoughts and realized that he was afraid of what we were to find.

"How do you feel, Erebos? Are all your powers still intact?" I asked him, afraid he might have lost his power during the Exchange when he gave part of himself to the Lessers.

"My body is well but I am confused. Here we are hunting for these blood-drinkers while the Lessers wait near their hills. Should we not train the Lessers prior to finding these blood-drinkers?"

"We cannot waste time, Erebos," I said sharply.

His face warned of apprehension. "What if the Fallen Stars come today? They are not fools. You know this. If they know such an army exists, they are probably keeping a close watch on this place."

I knew in my heart that the Fallen Stars would eventually come for them, but for some reason they were delaying their actions. Such an army was not meant to just sit here idly. "We are carrying out what the Fallen Stars have been unable to," I answered.

"This is where they sleep," Cahir said as he stopped in front of a hill. "They are buried beneath this hill. If you choose to wake the blood-drinkers, you will have to provide food for them," he acknowledged.

A thought then hit me. "Cahir, do they need to kill in order to feed?"

Cahir hissed. "No, my lady.... Some can stop drinking blood before their victim dies but I cannot guarantee it, especially since they have been underground for so long."

"Can they feed on the blood of the Lessers?" I asked, hopeful.

Erebos' look pierced mine as his eyes shifted in my direction. He looked surprised.

"You must be insane, Nephele. Are you telling me that we have come all this way for the Lessers and now you want to use them as bait for the blood-drinkers? What if the blood-drinkers kill them?" Erebos asked in rage.

"Cahir, you said that you would serve us wholeheartedly, right?" I asked him. He gave me a soft frightful smile.

"What are you doing, Nephele?" Erebos charged.

I approached Cahir, who stood next to one of the hills. I gently folded his hand in mine. "Will you allow one of the blood-drinkers to feed on you?"

He retracted his hand from mine instantly. "What are you saying?"

"All I am saying is that if you allow one of the blood-drinkers to feed on your blood, we will not have to bring all of the other Lessers here. Think of it this way—if he feeds on you and you don't die, we will know that the others can drink from the Lessers and they too shall live."

Cahir slowly bent down on his knees as he faced me. "Do what you will," he said. I kneeled alongside him so that my hands could comfortably caress his face. "Think of what I am offering you, you will be doing your kind a favor. I would not want to lead my own kind to their destruction if I could have done something that could have helped to avoid it."

He moved his fingers to touch the ashes that sat on the hill. Silence filled the air. He purposely lifted his right arm toward his face; he fixed his eyes on his wrist. He brought his wrist toward his mouth and ripped it open with his teeth. Without a single word, he watched as his blood poured over the ashes. Seconds later, he used his other hand to put pressure onto the wound, stopping the flow of blood.

I withdrew my presence from him, allowing him to stand on top of the hill alone. It wasn't long until the hill exploded, becoming nothing but dust.

Cahir's body was thrown to the side, landing on the ground. I was alarmed.

"Be ready in case it attacks," Erebos declared.

Once the dust settled, the decayed, colorless and lifeless body appeared. It stood upright. Instead of skin, a clear pasty substance covered its entire body. A few scraggly strands of black hair covered its scalp. There were gigantic holes where the creature's eyes and nose had once been. Its jaw dangled loosely from its mouth. Two of its upper teeth were longer than the rest, glaring brightly.

Cahir trembled with fright as he approached the blood-drinker; his lower jaw quivered. He drew his wrist closer to its mouth. The blood-drinker grabbed Cahir's wrist violently. It drank the blood carelessly, spilling it everywhere as the blood drained profusely from both sides of the blood-drinker's mouth. Erebos approached me.

Cahir's skin became pale as the blood-drinker drank his blood. Cahir muttered words that I couldn't understand as he stared at the creature drinking his blood. Unexpectedly, the creature tossed Cahir aside with such force that his body slammed up against an old tree that was nearby.

Skin grew over its body; the empty holes on its face were no longer void since its features returned to normal. It was mesmerizing to watch the transformation occur right before my eyes. In a short time, it became apparent that the creature was a male.

His red eyes shimmered like stars; his skin was of an olive pigmentation and his hair was dark. As his body changed, pieces of ragged clothing appeared, covering his waist and legs. He had the appearance of a well-built man.

I cautiously approached him, closely surveying every single detail of his body. He turned to me; his breathing was shallow.

"Wh-why did you come?" he asked with a stammering voice.

"Is...is Cahir dead?" Erebos asked the blood-drinker as he drew near.

The blood-drinker let out a mild laugh. "I might have been sleeping for a long time, but I know how to control my urges." He looked down at Cahir's body. "He isn't dead." He gave a menacing look and cracked his neck. "You have not yet answered my question. Why have you come?"

I sighed. "We have come to awaken you from your sleep."

"There must be more to your plan than just to awaken me, I am certain. As far as I remember we were doomed to stay in the Heart of Elysium forever and now, you appear and revive me." He smiled. "What is it that you want from me?"

"We have come for your allegiance. War is spreading throughout Elysium and we seek assistance from those willing to aid in the awakening of the Dark One," I responded.

"You seek the Diary of Lucifer?" he asked with a menacing voice.

"Yes," I replied.

"Is the Council still protecting the Diary?" he inquired.

"No. We had possession of the Diary, but it was stolen," Erebos added as he walked closer to the blood-drinker.

"Are you aware that there are four more books that Lucifer has written?" I asked him, curiously longing for his answer. Maybe he knew of the other powers the books possessed.

"Well, of these other books I don't know, but I am pretty sure you don't have the Book of Letters." His allegation was followed by a smile.

I was silent.

"I thought so. If you had the Book of Letters, you wouldn't be here," he groaned.

"We seek your allegiance to destroy those that oppose Lucifer and his ideals. We need to gather the books and their bearers in order to awake him from his sleep," I informed him.

"If we pledge allegiance to you, how are we to know that the Creator will not send us back here again?" He stepped forward, his eyes only inches from mine. "How can you guarantee that we will not be imprisoned here in the Heart of Elysium again?"

I knew what I was capable of doing to him and I was aware of the power inside of me, but he stirred up emotions in my heart that were unknown to me. He made me feel vulnerable. "We have an ally inside of Tristar," I divulged. "We can trust him to watch over your kind. You do not need to worry about returning to this place. Our armies are numerous and strong."

"Then why is it that you are seeking my kind?" the blood-drinker retorted.

"Will you join us?" Erebos asked impatiently. "We are not here to waste any more time."

"And I have not returned to waste mine," he proclaimed. "I will join with you. Even a slight chance of vengeance against the Creator is better than none at all."

"What is your name?" I asked.

"Bartholomew Winmore, king of Madbouseux. That is what the people called me during my reign in my human days," he answered.

Unexpectedly, he paced around us, looking at the other nearby hills. He strolled down to our right, approaching a very old, dead oak tree. He walked by Cahir's unconscious body, looked at the body in disgust and continued to head toward the tree. Once he was under the branches, he lowered himself to his knees and caressed the ground.

"I have a question for you," he shouted. "What will the other blood-drinkers feed on in order to awake from slumber?" His eyes were threatening as they drilled into mine. "You?"

I did not think twice before answering. "Him…" I pointed to Cahir. "Let them feed on him. Cahir has served his purpose already. He has led us to you." I waited for Erebos' approval.

"Are you sure you want to sacrifice him this way? He could still be useful," Erebos contested.

"I am more than certain. We have an army of Lessers waiting for us. Cahir's life is a small sacrifice compared to the greater honor." I observed that Cahir's blood was oozing from his wounded wrist.

Bartholomew's eyes were fixed on me, as he waited for a confirmation to allow the others to feed on Cahir.

"Do not just sit there. Feed him to the other blood-drinkers," I ordered as I came near to him.

"His blood won't be enough to keep us fed for long. There are ten of us in this region. More are scattered throughout the Heart," he said. "We will need more blood."

"When we leave the Heart of Elysium, we will come upon a village where you and your kind can feed at will, but right now, this is all that we have to offer," Erebos added.

"Again, I am afraid, this will not suffice," he said sharply. "They might have to feed on one that has the ability to heal fast and feels no pain." Without hesitating, he brought his wrist to his mouth and brutally sunk his teeth into it. He extended his arm; the blackish-colored blood dripped onto ground. Within moments, the ground caved in as the creature rose up from the ashes. Its physical features were very similar to Bartholomew before he had received the quota of blood to restore his body to its original design.

The blood-drinker was naked; dirt covered its entire body. The creature grabbed ahold of Bartholomew's blood-soaked wrist and drank zealously from it. Bartholomew obligingly let the blood-drinker feed. He hummed a tune as he watched the creature gulp his blood.

"Ah, ah, ah." He smirked. "Enough. You can feed on more at a later time."

I could tell this one was a woman. Her golden locks regained their color and her eyes were the color of hazel. Her skin was as pale as the moon, and her cheeks had a slight shade of red to them.

"I need to feed," she cried in a weak voice as she turned away from Bartholomew's wrist. "Why would you allow me to feed upon your blood? You know to drink a blood-drinker's blood is against the law," she said as she turned to face Erebos and me.

"Who are you?" she asked. "Are you the ones that have awakened us?"

"Yes, we are. This is Nephele and I am Erebos," Erebos replied. "We are your allies."

"They are with us," Bartholomew assured her.

"Why did I have to drink from you?" she asked Bartholomew.

"Nylora, desperate times call for desperate measures. We need to leave the Heart of Elysium and they have come to lead us out."

"We have been buried in the Heart of Elysium for hundreds of years. What is it that we are going back to? What does the world have left to offer us?" She gently placed her right hand on his face. Her skin had not yet fully restored to humanlike flesh; patches of gray wounds were scattered throughout her body.

"Lucifer is about to awake. The Diary has been found, but the Book of Letters is still missing. Do you not remember our days of glory, when I had the Book of Letters?" He smiled. "I'd say we have a lot to go back to."

"I hope their kind is trustworthy, Nephele," Erebos whispered. "If they become a hindrance to the tasks the Dark One requires of us, I will not hesitate to send them back to this place."

"And I would gladly help you," I added.

"Are we ready to carry on?" I asked Bartholomew and Nylora. "I believe you have been in this place long enough."

"Wait...wait...impatient Nephilins," Bartholomew chanted haltingly. "We must awaken the others."

Bartholomew and Nylora were unhurried as they examined the dark landscape, checking every hill and tree, searching for the location of the other blood-drinkers.

"I hear one in here, my lord," Nylora stated as she pressed her head against a small hill behind us.

"Ah! I can see that this one is starving," Bartholomew noted as he once again sank his teeth into his wrist; blood oozed out of the wound, dripping onto the ground.

The hill shook violently, exploding into dust. The blood-drinker forcefully snatched Bartholomew's wrist, gulping down his blood. Seven times the same act was repeated until all the awakened blood-drinkers in this area had been revived.

Erebos and I watched closely, observing the blood-drinkers as they awakened. Bartholomew healed quickly, showing no signs of weakness as the blood-drinkers fed off of him. Once all the blood-drinkers were fully restored, they would ask Bartholomew the same question: *Why did you feed us your blood?*

The joy of being alive again was explicitly painted on their faces as they rejoiced at the sight of each other's company. They greeted each other with exuberant hugs and handshakes.

XX

"My people—hear me!" Bartholomew shouted at the top of his lungs. The blood-drinkers attentively looked at him as he walked in our direction. "These are the ones that have come to our aid. They have revealed unto us that the Diary has been found." The other blood-drinkers let out loud chants. "These people said they are to make war against Tristar and the Creator. I say we join them in battle and take back the Book of Letters so we can once again live in full glory!"

They yelled frantically in agreement to his speech.

"Let us head back to where the Lessers are," Erebos suggested in a loud voice. "We cannot leave without them."

Nylora hastily approached us.

"Others? What others?" she asked.

"The Lessers—they await us not far from here," I responded. "They have also sided with us."

Bartholomew's face was stamped with anger. The veins on his neck popped, his hands fiercely clasping each other as he took heavy breaths. "By Lessers you mean the snakes that dwell here?" he asked.

"Yes," Erebos affirmed coldly.

"You do not really think that we are to stand next to those weaklings again, do you?" Nylora said with a disgusted look on her face.

"I do not see a reason why our union would not work," I said in aggravation.

"The reason why some people became snakes and others became blood-drinkers was simply because one kind was smarter, stronger and more skillful than the other. They are foolish and weak." Bartholomew's voice deepened. "What can we expect from creatures that eat dust and slither on their stomachs?" Bartholomew barked angrily. The other blood-drinkers laughed hysterically.

"They are no longer brainless creatures," Erebos retorted. "I have given them a mind of their own through the Dark Exchange. A part of me lives inside of them now. You just drank from one of them." Erebos pointed at Cahir's immobile body.

"They will only be useful when we need to feed, nothing more," Bartholomew contested. "Still, we refuse to fight alongside them, whether you like it or not."

"I guess we have an issue to solve now, don't we?" I implied. "Who will get what they want…"

Nylora raised her right eyebrow. "There are ten of us and two of you. I don't see a battle happening," Nylora retorted with a sneer.

Flames enveloped the blood-drinkers as Erebos moved his hands swiftly. "I think you are forgetting that I am a Fallen Star, commissioned by Lucifer to fulfill his desires," he shouted as the flames danced around the blood-drinkers.

"You are of lesser authority, Fallen Star. If Lucifer trusted you completely, he would have told you about us—about the Heart of Elysium. Instead, he told other Fallen Stars and kept you in the dark," Bartholomew shouted from behind the fire as the flames lost their intensity. "Do not forget that we also had a covenant with Lucifer, which gave us great powers, and once we get ahold of the Book of Letters, we will be sure to rid Elysium of your kind."

I was speechless when I saw Bartholomew had stopped the flames. "To tell you the truth, our allegiance lies with no one other than ourselves. We want the Book of Letters and we will find it. We've had the book before; we know what the book looks like. We don't need your help." The blood-drinkers synchronically walked toward us as Bartholomew spoke.

My body turned to shadow, hovering over the blood-drinkers. I released pain upon them. Scattered screams resounded as the ten were brought to their knees.

Erebos raised his right hand, swiftly moving his fingers. Grunts, moans and screams followed as the blood-drinkers were tortured with pain.

I changed back to physical form.

"Let us hope that after this little lesson, you will refrain from saying such foolish things," Erebos spoke in rage; his eyes were opened wide and fixed on every single one of the blood-drinkers. I had ceased my attack, while Erebos inflicted them all with torturous pain.

To our surprise, one by one, the blood-drinkers stood to their feet. "We may not have fed properly, but we still harbor great strength," one of the blood-drinkers with flaming red hair and green eyes said. "We are Madbouseux's strongest warriors and we will not take surrender lightly." His body disintegrated in the air, becoming a gray shadow. He moved around us in a circular motion. Erebos grabbed my hand as our bodies shifted to shadows. With all our speed, we flew away from them.

Behind us, I saw the blood-drinkers ferociously chasing us; their dragon-like wings were dark and rugged.

"Where are we headed to?" I asked Erebos as we made our way through the air.

"The Lessers…. They have allied to us. They will fight for us." His voice sounded apprehensive. "It would be foolish to try to defeat all these blood-drinkers by ourselves."

Bolts of light and fire passed us by, followed by the blood-drinkers' strong cries of rage. I was not accustomed to retreating from my foes, but this situation was particularly different. We were outnumbered. We headed toward the Lessers, not knowing what to expect once they saw the blood-drinkers.

Their bodies changed color as they flew. To my right, one blood-drinker assumed the form of a hand that grabbed me by the arm, snatched me, and pulled me against the ground. I reacted immediately, attacking the blood-drinker with my mind. I was released from the strong grasp as the hand vanished.

Above us, the Lessers appeared, flying in the direction of the blood-drinkers.

"I have called them out to fight," Erebos stated as we hastily flew. "I have given them wings also...to help them in battle..."

Confusion stirred inside of me. "The Lessers might die in battle here," I bellowed. "You should not have called them to fight before consulting with me."

"Forgive me, Nephele, but we are running out of time. We need to leave the Heart of Elysium," Erebos replied coldly.

The Lessers' speed and agility were incredible. Their wings resembled that of a vulture; rugged feathers with faded colors. Their faces were void of any emotion.

We turned to look at the Lessers the moment the battle cries arose.

"The Dark One never asked us to come to the Heart of Elysium. We have the Shadows, the Fallen Stars and the Lessers. Our army is strong enough already. We do not need this forsaken army. We should head out now," Erebos affirmed in rage.

As soon as those words came out of his mouth, I landed a punch on his face with all of my might; his body shot straight down to the ground. The impact of his body was so severe, it formed a crater.

"We are not turning back!" I yelled, approaching his body.

"Nephele, you do not want to fight me. You know what I am capable of." The dust that formed from the impact moved around him like a tornado. "Lucifer has commanded me to go into the kingdoms and command their rulers to fight for him. I will not allow your stubbornness to hinder me from fulfilling the task *Lucifer* has entrusted me with," he added.

I laughed. "Just because you are embodied inside of a king does not make you one, Erebos. Just because your kind fathered us, it does not give you the right to dictate our doings." Flames of fury burned inside of my heart. My loyalty did not lie with the Fallen Stars or the Shadows—my heart was loyal only to the Dark One. "I will face and destroy any who oppose Lucifer's wishes."

"Leave the Lessers and the blood-drinkers here or we are going to have a problem." The dust surrounded him like a blanket. With my gaze, I caused flames to engulf his body.

"We stay, we fight and take the Lessers with us, back to Elysium," I declared.

A heart-wrenching roar filled the air as the blood drinkers and the Lessers lightened the sky with their attacks.

"I am trying to save us, Nephele," Erebos shouted. "Stop this madness."

I ceased the fire when a loud roar echoed, followed by a putrid stench. Some unseen force tightened its grasp around me; I had never experienced such a feeling before. The pain I felt overwhelmed me from head to toe. My head felt as if it was about to explode.

"Capios," Erebos said. "I have the ability to create them." He walked toward me. Everything around me was growing dim. "It is time that you show respect to those that are superior to you. I am growing tired of your stubbornness. You are going to get us both killed if you do not listen to me.

"As the Capios' grasp tightens, you will soon wish for death and when you do, I will release you and you will follow my orders. I will not tolerate such stubborn actions from you anymore. Your devotion to the Dark One is clouding your judgment."

I felt the hands of the Capios pressing me down. They turned me onto my stomach and forced my face on the ground. Blood dripped from my nostrils and mouth. With every breath I took, ashes permeated my throat. Their growls were soft and shallow.

"Why do fools get caught up in the affairs of others?" a loud voice bellowed. The Capios let me loose; their growling faded. I lifted my head up and saw a man of high stature standing in front of me.

"I was wondering when I would see you again. You have some explaining to do," Erebos affirmed in a strong voice.

"Explaining?" The man's voice was unlike anything I had ever heard. He spoke every word peacefully, but with great authority. "Erebos, you were told by Lucifer to go about the kingdoms to gather their kings to fight alongside us, not to meddle in the affairs of Nephilins." A soft grin was stamped across the man's colorless face. His hair was short and dark and his eyes were gray like the ashes scattered along the ground. The rugged garments he wore were stained with blood.

"You are not in a position to inquire about what the Dark One has asked of me, Xavier," Erebos said. "You kept me in the dark all this time about this place...these creatures..."

"I never told you about this place and yet you have found it on your own," Xavier asserted sarcastically. "How mature of you, little brother!"

Xavier raised his right hand in the direction of the fight between the Lessers and blood-drinkers. "I see you have been playing with my puppets. You should have known better," Xavier said; Erebos scoffed in anger.

The blood-drinkers and the Lessers walked toward him like spellbound drones. Their eyes were glazed over with a white mist.

"What are you doing to them?" I asked him. "We are to use the Lessers and blood-drinkers against Elysium and in the conquering of the kingdoms." I approached him.

Xavier's laugh caused a great rage to rise within me. Who was this man?

"Little girl, these creatures do not concern you. Lucifer already had plans for them before you even knew they existed."

"I have accomplished that which you have ordered, Master," a broken voice cried out from behind me. Quickly, I looked over my shoulder to find Cahir dragging his broken body against the ash-covered ground.

"Master?" Erebos mumbled, confused. "How is he your master?"

"After the castle of Justicia fell in Elysium, I found Cahir lying desolate in the forest. When I saw the transformation he had gone through after the fall, I knew he could be useful. My good and faithful servant led you two to exactly where I wanted you to be."

I pondered on Xavier's claims about Cahir luring us to do his bidding. How could Lucifer have allowed such a thing?

"Why would you keep me in the dark like that, Xavier?" Erebos questioned him. A feeling of disappointment flowed with every word he uttered. "Can we not find loyalty in each other anymore?"

"Brother, after the fall I believe you have already realized that loyalty only existed during our days with the Creator. After those days, we have seen so much darkness, it is impossible to believe in loyalty, even amongst ourselves." Xavier walked to Cahir, who now stood next to the Lessers and the blood-drinkers. "Once I saw that the Lessers and the blood-drinkers were battling, I had to intervene. I could not risk losing them."

"You were not going to lose them. We had it—"

"Under control?" Xavier cut me off, letting out a sarcastic laugh. "If the Dark One wanted you to know about this place, he would have told you, Nephilin." He grunted. "I swear, of all the mistakes the Fallen Stars have made, sleeping with women was the worst of them all."

Out of anger I used my abilities to inflict pain inside of his head. With a single nonchalant movement of his right hand, he easily dodged my attack as if he could also see it coming. "I can see the red flashes that come out of you, Nephele. Do not be foolish enough to try to attack me with your cheap tricks.

Your rage is your greatest weaknesses. You should learn how to control it."

Cahir slithered closer to Xavier's feet. "Master, I ache. Please renew my strength." Drool poured from his mouth.

"I am fond of the name they have given you," Xavier said as he kneeled down; Cahir's eyes shot up toward him. "And I will gladly give you your strength back." He held up two of his fingers and placed them onto Cahir's throat. At his touch, Cahir's skin opened, creating a perfectly round wound; blood flowed like a running river. He choked on his own blood, writhing on the ground in desperation.

"Bartholomew and Nylora, please come and drink." They both walked toward the puddle of blood without hesitation. Their pace was slow and they stumbled as they walked.

They both knelt down and drank the blood that steadily poured out of Cahir's neck.

"Cahir has served his purpose. It is time for him to meet his fate," Xavier said as he approached Erebos and me.

I contemplated upon what I could do to escape, but in the midst of such great power, my abilities and tactics seemed inadequate.

"Do you know anything about the Book of Letters?" Xavier asked me with a grin.

"We know that the Book of Letters is not in Elysium, neither is the Book here in the Heart," Erebos implied.

"Little brother, I am completely aware that the Book is not here." He moved toward the Lessers, who were all standing as still as statues under his influence. "But I have been informed by our source inside of Tristar that they do not have the Book of Letters either. One of the book-bearers has possession of it. Only, the bearer of the book isn't aware of the power of the book he carries around."

A chill shot down my spine. The thought that the book-bearers had such a weapon in hand was frightening. An unexpected thought struck me.

"I remember when we arrived at the Prison, I saw three lines surrounded by a circle appear on the wall used to open the Prison, but the image rapidly faded," I stated. "No one knew what the image was. Never had I seen such sighting."

Xavier shot a worried look at Erebos and me.

"Afterward, when we headed back to Aloisio, in the middle of the battle, I found Devin, Ely and the book-bearers trying to escape," I added.

"The book is with the book-bearers. Let's hope they have not yet discovered the truth about the Book of Letters," Xavier mumbled.

"Do *you* know the truth about such mysterious object?" Erebos asked.

"Yes, I do," Xavier answered in an assertive tone. "Not only of the Book of Letters but the truth of all other books as well. Lucifer wrote all five books while he still lived in Tristar. The writings on each book are unknown and will only be unveiled once the books are opened and read by the book-bearers. He never revealed the things he had written on these books. Before Lucifer declared war against Tristar, he gathered the Stars and explained the purpose of each book."

Xavier sighed.

"All five books are crucial in order to give Lucifer a body when he awakens. The Diary represents Lucifer's heart, the Book of the Light Bearer holds Lucifer's mind; the Book of the Destroyer, being the third book, represents Lucifer's arms. The fourth book, the Book of the Enlightened, represents Lucifer's legs, and lastly, the fifth book, the Book of the Justifier, represents Lucifer's chest."

"So...when they are all read, Lucifer will have a full body..." Erebos sounded surprised, his mind trying to understand this new information.

"That is why all the book-bearers need to read the writings on the books..." My voice trailed off as I spoke.

"We plan on using the Dark Exchange on the book-bearers. The same curse used to give the Lessers a mind of their own. We will try to penetrate their minds, forcing them to open and read the books," Erebos asserted.

"That sounds like a good plan, but we need more than just a curse to do this. This is why I brought you to me!" Xavier smiled, his eyes meeting mine. "Nephele, you are not afraid of taking risks and pursuing the unachievable to obtain what your heart desires." He placed his right hand on Erebos' shoulder. "Whereas you, little brother, you are strong and you willingly follow Nephele's desires. A living proof of this is how you risked so much by coming here."

"How do we know which book-bearer holds the Book of Letters?" I asked.

"You claimed that you caught sight of three lines inside a circle on the wall back in Justicia, correct?"

I nodded.

"Each book is marked by a symbol. The Diary is a circle with one line, the Book of the Light Bearer has a circle with two lines…"

"The third book is the Book of Letters…" Erebos affirmed in a thoughtful tone.

Xavier gave me an evil grin. "What better way to retrieve not only the Book of Letters and all other books than to send out Capios," he said, shooting a thoughtful gaze at Erebos.

Erebos closed his eyes and in an instant, loud growls and howls resounded. On the ashy ground, I caught sight of the Capios' footprints. They seemed to be rambling around.

"Good. We send the Capios throughout Elysium to snatch the book-bearers," I said with a smile.

"Capios," Xavier shouted. "Leave this place and find me the book-bearers. Bring them to me alive and unspoiled. They hold something that is dear to us and we need it back."

The growls faded; the putrid smell vanished.

"What about them?" I nodded my head toward the Lessers and the blood-drinkers. "What are you going to do with them?" I asked Xavier.

"They are under my command now, Nephele," Xavier said boldly as he walked toward the blood-drinkers and Lessers.

An unexpected laugh resounded. "Your command, Xavier?" Bartholomew retorted snidely. My eyes darted in his direction.

"I was wondering how long we had to keep on pretending to be under his influence," Nylora said as she stretched her arms upward. "My body was growing numb." She gave Bartholomew a smile.

Xavier angrily looked at the blood-drinkers. The Lessers remained motionless, their breathing shallow.

"How dare you try to fool me?" Xavier questioned the blood-drinkers with a loud voice.

"The moment you tried to force us to fight for you, I realized there was no other choice," Bartholomew said with a smirk. The blood-drinkers closed in on us, walking in perfect synchronism.

"This kind of action is typical of your kind...the Fallen Stars have always believed that they had the right to order us around. Well, things have changed, Xavier. I hope you and your friends have enjoyed your stay here in the Heart of Elysium, because this is where you will sleep for the rest of your days."

Before the last words drifted out of Bartholomew's mouth, the blood-drinkers' eyes turned white and a red mist enveloped us.

Torturous pain raced through my body. I contained my urge to scream. A throbbing ringing sound echoed in my head. I tried to release my attack, but my body did not respond.

"You scum...you..." My mouth stopped responding to my command before I was able to finish speaking.

As my vision dimmed, I caught sight of Erebos and Xavier writhing in pain.

My body thudded to the ground as I lost control of my arms and legs. With every breath I took, ashes traveled their way inside of my nostrils.

My eyelids closed on me as I took in one last breath.

As I succumbed to the darkness that took me, a vivid image of Isaac filled my mind.

In his hand, he held a silver sword. The sword's blade was long and thin, its grip as black as the night.

I struggled to stand to my feet, realizing that some unseen force was pinning me to the ground. I desperately tried to move my hands with the hope that I would break free from whatever had ahold of me, but my attempt was folly.

Isaac strolled in my direction; his wings expanded, revealing their pearly white color. At every step, the sword Isaac held in hand shone with a vivid light. There was nothing around us but pure darkness.

My body was still unresponsive to my commands. I was frozen before my enemy like a lamb out to slaughter.

Rage and fear tried to find their way inside of me, attempting to take me over, but I refused to surrender to these feelings.

Isaac got on his knees next to me and I feebly clenched my fists in an attempt to punch him, but my arms didn't move.

My eyes looked up into his cold gaze.

Brusquely, the blade of his sword pierced the back of my left hand. I tried to scream, but there was no sound coming out of me. My body trembled as the pain coursed its way from my hand to my arm.

The only weapon that had the ability to kill a Nephilin was a sword or a spear. This pain was different from any other I had ever experienced. I felt a sharp pain spreading inside of me, rushing through my veins.

The feeling I was enduring was excruciating. My organs felt as though they were being burned from the inside out. Sweat streamed down my face.

Isaac placed his right foot on my head, crushing my face to the ground. I took in heavy breaths; my eyes couldn't see anything but the darkness.

The coldness of the blade invaded my chest, followed by an unbearable pain. I groaned, holding back my screams. In a matter of seconds, my entire body was numb.

My teeth clenched as my heart accelerated in my chest, but the beating progressively slowed its pace and became nothing but a soft murmur.

I felt the pressure from Isaac's foot leave my head. Moments later, I felt him breathing on my neck.

"You see…even with all of your dark powers, Nephele, in the end, you will never win," Isaac whispered in my ear.

All faded as I surrendered to the weakness that had taken me.

"I KNEW THE DARKNESS WAS STRONG AND THE TIME I HAD SPENT IN THE SHADOWS SHOWED ME THAT POWER IS A MERE FORCE RULED AND YIELDED BY WISDOM."

ISAAC KHAN

ACKNOWLEDGMENTS

God, I would have never been able to write this without you. Thank you!

It would be extremely selfish of me not to mention the people that helped me on the birth of my first novel.

I can't imagine how someone could get through all this process without a family. Mom, Deborah, Dad, and Carlos, you guys are amazing. Thank you for supporting me and all my crazy ideas.

My friends, how I could have gotten this far without your words of encouragement and your willingness to help me "see the bigger picture" is beyond me. Thank you for believing in me all these years.

A huge thank you to Valentina Gaines for all the suggestions and corrections. Your efforts have not been in vain. Thank you for being so in tune with the story.

My dear friend and author, Janet DeAngelo. Thank you for loving these characters as much as I do. Your restless dedication to this story has inspired me in so many levels. I love you.

Pastor Sandra Santos and all my mentors and pastors, a huge thank you. Your words of wisdom, encouragement, and your dedication have inspired me beyond words.

Thank you to my "first readers," Ronaldo Alves, Fernanda Alves, Luiza Aquino, Iggy Villaverde, Mariana Debossan, Mariana Novaes, Lorrayne Romeiro, Junior Almeida, Jorge Trindade, Yuri Pradines, Daniel Junior, Sydney Giers, Rosalie Galante, Josiane Costa, Peter Batarseh, Daniel Batarseh, Flavia

Duddey, Hannah Lemes, Josh Cabral, and Rafaela Melo. Your input and encouraging words have made all the difference.

This story would never be what it is if it wasn't for all the amazing music that inspired me along the way!

Howard Shore, John Williams, Muse, Linkin Park, Evanescence, James Newton Howard, Alexandre Desplat, James Horner, Hans Zimmer, Fever Ray, Florence and The Machine, Red, Atticus Ross, Harry Gregson-Williams, Nicholas Hooper, Two Steps from Hell, Within Temptation.

You have all helped me overcome writer's block.

A huge thank you to all the readers. Thank you for believing Isaac and all the other characters are worthy of your time, attention, and love.

Thank you for embarking on this journey.

ABOUT THE AUTHOR

J.D.Netto (Jorge de Oliveira Netto) is Brazilian-born. Raised in Framingham, MA, J.D.Netto always had an eye for epic fantasy and storytelling. At an early age, J.D.Netto had the habit of locking himself in his room, turning on any soundtrack he could find, and there he wrote for hours. During his senior year in high school, J.D.Netto had an idea that changed his life: "What if Lucifer had a diary? What if the diary was a secret? What if the secret was a reality?" These simple questions led J.D.Netto to write for six consecutive years, creating the world of Elysium. Apart from writing, J.D.Netto is a graphic designer, musician and illustrator.

http://www.thewhispersofthefallen.com

Lightning Source UK Ltd.
Milton Keynes UK
UKOW02f2109140115

244502UK00004B/159/P